THE TREASURE OF ST. PAUL

THE TREASURE OF ST. PAUL

Karla Brandenburg

Writers Club Press
San Jose New York Lincoln Shanghai

The Treasure of St. Paul

All Rights Reserved © 2002 by Karla Brandenburg

No part of this book may be reproduced or transmitted in any form or by any means, graphic, electronic, or mechanical, including photocopying, recording, taping, or by any information storage retrieval system, without the permission in writing from the publisher.

Writers Club Press
an imprint of iUniverse, Inc.

For information address:
iUniverse, Inc.
5220 S. 16th St., Suite 200
Lincoln, NE 68512
www.iuniverse.com

Any resemblance to actual people and events is purely coincidental. This is a work of fiction.

ISBN: 0-595-23363-5

Printed in the United States of America

CHAPTER 1

Kira dreamed of a dark man, sifting debris through a sieve, crouching in a dark alcove cut into the earth. She could sense the simple pleasure of his work—an indulgence to allay his anxieties.

To be as one with the earth.

In her sleep, her brow creased as she witnessed the approach of another man, his features distorted into ambiguity. She could see the dark man's shoulders tense, feel his agitation.

"You should be in the lab," she heard the intruder say.

"Maybe you'd like to do this?" the dark man suggested, rising to his feet, wiping a sleeve across his glistening forehead. Reaching his full height, he stood nearly six inches taller than his adversary.

"That's what the laborers and students are for." The shorter man leaned against the wall, folding his arms and crossing one leg over the other.

The dark man peeled off his gloves. "There is plenty of work for everyone, and some that is being neglected."

"There are more than enough hands to do my work."

"Then it is no longer your work, is it?"

The other man straightened, trying to reduce the difference in height. Supporting himself with both hands, he leaned against the wall. "It will all be mine one day."

"And what would you do with it?" the dark man challenged, spreading his legs and putting his hands to his hips.

An old man stepped up between the two. "It is mine to give," he reminded them.

"You would take from me what is mine?" the second man protested.

"I would spare you from an unwanted burden." The elder stood beside the dark man, father and son united in their common interest.

The second man turned on his heel and walked back into the tunnels of earth, pounding at dirt covered walls as he passed through. "I will have what is mine."

The dark man's father laid a reassuring hand on his son's shoulder. "He will soon tire of the search and be off again."

"I wish I could be sure."

In the dream, Kira heard two short beeps from a wristwatch and watched the dark man come into focus, walking into a sun-splashed courtyard below the earth's surface.

He reminded her of a picture she'd seen in a history book of Marcus Aurelius, loose curls shortening the length of his black hair, piercing black eyes set deep into his tanned face.

"Lay down your tools," he shouted.

Cupping his hands to his mouth he shouted once more. "Lay down your tools." He tugged at his sweat drenched shirt, touching his chin to the collar to stop a tiny silver trail.

She was aware of people passing, escaping from the tomb, climbing Jacob's ladder up into the clear blue sky.

Kira twisted uncomfortably in the bed, her eyes squeezed tightly shut.

Something's wrong.

The dark man touched a piece of the wooden framework that supported the tenuous walls of a villa long buried beneath the earth's surface. He pulled on one of the support beams to test its strength and then searched the post with his hands for weaknesses. Satisfied, he turned to leave.

Then he saw the rope.

He dropped to one knee and picked up the snakelike coil. Kira felt the tremor of apprehension. She followed his visual inspection of the ground inside the tunnel and then watched with him, frozen in disbelief as another rope suddenly pulled taut.

And then the earth trembled.

A cloud rolled out of the tunnel. In her sleep, Kira coughed, tasting the dust that filled his nostrils, feeling the cold grip of terror around his heart.

With the sounds of breaking wood came cries of panic and the landslide of displaced debris rushing to fill the void.

"Father!" the dark man called out, running blindly back into the tunnel.

He stumbled, falling to the floor and coming face to face with another man on the ground.

"Help me." The words sounded hollow, muted by the earth that closed in around the two men.

The dark man pulled a trowel from his belt, digging through the rubble to provide the trapped man room to maneuver out from under the beam that held its prisoner.

He positioned himself over the broken wood and wrapped his arms around the support, grunting as he struggled to lift it.

Kira felt the flexion of his muscles, the pain of exertion.

A thrill of adrenalin.

From behind came excited voices of people coming to help. Hands reached in to pull the trapped man free.

"Papa!" the dark man shouted into the clouds of dust again, his voice hoarse. He clamored further into the tunnel, shoveling back handfuls of loosened dirt, coughing as the rushing earth tried to suffocate him.

Kira's breathing had become labored, living the events of the dream. And then a tear fell from her eyes when the dark man found his father.

"No," she moaned in her sleep.

"NOOOOOOO!" The dark man's agonized cry echoed in her dream, dislodging caches of earth.

Her eyes popped open and she sat bolt upright in bed, fighting for air. "Not dead," she choked, tears streaming down her face.

You must help him.

Not sure if she was awake or still dreaming, she closed her eyes again until her breathing returned to normal and the images faded.

Pulling her legs up to her chest, she lay her head on her knees and cried.

CHAPTER 2

Watching the gentle rise and fall of hills transfigure into the dirty overcrowded buildings of Naples, Kira felt increasing apprehension over her decision to go on to Herculaneum.

She reached for her journal, the letter from home bookmarking the entries that chronicled the beginning of her quest to Italy.

June 12. That was the day she sat with Maeve Ryan, sharing a bottle of wine and hearing the stories about the excavation near Pompeii. That was the day she discovered the clue that inflamed her imagination until she was certain she had unlocked the secret of the Holy Grail. She read the words again, that page of her journal becoming more dog-eared.

> *She spoke of the Casa del Fioretti and of Herculaneum. Of the time of the volcano and a visit from St. Paul. Like an old Irish storyteller, she sat back with her eyes closed, feeling the effects of the wine as much as I was, I'm sure.*
>
> *It began as a vague remembrance, a detail that had been unearthed during the excavations, and then her religious background began its train of free association. It was difficult to contain my excitement once my imagination took over. The more this Irish Catholic woman told me about St. Paul, the more it began to make sense to me.*
>
> *The bright light that blinded him that day on the road to Damascus, the miracles he performed on Malta and the extraordinary*

events that followed him after that day. I couldn't help but relate the story to the legends of the grail. Blinding light, miracles, supernatural phenomenon.

Was it possible? A treasure, ultimately buried by the hand of God under the cataclysm of the volcanic eruption.

It must have been the wine, or maybe it was the mood of the night, sitting in an English garden drinking wine with a kindred soul, that made me think of the grail. This woman has ignited my imagination, making me wonder if, in fact, the grail could exist.

Maybe its just the effects of the wine, maybe its an excuse not to go home. If, in the clear headed light of day, my thinking doesn't return to the logical and rational, maybe I'll make application to Herculaneum and return with her to Italy.

The entry on June 13 was the list of "cons," reasons Kira should return home, marked by the letter that had arrived so timely. It was guilt that made it all seem so unreal on that following day.

But it was the need to escape that had driven her to England in the first place and more than the guilt, the letter renewed that point with greater emphasis.

A reply was in order, yet she couldn't bring herself to answer. The marriage proposal from Joe Cochran was forthcoming; his letters grew increasingly nearer the subject and increasingly critical of her impulsive trip to Europe in search of a "romantic invention."

Kira Ellison was 32 years old and six-foot-one inches tall. The men that weren't intimidated by her height were usually motivated by curiosity, regarding her more as a freak of nature. Although Joe had always been a very good friend, his relationship with her had been lukewarm at best. It wasn't that she was against marriage; it was the lack of ardor that made her think there must be something better.

The moment she had seen the ad in her archeology magazine she saw her way out. She had signed on for two weeks at an archeological site near Cadbury Castle—Camelot. A vacation abroad could provide her with new material for the junior high school students she taught along with a fresh, firsthand perspective on European history.

The train was slowing, approaching the Stazione Centrale. She closed the book in her lap and looked out the window, watching a man walking along the sidewalk just ahead of the train.

He was easily taller than she was even though Kira stood shoulder to shoulder with most of the male population. Somehow she had expected the Italian population to be more diminutive.

His hair hung in loose, black curls to his collar, his shoulders broad beneath a blue plaid cotton shirt. Each stride commanded attention, his head held high and proud. He reminded her of the dark man she dreamt about the night before.

The dream was still fresh in her memory, bringing back the anxiety. She had spent the first hour on the train from Rome analyzing what could have sparked such a dream, finally interpreting the dark man as herself, associating the loss of his father with her own recent loss and attributing the location to her expected destination. She knew the dark man too well; his thoughts had mirrored her own.

While the train wheels squealed into the Stazione Centrale, Kira tucked her journal into her backpack and reached for the purse she bought to hold her new reference books.

People began bouncing off one another, pulling out luggage in anticipation of getting off the train. Kira clutched her backpack tightly wishing, as she averted the stares of enterprising Neopolitans, that she had heeded the advice to travel in a group.

With a jerk, the train came to a stop. Using the foreward momentum, Kira pulled herself to her feet.

In the crush of people that pushed her through the narrow door and out onto the platform, an invisible hand reached out to pinch her, squeezing her bottom appreciatively.

She squeaked, turning to locate the offender but saw only the scattering crowd of people dispersing in all directions. From behind her came a tug at her shoulder and then a small Italian was running through the station with her purse—the book bag.

She lifted an arm to call out and then reconsidered, intimidated by her lack of command over the language and the unfamiliar environment.

"It's only books," she said quietly, her concern growing.

She abandoned all thoughts of visiting the Museo Archeologico Nazionale. All the warnings of traveling alone in Southern Italy which she had previously ignored were being perfectly illustrated for her now.

"Circumvesuviana," she reminded herself, looking for the train that would complete the last leg of her journey.

"Make sure ye get the right train," Maeve had warned her. "Ye dinna want ta end up in Torre del Greco. 'Tis easy ta take the wrong train."

But which was the right train? She turned her head in search of a sign, colliding sharply against a broad male chest.

"Oh! I'm so sorry!" she apologized, stepping back to gather her wits. Looking at his face, she gasped.

You must help him.

He was indeed taller than she was. His black eyes looked right through her, set deep in an otherwise expressionless face. "Are you all right?" he asked in nearly perfect English, reaching out a solicitous hand to steady her.

She shied away, unnerved by the flesh and blood incarnation of her dream. She pulled her backpack tightly to her, staring at the dark man.

"You're okay," she whispered with a sudden intake of air.

The corners of his eyes softened and he brushed at the front of his shirt, his mouth twitching with amusement. "Yes, I'm fine. Not so easily bruised."

She backpedaled, frightened. As she stared at him, she wondered if the nightmare had been a premonition. "Your father?" She asked the question before she realized she had spoken.

He tilted his head warily, his mouth firmly set into a scowl. He squinted his eyes before he finally asked, "Do I know you?"

Turning away, she saw a conductor standing on the platform and started toward him, but the dark man reached out to hold her back.

He released her immediately, pulling back as if he had received a jolt of electricity. They stood staring at each other, neither of them knowing quite what to say.

You must help him.

When she heard the words in the dream, she thought they had been the dark man's thoughts as he reached out for his father. Now she wondered if she had gotten it backward.

In her sleep, she had shared this man's deepest emotions. Standing face to face with him, she felt like a voyeur, much like waking from an erotic dream and seeing the subject of her desire standing before her.

Flustered, Kira turned her head and continued down the platform. "Excuse me," she called out, holding up a hand to attract the conductor's attention. "Can you help me?"

He began a colorful tirade in rapid Italian dialect accompanied by an orchestration of his arms that left Kira baffled.

"Scuzi," Kira started again. She waved her hand toward the trains, the little bit of Italian she did know abandoning her. "Ercolano?"

"You are looking for a train to Ercolano?"

She turned slowly, half afraid to acknowledge the dark man. Forcing a smile, she pushed her glasses back up the bridge of her nose. "Do you know which train I should take?" she asked politely.

"I am going there myself," he offered, bowing his head slightly.

"Oh." She looked back at the conductor nervously.

The conductor smiled benignly, tipping his hat to the man behind Kira. "Padrone," he greeted. He nodded toward Kira, speaking his

Italian more slowly. "She is so tall! But her hair—it shines like the sun."

She was less surprised that she understood what he said than by the reaction of the dark man. "Padrone," as he had been called, flinched, and his fingers began counting off against his thumb, nails clicking as they passed in turn.

He extended an arm, directing her toward the train. "You are American?" The question sounded more like an accusation.

"Yes."

"I spent some time at the University of Arizona."

"Oh? I've never been there." His sudden materialization caught her off guard. Face to face with a stranger she felt she knew as well as she knew herself, her normal defenses were paralyzed.

"You are going to Herculaneum?"

Kira climbed into the train ahead of him. "Why do you say that?"

"We do not get many visitors to Ercolano—except for the excavations."

"It's very good of you to direct me to the right train."

"I would advise you not to travel alone if you can avoid it," he suggested coolly. "Are you meeting someone in Ercolano?"

She bristled with the patronizing tone of his question. "You've been very kind. Thank you for your help."

A flicker of something, amusement? registered behind his dark eyes at her dismissal. He proffered a slight nod of his head without taking his eyes from her. Kira returned the gesture and resumed her search for a seat.

Beside a window, a gaunt looking man sat alone. His blond hair curled slightly where it had grown just to the nape of his neck. Eager to escape from the dark Italian, Kira stopped beside the seat. "Scuzi," she began hesitantly, smiling and motioning to the seat.

"Je vous en prie," he offered, standing.

"French," she noted half to herself.

"Yes," he answered in English. "*Americaine*?"

"*Oui*," she answered, exhausting the extent of her French vocabulary.

"You are traveling alone?" His accent reflected the intonations of a British tutor.

"I'm joining a party in Ercolano," she replied, taking the seat.

"I am Jean-Marc Lavasseur." He resumed his seat, extending a hand.

"Kira Ellison."

"You are going to Herculaneum?"

Kira smiled, her transparency now obvious even to her. "I'm joining a private excavation at the Casa del Fioretti."

Jean-Marc reached into his pocket and pulled out his business card. "Then we will be working together."

"You're going there, too?"

"Welcome to the past," he said while the train lurched forward.

"Departement des antiquites grecques, etrusques, et romaines," she read from the card. "The Louvre?"

He nodded, pleased that he had impressed her. "I come to learn."

"Is this your first trip here?"

He shook his head. "*Non*, I go back to Paris one weekend each month. I have come here it is four months."

"Tell me about the site."

"Herculaneum is buried 20 meters below the city."

"I remember reading that." Kira leaned back in her seat, unconsciously reaching for the purse containing her books that was no longer there and then turning toward the Frenchman, ready to glean whatever knowledge he was willing to share.

"The first discoveries remain hidden beneath the streets of Ercolano. There are doors in the city that lead down through the first tunnels, but these excavations are necessarily limited because of the dense population above."

"And the public excavations?"

He waved an arm. "*Formidable* examples of architecture, engineering. These buildings still have roofs. In Pompeii there are not so much."

"Would you go with me into the public excavations? And I was really hoping to see the Museo in Naples."

Jean-Marc threw back his shoulders. "Je suis marié!"

Kira blushed. "I didn't mean to suggest…its just that everyone keeps telling me not to go out on my own."

"But of course," he laughed. "I will assist you in finding a suitable guide."

"In the meantime, may I impose on your company until we reach the Casa del Fioretti?"

"I am honored."

Kira looked up to see the dark Italian walking back down the aisle.

"You have met Il Padrone?" Jean-Marc observed.

She pulled at a flap of her backpack and turned her attention back to the Frenchman. "Not formally. Who is he?"

Jean-Marc nodded in his direction. "Dominic Fioretti. It is his excavation."

Kira's mouth fell open in surprise. "Then who is Franco Fioretti? He's the one who accepted my application."

"His brother. Franco is been back only a short time."

"Yes, I know. He was in England."

"You will have met Franco?" Jean-Marc was reevaluating Kira with a hint of amusement.

"No. I got to the site just after he left, but everyone talked about him. He has quite a reputation."

Jean-Marc laughed. "He is very…" he seesawed a hand while struggling for the correct word, "*aimable*. You understand?"

Kira felt the rising temperature of her cheeks again, tightening the flap on her backpack once more. "They say he is a Greco-Roman specialist."

"You would be, too, if you grew up in such a place."

"You don't think much of him."

"I do not work much with him."

The train began to slow. Tall buildings crowded the streets, centuries of dust tarnishing crevices and adding gloom to the dark avenues. Laundry hung between the balconies like flags.

Mt. Vesuvius loomed along the horizon. "I'm told the volcano has been dormant since World War II," Kira commented, her mind sifting through the information she had read preparing for her arrival.

World War II. Hitler had been searching for religious artifacts, and Mussolini had financed some of the excavations of Herculaneum before the volcano erupted again. She put a hand to her shoulder once more and then caught herself again, shaking her head angrily over the lost books.

Still, the information clicked into place. Could the grail really exist? If only it would manifest itself the way…

"Their father," she asked Jean-Marc, recalling the dream. "Is he dead?"

Jean-Marc crossed himself. "Repose en paix."

❧   ❧   ❧

Dominic settled into one of the compartments on the train, satisfied that the girl at least had an escort. Another man made a move to join Dominic and then thought better of it when met with a chilling glare.

His mood softened thinking of her. She was lovely. He had always thought that a woman with hair like the sun should be blond, and yet the golden brown shades of hers had impressed him immediately, as it had the conductor on the platform.

He cursed an overactive imagination. It was no more than a joke his father liked to tease him with, this woman who was the sun. But how had she known about his father?

A fresh stab of pain pierced his grief stricken heart and he caught his breath. Vengeance would be swift when he ferreted out the murderer. His thoughts clouded red with anger and through them he saw her face again, breaking through like the sun that follows a storm. Without thinking, he closed his eyes to absorb the warmth.

It was the first moment of serenity he had felt since his father's passing, a moment he quickly escaped. He had no time for whimsy. Until he found who plotted against his father's life, he could not allow himself to be distracted. There was little doubt that his own life depended on finding the answer.

CHAPTER 3

She followed Jean-Marc into the locanda, walking past him as he opened the door for her.

The symmetry of the entry showed the design of the house to be U-shaped. A curved staircase rose up from the foyer to an avenue marked by doors. Below, a corridor disappeared behind the staircase on the main floor to the rear of the house and, at the other end of the foyer, another disappeared into the recesses.

There was a dome overhead that let the sunlight pour into the bright entrance setting off sparks of light in the marble all around. On the floor, a carefully designed mosaic gave the effect of an oriental carpet.

A blond girl came walking through one of the corridors and into the foyer, bright blue eyes suddenly alert on the new arrival. She did a little hop, her hair bouncing against her shoulders, and then walked a little faster toward Kira. "You must be the new girl. I'm Laura."

Kira nodded in her direction, feeling the appraisal of her new companion.

"Boy I bet someone's always trying to recruit you for a basketball game," she commented. "Do you speak English?"

Kira looked at Jean-Marc for reassurance.

"I will leave you in Laura's care," he said. He gave a little bow and then proceeded to jog up the staircase.

"Your room's next to mine," Laura volunteered. "It's an adjoining suite. Maybe the rest of your luggage has already arrived."

"This is all I brought," Kira told her, holding out her backpack.

Laura walked sideways up the marble staircase, keeping a disbelieving eye on Kira. "Italian men appreciate women. If you want to get pinched, you're going to have to wear something other than baggy sweaters and jeans."

"And if I don't want to get pinched?"

Ahead of her, Laura was opening a door along the hallway overlooking the foyer. Picking up her pace, Kira hurried up the remaining stairs.

"Married?" Laura asked.

"No."

"Engaged, then?"

"Does your world revolve around men?" Kira asked shortly, looking around her new living quarters until her eyes rested on Laura once again. "Do you know what was happening in the world when Mt. Vesuvius erupted? Doesn't this site mean something other to you than Italian men?"

Laura plopped down on the white coverlet of the double bed. "Well...no..."

"Christianity was spreading. Persecution was beginning. Rome was about to burn."

Laura leaned back on her hands with a disinterested look on her face. "No kidding?"

Kira leaned on a writing desk to look out the window across a landscape of vineyards and trees, the fresh scent of lemons rising up to greet her. She turned slowly back around to look at her American companion. "Why are you here? Other than for the men, of course."

"Mosaics. I'm going on to Ravenna to study when I'm done here." She hopped off the bed and pointed toward their common door.

"My room's through there," then she nodded toward the corridor, "or through the hall."

A small woman appeared in the open doorway, clearing her throat. She looked uncertainly at Laura and then addressed Kira.

"I am Anna Giannini. If you require my services, please feel free to call on me." She was dressed in a dark blue linen suit, her dark hair streaked with gray and tied into a knot at the back of her neck. Her English was heavily accented, each word spoken deliberately. "Signore Franco would like to meet with you when you have made yourself comfortable."

"What's the rush?" Laura asked impertinently.

"Ché?" the small woman asked, prompting Laura for explanation.

Turning her head and waving it off, Laura went to the window beside Kira.

"Where would I find him?" Kira asked politely.

"In the study. It is the first door at the bottom of the stairs," Anna replied. "Do you find everything you require?"

"She only just got here," Laura snapped. "She hasn't had time to do anything except drop her pack."

"I *would* like to make a phone call," Kira told Anna.

"I will assist you after you have seen Il Signore," she offered.

"Wouldn't want to keep Il Signore waiting now would we?" Laura said snidely.

Anna kept her eyes on Laura, bowing and then disappearing quietly down the corridor.

Laura walked back over to the door and slammed it shut. "She attends their every need," she said sarcastically, and then a smile spread across her face as she finished her thought, "although I'm not sure that it wouldn't have its merits. You know some of the superstitious types say that Dominic is really one of the statues come to life to reclaim what was his. He certainly has the look."

"And the other? Is he made of stone too?"

She sighed. "Now there's a man. The dark hair, the blue eyes." She looked at Kira warily. "So what would you do if a handsome Italian were to flirt with you?"

Kira smiled. "He's all yours."

Laura breezed over to the common door. "I'll let you get settled so you can answer your summons."

❦   ❦   ❦

Kira floated down the curved series of steps overwhelmed by her lavish accommodations.

She craned to look down the corridor at the closed door of the study where the Signor of the Casa attended his guests. Her hand slid off the polished wood of the banister as she arrived back in the foyer.

Doric columns lined the passage to the rooms beyond. The house had the feel of a museum. Two leather wing chairs sat outside the door in front of her, reminding her that this was still a place of business, even if it was their home.

Kira let her hand fall against the door, suddenly nervous at the prospect of meeting the man who owned all this.

"*Entrata*," The lilt of the single Italian word was only loud enough to penetrate the solid door although its resonance seemed to echo inside the room after the door gave way to a gentle push.

"Ah, Miss Ell-ee-sone." Kira smiled at the mispronunciation of her surname twisted into Italian. "Please sit down."

The room was dark. One small window was overshadowed by the wooden bookshelves that cloaked the walls.

Occupying their own sections of the bookshelves behind the big oak desk a bronze statue of the patron saint, Hercules, and a beautifully chiseled Aphrodite graced the study. Atop the desk was a large sculpture of Priapus, his eternally erect phallus standing at attention.

The strong Roman nose, the long face and the small mouth of the model on the desk had been handed down through generations to the man seated behind the desk. Franco Fioretti looked up from an array of photographs scattered across the top of the desk, a magnifying glass in his hand. His eyes sparkled like mountain lakes reflecting the first snow fall. "You are a history teacher, no?"

"Yes."

"You are much more pretty than I think for such a dreary occupation."

Kira shifted uncomfortably in her chair. "You will excuse me for asking, but if you find history dreary, why would you sponsor an excavation?"

His broad chest expanded with a cleansing intake of air. "But you misunderstand me. Here history comes to life, no? In a classroom, it is much more…how can I say…difficult to appreciate?"

Kira crossed her legs and wiped the heels of her hands on her jeans. "I would hope my students don't share your opinion. Perhaps my experience here will help me to breathe a little more life into their lessons."

"We are honored to have you." An enigmatic smile took years off her first guess at his age. "Let me show you some of my pictures, a preview." He waved to Kira to come around the desk.

Kira leaned anxiously across the desk reaching for some of the photographs.

A mosaic and a fresco were easily identifiable. She reached out to pull more toward her, but Franco caught her hand.

His quick movement mixed the scent of his cologne with the still air in the study, his warm hand closing around Kira's. "You are most enthusiastic," he said in a deep, honeyed voice.

She pulled back, startled, when a flash of light on metal caught her eye. Franco was sitting in a wheelchair. Her eyes immediately darted back to his face, flushing when he met her stare.

"Is something wrong?" His words were slow and measured. His hand tightening around hers.

"I'm sorry," she struggled to find appropriate words. "I didn't realize…"

"That I am a cripple?" he finished.

Her mouth hung open limply, waiting for the words to walk out and rescue her. Instead, she closed the escape route and tried to smile.

"An unfortunate accident," he explained, "but not permanent. I assure you I am quite healthy."

❦   ❦   ❦

Large, leaded glass windows allowed the sunlight to flood his work room tucked back on the family side of the horseshoe. Dominic sat alone at the long metal table, picking through debris for the smaller testaments that the excavation yielded. Instead of seeing fragments, though, he was seeing suspects. A murderer still walked through the corridors of his home.

With an exasperated grunt, he pushed away from the table and yanked off his rubber gloves, unable to concentrate. He needed to go below, to the quiet of the earth. Nothing else would ease his temper.

Long strides carried him purposefully down the corridor to the foyer, pausing a moment as he neared the study. The muscles along his jaw tightened, irritation with his brother adding to his aggravation. How much longer would it be before Franco would be able to resume his travels and leave Dominic to his work? And then there was Paolo. To have them both home at the same time required more patience than he would ever be able to possess, and with the recent string of events, more trust than he was willing to offer.

He advanced on the closed door of the study, eager to learn whose voices he heard plotting. With a strength borne of animosity, he threw the door open, rocking a statuette of a satyr precariously mounted on a pedestal just inside the room. He struggled for composure, completely unprepared for the sight before him.

She stood leaning beside Franco, a faint blush coloring her cheeks like pink summer roses. Her complexion turned a shade redder, withdrawing her hand from Franco's grasp while she straightened to acknowledge Dominic's entrance into the room.

"Ahh. My brother Dominic," Franco purred in a manner all too familiar to his younger brother.

Dominic watched her straighten her shoulders, nodding once, slowly in recognition.

"This is Kira Ellison," Franco continued. "She has come to us from Cadbury Castle in England."

With the explanation, all the pieces fell into place. The younger Fioretti sauntered into the room, squinting at the tall woman with the golden hair who knocked the wind out of him at the train station. His anger intensified considering how he had allowed thoughts of this woman to ease his troubled mind. It was foolishness to believe his father's taunting of the woman who would find the grail, the woman who would be like the sun.

"I begin to understand." He took measured steps toward Kira, gauging his own reaction. With steely reserve, he stepped close beside her, daring her to move.

"My brother studied radiocarbon dating in America," Franco continued, unfazed. "He oversees all the work done below."

Kira sunk back against the bookcase as if being pressed by some unseen force.

"I have very little patience for fortune hunters," Dominic stated flatly. "I hope my brother has not misled you. I know how persuasive he can be."

He recognized a spark of indignance in her eyes as she took a contumacious step forward. "I'm afraid I don't understand."

Turning, Dominic took the figure of Priapus from the desk into his hands and then looked to Franco. How alike the two were. There were no women safe from Franco's desires. "I am surprised Franco did not tell you how difficult I can be, especially with women who are not here to learn."

"And why else would I be here?" she challenged.

"She has her credentials." Franco straightened in his chair, watching his brother with renewed interest.

"I'm certain she does." Dominic returned the attention of his dark eyes to Kira, making his own inferences as to what credentials Franco would seek out.

Kira's fingers curled into the palms of her hands. "You don't think a woman could possess any intelligence?" She contested.

Dominic's expression remained unchanged, but his eyes swept casually over her, sliding down to assess the long legs hidden beneath blue denim, returning slowly upward to her face. He locked onto her eyes once more, only to find his thoughts distracted by the color of her golden brown hair, the color of the sun. He surprised himself by wanting to believe in her innocence. What a relief it would be to have an intelligent woman working in the excavation. And just maybe….

He took another step, challenging her with his proximity. He bit the insides of his cheeks marveling at the girl's temerity. "An excavation is not an easy place for a woman to work," he finally said.

Her head was tilted only slightly, her eyes holding his resolutely to rebuff the insult he threw at her. "I have experience," she replied more tersely, not giving any ground.

Dominic raised an eyebrow speculatively. "Doing what?"

"Let her be, Dominic," Franco warned in Italian, his voice low and threatening.

"You may be required to do some digging," Dominic suggested, noting the protective tone of Franco's voice.

Kira bit her bottom lip, her temper seething dangerously close to the surface. "That's why I'm here."

The woman had spirit.

Franco forced a cough, amused by Dominic's feigned overreaction. "I will suggest that you visit Anna, Miss Elleesone. You will find her in the office across the hall." He maneuvered his wheelchair around the desk as he spoke until he came to a stop beside his brother. "She will have some guidelines for you and will be able to answer any questions you may have while you are here." He looked at Dominic, daring him to say something further and then he nodded a dismissal. "Thank you for coming."

The two men watched her walk out, flustered and red faced, each in his own way admiring the lovely woman who had come into their home.

This was not the time to lose ground to Franco. The minute the door closed behind her, Dominic turned on his brother. "How could you be so foolish?" he shouted. He paced around the study like a lion trapped in a cage, black eyes flashing, his dark curls flying with every movement of his head.

"We have lost many workers. She has archeological experience—at Cadbury Castle. She paid the fee. Maybe you do not realize what it means to lose so many workers."

"I am fully aware," Dominic barked back at his brother. "This is my excavation now." He thumped his chest for emphasis, leaning over and daring his brother to contradict him. "This is not the time to be parading another of your women through the site."

Franco watched his brother speculatively. "And if I told you this was the first time I met her?"

"You just told me she followed you from England. I wish you would leave your women in the bedroom where they belong." He threw his hands in the air seeking supplication from above before he continued his tirade. "Maybe you are not aware of the rebuilding we have to do below, of both the site and of the morale. That idiot Carlo took half the laborers with him with his wild stories of Papa haunting the excavation. Now they all think they've seen a ghost."

Franco turned the wheelchair away from his brother, looking through the window without a discernible focal point. His voice took on a guarded hush. "And what of this ghost?"

Dominic's shoulders slumped as he collapsed into the chair, hitting his forehead with the palms of his hands. "Papa is dead, Franco."

"But did you look?" With one hand, he expertly spun a wheel so that he faced his brother again.

"Of course I looked. Carlo is an old fool."

"And the others?"

Dominic leveled his eyes on his brother. "It only takes one to get them started."

Franco pressed his fingers together. "Still, he did see something."

"There is no ghost!" Dominic roared, his voice rattling the statues secreted in the bookshelves. He turned away from his brother, wishing he could turn away from his pain and anger as easily. "We need archeologists, Franco, not playmates."

"You want this one for yourself, perhaps?" Franco taunted.

Slamming his hands on the top of the desk, Dominic rose threateningly. The words of protest froze in his throat, thinking back to the ease with which Franco could insinuate himself into a woman's good graces. Even crippled as he was, Kira stood beside him with her hand in his only moment's before, that pretty blush coloring her cheeks.

Why did it always have to come down to this?

"Perhaps she is the light of your life," Franco teased, rolling around to meet his brother behind the desk again, "the one Papa always teased you about." He laid his head back and laughed at finding his younger brother's weakness.

Dominic leaned on the desk, bringing his face level with his brother's. In a deep voice, he growled his retort. "I have no intention of accepting your cast-offs, brother, but rest assured," he paused as he turned to leave the room, "we shall soon discover if she is, in fact, here to work."

Across the hall she sat in Anna's office, talking on the telephone. A fresh wave of anger washed over him at his failure to hide the interest she had sparked in him.

He forced his attention away from her with a sharp turn of his head, looking instead toward the open room at the rear of the casa.

His mood shifted sharply at the sight of two laborers moving through the dining room at breakneck pace in his direction.

"*Santa Maria, Madre de Dio!*" he cursed, moving into the center of the hallway, arms outstretched to intercept the frightened men. "What is this?" he thundered

"Aiyyyyyy!" The first man shrieked in terror as Dominic's hands closed around him. The second man tripped and fell at the foot of one of the columns, grabbing hold of it tightly.

"Il Signore," the laborer in his arms blubbered, looking over his shoulder and crossing himself.

"Humberto!" Dominic scolded, shaking the frightened worker. "Tell me what happened!"

Humberto looked at his employer with wide eyes. "Il Signore," he whispered, again. "I saw your father."

"My father is dead." Dominic's voice echoed with the force of his affirmation.

"Dead too soon," Humberto whispered. "His spirit walks." He pushed away from Dominic and ran toward the foyer.

The other laborer still lay on the floor, trembling, arms wrapped tightly around his anchor.

Dominic rolled his eyes impatiently. "And what is it you think you saw?" he barked.

Letting go of the pillar, the other man waved his arms wildly, the fear in his eyes evident. "There was a flash of light and a great sighing from the walls."

Dominic waved him away, peremptorily dismissing his testimony.

The second laborer scrambled to his feet and hurried past Il Padrone, bowing and crossing himself as he left.

※ ※ ※

Kira tapped her foot, nervously waiting for the overseas connection to complete. She closed her eyes and took another deep breath.

The man was far too antagonistic. In his anger he looked like the devil incarnate, a sharp contrast to his brother's rakish good looks.

"Hello?"

The sound of her brother's voice flooded her with the comforts of home. "Hi, Greg. I'm so glad to hear your voice."

"Kira! I was just getting ready for work. You're not at the airport already, are you?"

She blew out a slow sigh, preparing for his reaction to her news. "No, I'm in Italy."

"Italy!" She winced, hearing the disapproval in his voice. "What are you doing in Italy?"

"Well...Can you pick up my mail for a couple more weeks?"

"How many weeks?"

She cowered, almost afraid to tell him. "Six?"

"Kira!"

She held up her free arm, shrugging her shoulders. "It's not like its a big deal. What—one extra step out the front door? I'll wire you more money for my bills."

"That's not the point." He was quiet for a few minutes but the sound of children in the background fighting for their father's attention filled the void. "What are you doing in Italy?" She could hear the control he fought to hold over his tone.

In the corridor outside Anna Giannini's office there were excited voices, a man speaking in quick, breathy tones. "Well, I met someone in England." Dominic Fioretti appeared in the hallway, looking at her accusingly. She turned her back to him and lowered her voice, cupping the phone with one hand. "I met someone," she continued. "I'm testing a theory."

"Not more of that Holy Grail crap? You weren't really serious about that, were you?"

Kira winced, knowing how foolish she sounded. "Actually, there's a chance it's here." She held up a hand to brook the ensuing argument. "Hear me out. I wasn't serious when I went to England, but I met a woman who piqued my curiosity. I had to come."

"But Italy? Aren't you reaching a little bit? Joe's not going to wait forever."

"All the better," she muttered.

"Aw c'mon. What's wrong with Joe? Honestly, Kira. It isn't as if you have the whole male population panting after you. What's wrong with him, anyway?"

"Haven't we had this discussion?"

"You're thirty-two, you're not getting any younger."

"And he's not getting any older." Kira smiled indulgently. "Why ruin a perfectly good friendship? I want the man I marry to be a little more…" She looked out toward the corridor again, checking to be sure Dominic had left. "Joe wants someone to mother him and wait on him. And what is it with you men that you can't believe a woman capable of any intelligence?" She spoke the last words louder than was necessary, watching the corridor for looming shadows.

She heard him chuckle. "Bet you're glad you taught that English as a Second Language class now."

"Thank you, Mrs. DeLuca." She smiled, wishing her brother was standing beside her instead of on the phone thousands of miles away. "I miss you Greg."

"Don't miss me, miss Joe. What am I supposed to say to him?"

"Don't tell him anything."

"And when he asks where you are?"

She threw a hand in the air. "Tell him I threw myself into a volcano."

She pictured her brother pacing around his bedroom in the duplex, half dressed while he tried to think of something supportive to say in spite of his objections. "There obviously isn't anything I can do about it. You're there and I'm here." Again came that sigh she recognized so well. She smiled.

The resignation came through in his voice. "I hope you find what you're looking for. Look, I have to get going or I'll be late for work. Geez—I'm late already."

"Let me tell you where I'm staying."

Hanging up the phone, she knew he was right. Joe deserved the courtesy of a phone call at least. If she waited a few more minutes maybe she'd miss him. A frown of resignation creased her brow realizing she couldn't put off the inevitable forever.

Pulling her address book from her pocket, Kira looked up the phone number. She knew almost every phone number she dialed on a regular basis—every number except Joe's.

Kira took another deep breath and began punching in the string of numbers that would connect her overseas again.

"Hello?" came his sleepy voice.

"It's Kira," she announced, tapping her fingers on the desk. She was smiling again, glad to hear his voice after all. "How's everything?"

"Fine. When are you coming in?"

She took a deep breath and closed her eyes. "Next month."

"Next month! I thought you were done in England."

"I'm in Italy."

"Italy?"

She looked at the phone in her hands, checking for loose pieces. "Can you hear me all right? You're repeating everything I say."

"You were looking for Arthurian relics," he reminded her sharply. "Those are in England."

She sat down behind Anna's desk and held her head with one hand, leaning on her elbow. "No, the Holy Grail is a religious artifact. Look, I met this lady—Maeve Ryan. She came from this site, here in Italy—its near Pompeii—Oh you wouldn't understand."

"Kira, I need you here."

Closing her eyes again, she could see Joe, his thin blond hair—the round face. She opened her eyes sharply, resenting the way he needed her. "It would be stupid to come home when I'm so close."

"You said yourself there was nothing in England. You've had your little vacation; now, don't you think it's time to come home?"

The imperious tone of his voice sent off the same old irritation. "This is more than just a little vacation." Her free hand went to her hip.

"You should have plenty of things to tell your history class. Exactly what do you expect to find in Italy?"

"I don't know, but the possibility exists of either the grail or other significant finds." She looked around the room, searching for something to distract her. Her fingers curled into her palm again.

"There's something I want to talk to you about, Kira, and I had hoped to say it to you in person. You know how fond I am of you..."

"I'll be home next month. It can wait."

"We're not getting any younger. I really think we should discuss it. Kira..."

She tapped at the receiver. "I think we're losing the connection, Joe. I can hardly hear you. If its that important I think you should wait until I get home."

He laughed, not fooled with her ruse. "I guess it'll have to."

She smiled, relieved. "I'll be in touch."

She returned the phone quickly to its resting place hunching her shoulders to protect herself from the images of a future with Joe Cochran.

"Kirie?"

Kira lifted her head, and smiled. She rose from behind the desk and walked out to meet Maeve Ryan. "I am so glad to see a friendly face!"

Maeve held out her hands, offering a matronly smile. A brown headband held the mousy hues of her hair off her face. Her clothes were covered with dust. "You've had some trouble, then?"

Kira checked the corridor, half expecting to see the dark satyr lingering behind one of the pillars. "Well, no."

"Aye, I suppose I know what ye mean. Things are a bit different since I've been back meself." She cocked her head to one side. "Come sit with me."

A large open room lay at the end of the corridor. Tiled floors and elaborate light fixtures indicated that it had been a ballroom once. Now it was dotted with tables and chairs peopled by smudged workers.

Maeve directed Kira to a table, pulling up her own chair.

Kira looked at the people around her, noticing the furtive looks. "Are they always such a cheerful bunch?"

"'Tis only that they're frightened."

Kira looked directly at Maeve, noticing that she, too, was perhaps a little paler than the last time they met. "Why would they be frightened?"

Maeve waved a hand carelessly in front of her face, dismissing the notion. "They're a superstitious lot, they are. They'll be right enough when Il Padrone comes back up."

"What's he doing?"

"Just havin' a look below, to see that all is as it should be, isn't he."

"Then they don't know who did it?"

Maeve was unable to mask her surprise. "Did what?"

"The cave-in."

"While we were in England? I've been told it was an accident. Have they told ye different?"

Kira studied her fingernails nervously. "No. Actually they haven't said anything."

Maeve leaned over the table conspiratorially. "But you'll have heard something different maybe?"

"What's he looking for?" Kira dodged.

Maeve sat back, her skin nearly as ashy as the dust that covered it. "His father."

"But I thought his father was dead."
"Aye, he is."

CHAPTER 4

❈

Kira woke to the sounds of singing in the streets of Ercolano. Outside the casa, vendors called out to their customers, describing the contents of their carts with lilting tunes and singsong chants.

She listened to the voices carrying through the early morning, blending together and challenging each other at the same time. Smiling to herself, she thought how much more enjoyable it was to wake to the sound of human song than to the obnoxious buzzing of an alarm clock.

From below came the smell of freshly brewed coffee. In the hallway outside her room, Kira heard other guests descending, prompting her to dress quickly for her initiation into the excavation.

Opening her door, she found Laura leaning on the balustrade overlooking the foyer, slender legs stretching down to white anklets and gym shoes. "Isn't it uncomfortable to work in a skirt?" Kira asked.

"Depends on what kind of work you're doing." Laura winked and started down the staircase.

Kira followed the younger girl through the length of columns past Franco's office and into the dining area.

Curious eyes followed the new arrival to her table. "How does it feel to be the new kid on the block?" Laura nudged with an elbow. "How tall are you, anyway?"

"Taller than most." It was a common question, but people were often more shocked by the answer than the supposition.

"Educate me," Kira challenged. "Tell me about the work."

Laura waved a hand flippantly in the air. "Work is work. You dig, you get dusty, you get muddy. Sometimes you find something." Her hair fell in front of her face while she bent over her plate, concentrating on spearing some grapes with her fork.

Jean-Marc pulled a chair up backwards to their table and set down his plate. "May I join you?"

When Dominic Fioretti entered a room, even the air seemed to come to attention. Feeling the change, Kira turned to see him standing in the entryway.

"Buona Sera," he greeted the gathering. His gaze rested momentarily on Kira. Continuing in Italian, he gestured toward Kira, her grasp of the language good enough to interpret his introduction of her to the group

She rose to only three-quarters and quickly resumed her seat, hazarding a glimpse under veiled eyelashes at her host. He approached each table in turn, greeting the workers and addressing their progress individually.

When he reached her table, he spoke to Kira's companions first. "Laura, you are with the mosaicist? I am sure you will find her work most fascinating."

"Most fascinating," she echoed somewhat short of enthusiastically.

He paid little attention to Laura, either not hearing or not caring that she seemed less than thrilled with her assignment.

"Monsieur," he addressed Jean-Marc, "Comment ca va? Qu'est ce que tu decouvrit?" he demanded in French.

Jean-Marc looked at Kira and then back at Dominic before responding in English as a courtesy. "I believe we see today."

"Bene, bene. And you, Miss Ellison, somewhat different than your classroom, I expect."

"I am anxious to see Pompeii."

"Then you are at the wrong site," he stated flatly.

Jean-Marc jumped to the defense. "And yet it is all part of the same disaster."

Dominic flashed a condescending smile at Kira which only served to enhance the sardonic image. "It seems you have *another* admirer. Perhaps you can observe Monsieur Lavasseur today until you become more familiar with our work here."

"Another admirer?" Laura echoed quietly, looking suspiciously at Kira.

"Give me a break," Kira retorted under her breath.

The Frenchman rose to his feet, inviting Kira to follow. Accepting the challenge, she bumped the table in her hurry and upset a vase. It fell to the floor, shattering irreparably. Kira covered her face with her hands in horror before she fell to her knees to begin collecting the shards of pottery.

"Leave it," Dominic waved testily. "You should realize that we are surrounded by treasures, Miss Ellison. Please use more care."

"It was an accident," Laura defended.

"A very unfortunate accident," Dominic agreed.

Jean-Marc knelt beside Kira and laid a hand on her shoulder. "What do you see in these pieces?" he whispered, cocking an eyebrow in the direction of the fragments.

Stopping to examine a piece of the broken vase, Kira turned it over in her hands, running her fingers along the sharp edges of a cheap decoration. "At least this can be replaced. I'd be happy to pay for a new one," she offered, offering the pieces up to Dominic.

Dominic raised one eyebrow. "It will not be necessary."

With his departure, she left the pieces on the floor and rose to stand beside Jean-Marc, his smile belying his amusement. "Let me take you down to our corner of Herculaneum," he invited, motioning through an arch.

Outside the dining room, a courtyard joined the two sections of the house, a great chasm laying open the villa below.

Kira held her breath descending wooden steps anchored into the volcanic debris.

Tiered walls were dug out of the earth, the garden section marking the floor below. "You can see the levels clearly," Jean-Marc said, pointing to the wall of earth as they descended. "At the top is the lava, the final stage. The next layer is from the surge." He threw his hands up in the air recreating the eruption of the volcano. "And at the bottom is the ash."

Scaffolding ran the length of the second story of the underground villa. "These are the cubicolas," Jean-Marc continued. "Below them is the triclinium." He pointed down through an arch in the earth that ran beneath the Casa overhead. "Here is the atrium and the tablinum. Here I work."

Approaching the floor of the excavation, Kira noted every protrusion along the path, reaching out to touch half-buried columns before passing through into the tunnels. The floor below changed from dirt into marble.

Kira stopped, overcome by the impressions of the cave-in from her dream. She had seen Dominic standing where she was now—seen the subterranean garden and the walls of a villa carved out of the earth's crust.

"Something is wrong?" Jean-Marc asked.

Kira shook her head and shrugged her shoulders to throw off the mantle of dread.

"Claustrophobia? This is the right word?" he suggested.

"No," she answered firmly. "Deja vu." She smiled at her guide. "You understand?"

Reassured, he motioned for her to go ahead of him.

She ducked through an opening and passed into a room carved out of the volcanic rock. A string of lights illuminated the dark chamber. The air was heavy with dust, and yet it seemed to carry the scent of a beach—sand and silt. In spite of the warmth of Italian summer, Kira shivered.

"This is the tablinum," Jean-Marc continued, brushing his blond hair off his thin face. "Il Padrone believes we will find many interesting pieces here."

"Il Padrone is hopeful, at any rate." Dominic Fioretti's voice echoed behind them. "But it is hard work, and requires much patience. Maybe you would prefer to observe."

"I came to work," Kira bristled, refusing to be intimidated.

"Anything that is uncovered must be carefully catalogued and reported to me," he instructed. "Everything is sifted for even the smallest fragments. Are you familiar with these procedures?"

Kira's nostrils flared and she took a deep breath. She crossed the chamber and pointed to a mound protruding from the wall. "Furniture?" She reached down and picked up a piece of lava that glistened under the artificial lights. "Silver—maybe a spoon? Should I hand each to you as I find them?"

Dominic motioned to the wall beside him, seemingly unmoved by her demonstration of temper. "Why don't you work here. We are trying to clean this mural."

Kira assessed the dirty wall beside Il Padrone. There had been no murals at the excavation in England, but she had seen workers clean painted areas with brushes. She reached into the tool pack around her waist.

"I would suggest a paintbrush for this area," he said, echoing her thoughts.

She withdrew her hand from her tool pack, flaunting what she already held. "Like this one?"

Behind his back, the fingers on his hands began clicking as each nail struck against his thumb. Dominic turned quickly on his heel and ducked back out and into the open courtyard.

Jean-Marc was masking a smile as he shrugged his shoulders. "Everything we find belongs to the Italian government," he explained. "Il Padrone is not always a patient teacher, but he is a very good archeologist."

He reached down to right a bucket on the floor in front of the furniture mound, uncovering the tools that lay waiting for his return. Pulling out a work-worn trowel he placed a loving hand to the lump in front of him. "You must understand. There are those that come who search only for immediate treasure. They have no interest in the history."

Kira turned her attention to the wall. "Isn't it possible to appreciate both the history and the potential treasures?"

She could feel his eyes on her back. "I do not believe the Treasure of St. Paul truly exists." His words hung heavily in the still air.

Kira turned around sharply. "What?"

He shrugged his shoulders. "He was very poor when he traveled to Rome—a prisoner. What could he leave behind?" He began to scrape away at the bulky shape before him.

"What are you talking about?" She prodded.

He shrugged his shoulders again. "It is only a story. I thought maybe you had heard it."

But Kira's heartbeat had quickened. She wasn't the only one who had formulated a theory about St. Paul.

❦ ❦ ❦

"Lay down your tools," came the muted echo through the dig. Kira eagerly returned her brush to her belt and followed the throng of excavators to the dining room where they assembled around the tables. The kitchen staff was laying out food and drink for the hungry workers.

Voices chattered freely, marked by frequent bursts of laughter. The absence of the brothers evinced a different personality from the group assembled.

Laura bounded through the dining room searching out her new companion. "So what did *you* find today?"

"A painted wall. How about you?"

"More pretty tiles stuck in the wall," she sighed.

"Do you think there could be Christian artifacts here?"

"In this place?" Laura remarked. "Not likely. Haven't you seen the blatant hedonism?"

"They uncovered the mark of a cross at Herculaneum," Kira pointed out.

"A shelf brace," Jean-Marc said, pulling out a seat at the table.

Kira folded her arms in front of her, leaning over the table. "But the nail holes were top and bottom, not on each side."

"It is certainly noteworthy," he agreed, "but very unlikely."

"And what about the Pater Noster at Pompeii," Kira persisted. "All this was buried at the very dawn of Christianity. Certainly the evidence will be slim. Consider the times they were living in. That's what makes the discovery so significant." She turned her chair to face Jean-Marc. "You mentioned the Treasure of St. Paul. He was here. Wouldn't that indicate the possibility of Christian artifacts?"

Maeve Ryan joined the small group. "You'll find the artifacts here quite different from those at Cadbury."

"I'm counting on that." Kira replied.

Maeve looked skeptically at the people gathered around the table. "Is it treasure yer lookin' for?"

Laura leaned forward on the table, intrigued by the turn in the conversation.

"I would hope to find *something*, whether valuable or not seems hardly relevant at this point," Kira maintained. "Just imagine the significance of Christian discoveries."

Laura sat back again, disappointed. "You really did come to dig, didn't you?"

Her three companions gave Laura identical looks of reproach. "What?" she asked, shrugging her shoulders in defense.

A hush fell across the convivial group. Kira looked up to see Dominic standing on the edge of the excavation pulling gloves off his hands and talking animatedly with another man.

He looked vacantly into the dining room while he listened to what the other man had to say and then lifted his head slightly and squinted when he saw Kira. Nodding and waving a hand impatiently at the man beside him, Dominic made his way into the casa.

Jean-Marc acknowledged him amiably with a nod of his head, saluting with a fork full of pasta while the three women pretended not to notice.

"You are making our new arrival at home?" he asked Kira's companions.

"But we're old friends now, aren't we, Kirie?" Maeve answered.

He squinted at Kira again. "Oh course, I'd almost forgotten that you were in England, too. Naturally Kira would not have met one without meeting the other."

Before Kira could contradict him, they were interrupted by the man who had been standing outside with Dominic. Following close on Il Padrone's heels, he now stood beside Dominic once more, waving his arms effusively as he spewed out rapid Italian dialect.

He was a young man, his dark, short cropped hair greased down showing rows where he had pulled a comb through it. His eyes were set wide apart under bushy eyebrows. Kira stared at him, not quite recognizing what she found so familiar about his appearance.

Dominic responded brusquely to the other man's complaints in the same, barely intelligible speech patterns, waving to the quartet at the table.

Wide, thick lips, grinned lasciviously while he bowed, paying particular attention to Laura, who returned a coquettish smile.

Dominic cuffed the young man across the back of the head, displacing a strand of greasy hair. With a flourish of his hands and grumbles of Italian, he grabbed the younger man by the arm, escorting him down the corridor.

"What was that all about?" Kira asked.

"Now there's a bad sort, he is," Maeve muttered. "Don't be paying any mind to Paolo, Kira. Like as not he'll be gone in a day or two after he's worn out his welcome with Il Padrone."

Laura got up from her seat. "I think I'll go upstairs and rest for a bit." She avoided meeting the eyes of the others at the table and slinked out of the dining room.

"Not exactly the welcoming type, our Padrone," Kira observed.

"You have the disadvantage of arriving after Laura," Jean-Marc pointed out, nodding toward the lithe blond retreating down the corridor. "I thought you did not meet Franco in England?"

"She didna," Maeve answered for Kira.

Jean-Marc rubbed the blond stubble pushing out along his chin, at first puzzled until a slow smile raised the corners of his mouth. He nodded toward Maeve, raising one eyebrow with a knowing look. He nodded in the direction Dominic had departed. "He is most anxious for Kira's comfort."

Maeve responded with a smirk. "I hadna thought of it before," she confessed. "Quite the professional, our Padrone." She winked at Kira. "He doesna usually take a personal interest in the students that come."

"I'm afraid he doesn't care very much for me," Kira agreed.

"He cares very much, I think," Jean-Marc corrected her, "can be *jalousie? Tu sais?*" he asked Maeve for confirmation of his choice of words.

Maeve smiled, Kira's expression reflecting her distress at the idea that Dominic could be jealous on her behalf.

Kira shook her head vehemently. "Now you're going to tell me he *likes* me?" She held up her hands to fend off any further comment.

"His attitude toward me has been nothing less than strictly formal. I just came to dig. That's all." And yet she thought of the dark man in her dream, handsome, vulnerable. Alone. "Look. I'm only going to be here six weeks." Her face flushed bright red.

Maeve and Jean-Marc exchanged amused looks.

"Ye do not need to convince me," Maeve assured her. "I was with ye at Cadbury Castle. I saw ye turn 'em away right enough then, didn't I?"

Kira relaxed, her color slowly returning to normal.

"On the other hand," Maeve continued, "for Dominic, 'strictly formal' is more attention than he offers most, especially since the accident."

"Then I'm sure he'll walk right up and propose marriage tomorrow," Kira said sarcastically. "Sorry, I'm already engaged."

"That's not what ye told me at Cadbury Castle," Maeve reminded her with a wry grin. "As I recall, ye told me that was what ye were trying to avoid."

Jean-Marc raised a hand to his mouth to hide the smile he couldn't suppress.

"Then why would I take up with someone else?"

Maeve leaned across the table looking directly into Kira's eyes. "We had a lot to drink that night in England, Kirie. Ye told me much more than ye probably meant to." She gave Jean-Marc a quick conspiratorial look. "Maybe you'll find that somethin' better in our Padrone, do ye think?"

Kira felt the heat rising from her neck into her face once more. "I said I thought there must be something more out there. I didn't mean to imply that I was actively looking for it," she said in a husky voice.

"I did no' think ye were." She reached across, taking Kira's clenched hands into her own. "But if opportunity is knockin' should ye not answer?"

Kira looked nervously at Jean-Marc, who pretended not be listening, before answering quietly. "I'm not in the market for a summer romance. It's far too easy to think you're in love with a stranger for a few days, but it never withstands the test of time."

Jean-Marc drained his glass and rose from the table, inclining slightly toward the table as he left. "Anything is possible."

CHAPTER 5

❦

Closing the door to her room, Kira sat down behind the desk to transfer the events of the day into her journal.

Her eyes gravitated to the mountain outside the window with the stirring of the chintz curtains in front of a warm breeze. A rainbow of colors lit the horizon with the setting sun.

Kira placed her glasses beside the journal on her desk and rubbed her tired, hazel eyes. She picked up the letter from Joe Cochran absently, sliding it into the back of her journal. There was no need to reply since she had spoken to him on the phone. She was thousands of miles away and drifting farther.

The carefree lifestyle of the people who lived in the shadow of Vesuvius was having an effect on her. Sheltered within the walls of the Casa del Fioretti, she could watch the people from the safety of her window, listen to their passionate conversations that conveyed the idea that everything they did was the most important thing they would ever do.

Kira thought of le fratelli Fioretti: Franco so handsome and rakish, and then there was Dominic. Aside from pointed ears and a tail, he looked very much like the satyr he had nearly unseated in the study below.

She continued to use Laura's analogy to the statues, seeing Franco as the figure of Priapus, playfully seductive, handsome and charming and forthright with his intentions.

Dominic was the satyr, his motives more subtle and yet still she felt the strong undercurrent of sexuality that surrounded him. Here was a man who made it quite clear that he did not believe women capable of any intelligence.

Kira scoffed at her daydreaming, chiding herself for even entertaining notions of a short-term romance; that's all that it could be, so far from home. How easy it would be to believe yourself in love for a few short weeks. For one of those involved it would be infatuation that would pass, for the other a broken heart. She would have to make sure Maeve and Jean-Marc didn't make any attempts at matchmaking. That wasn't what she had come for.

Shaking herself from the conducive effect of her surroundings to flights of fancy, Kira found that nature was demanding her immediate attention.

She moved mechanically from her room to the toilet down the hall as naturally as if she were in her own home oblivious to the dark shadows that hung threateningly along the corridor.

Inhaling deeply, Kira breathed in the earthy smell that the Casa retained. She took careful, measured steps back to her room as her now alert senses sharpened.

The hair on the back of her neck reacted like a frightened porcupine, nerve endings sending small jolts of electricity rippling all across her skin. Her ears focused on the sound that triggered the little guns. She wrapped herself in her arms to shake off the resultant chill.

The almost silent footfall stopped, followed by the deep hum of a man speaking. The sound seemed to be carrying from somewhere below. She reached for the cool wood of the intricately carved railing and leaned over, peering into the darkness. Silence assaulted her straining ears, broken by a sigh—female? and the closing of a door.

She resisted the impulse to investigate, common sense flashing warnings like a semaphore desperately signaling her to stay clear. She looked down at the oversized T-shirt that modestly covered her and walked back into her room.

Settling on the edge of the bed, she noticed something on the floor and bent down to pick it up. It was velvet to the touch marking a trail from the door. Holding it up to her nose she breathed in the delicate scent of rose petals. Shrugging her shoulders, she turned over in the bed to pull the covers up and found the stripped stem lying on the pillow. Jumping back, she stared at the thorns.

The prospect of sleep leaped farther away. Kira moved quietly across the dark room and pulled on a pair of pants, slinking out of the room and back into the dark hallway.

With one hand still on her door knob, she hesitated a moment, wondering where she was intending to go. In her violated room she saw her journal laying on the desk and then she remembered the quest. She had come to test a theory.

With her destination now clearly in mind, Kira skipped down the staircase, the ticking of a clock echoing in the empty foyer like the beating of her heart. Her bare feet caressed the thin carpeting silently, her path lit by the brilliance of the moon shining down through the glass panes of the dome overhead.

Past the watching columns of the corridor and through the dining room, Kira found herself in the courtyard. She looked nervously across to the other wing of the house where the brothers kept their privacy.

"Get a grip," she scolded herself quietly.

She scurried down the staircase and into the earth. Kira let her fingers trail against the rough rock of the excavation.

Nearly two thousand years earlier, St. Paul had walked through this house. Was it possible he had left the infamous grail of Christ?

"Idiot," she cursed, realizing she hadn't brought a light to find her way through the pyroclastic tunnels.

But then she remembered Jean-Marc turning over his bucket of tools, just like the archaeologists she had seen in England.

Squinting into the darkness, she saw the glint of metal. She reached out for it tentatively and turned the pail over carefully to uncover a flashlight among the tools.

The earth crumbled loosely between her toes, making footing unsure. She crept downward, pointing the beam of light ahead. The dirt cleared away to the marble when she reached the floor of the house below, cool and hard under her feet. In the glare of the flashlight, the tunnel was alien and uninviting. Determined, she passed through to the tablinum.

Archways and walls still crusted with layers of mud remained waiting for the embrace of the archaeologists that would return with the light of day.

Kira reached out a hand for the wall and felt her fingers tingle at the touch of the rough surface. From behind her came the sound of sliding dirt. Wheeling around, the beam of light illuminated the entrance of the dark atrium. "Is anyone there?" she called out nervously. The beam of light wavered uncertainly in the silence that followed. She formulated the words in Italian in her mind before speaking them again.

"My imagination," she whispered to herself.

"Il sole." The words could have been her imagination they were spoken so faintly. Kira backed away, turning as she fumbled back into the courtyard, and ran up to the upper level of the excavation to return the flashlight.

She emerged from the tomb to the courtyard above, gulping in the fresh night air.

"Trouble sleeping?" The moonlight glistened off the wheels of the great chair that mobilized Franco, his handsome face hidden in the shadows.

She smiled sheepishly. "Chasing demons," she laughed.

"It is not safe to go down alone, especially in the dark," he cautioned. "You do not know when one of your demons may catch up with you."

Kira shivered in the dark courtyard. "I don't believe in ghosts."

"There is more to fear than ghosts in an excavation." He took hold of the wheels beside him. "I will see you safely back inside."

Franco's chair moved silently across the carpet until it reached the tiles of the foyer, stopping at the bottom of the rising stairs. "Why do you go down at this time of night?" he asked.

Kira thought back to the list of regulations she had received from Anna Giannini and flushed nervously under the spotlight of the moon. "I don't know," she told him honestly. "It will not happen again. I'm sorry, Signore Fioretti."

※ ※ ※

Dominic crouched over a sieve, idly fingering through the contents before nodding his approval. Returning to his full height, he looked at the crumbling walls with a sense of pride. Many years of hard labor had finally uncovered the home of his ancestors, hidden for nearly two thousand years. It was his heritage. These were his heirlooms.

He returned inevitably to the atrium, still expecting to see his father and perhaps hoping that there was a ghost so he could lay it to rest.

That the lawyer had buried their father before Dominic and his brother were released from the hospital was inexcusable. The walls around him seemed to echo his profound sadness while Dominic wondered how many people had been there to mourn Enzio Fioretti's passing.

From the warmth of the sun, Dominic passed into the artificial lighting of interior rooms still being carved out of the volcanic rock. He caressed the walls lovingly letting the sharp edges of hardened magma soothe his grief. From his vantage point, he could just see Kira and it made him uncertain once again.

She had indeed come to work, brushing back mud, tracing the crack in the wall. The work was tedious and progress was slow, yet she remained to her task. Each chunk of long-hardened mud that fell to the ground raised a cloud that made breathing difficult. Covered with dust, she reminded him of a jewel, waiting to be discovered. Or perhaps the grail…could she be the one?

With a turn of his head, he listed to muffled echoes of excited voices from other rooms as objects moved from their graves into conservation stages, a process Maeve would be seeing to today. Dominic closed his eyes and shook his head, wondering if he would ever be able to trust anyone again.

Across the chamber, a sheet of igneous rock fell to the earth. "Enfin," Jean-Marc sighed. His effort had finally exposed the expected piece of furniture.

"Padrone," Jean-Marc called out.

"Qu'est-ce que c'est?" He responded in French, ducking under a brace in the ceiling overhead that divided the two rooms.

"Une armoire." Jean-Marc replied, "Un stipo," he repeated in Italian.

"A cupboard?" Kira gasped, stepping back from her wall.

"Oui," Jean-Marc shook his head effusively in reply. "Comme elle est exquise." He caressed the carvings in the wood as if discovering a lost lover.

Kira stepped in front of Dominic, following the inlaid designs with her own hands in wonder at the workmanship. Jean-Marc's handiwork exposed the corners of the doors, the rest of the cupboard still encased in rock. The lower section had not withstood the advance of the surge. Wood was splintered away laying open a compartment filled with lava.

"Le Pitturas," Dominic commanded, calling for the photographer. "Excuse me, Miss Ellison." He nodded toward the wall where she had been working and lifted his eyebrows, dismissing her. Sheepishly, she obeyed, returning to the mural that she was uncovering.

Neapolitan workers came through with their shovels, cleaning debris from the floor.

※　　　　　※　　　　　※

Mortified by her forthrightness, Kira laid her hands against the wall to steady their trembling. She squeezed her eyes shut and felt a magnetic pull refusing to let her move away. Before her closed eyes, she saw a gleaming golden cup.

Her eyes popped open and she filled her lungs with air, realizing that she hadn't taken a breath for several seconds. She suddenly felt very anxious to attack her task.

With her trowel, Kira scraped off another chunk of mud. The colors of the fresco seeped into a crack in the wall. She followed the fault with her fingers.

Another scrap fell to the ground and she brushed the crevice delicately. The crack had taken a corner. She scraped off another section, working faster now. It no longer represented a fault. "Padrone," she called out uncertainly.

The guttural sound that came from his throat displayed his displeasure with her boldness. A distracted glance in Kira's direction showed a spark of interest when he saw the line. "What is this?" He approached and leaned forward to examine the crevice in the wall.

His eyes wandered from the wall to Kira's face. His expression carefully masked, Kira became alarmed that he would relieve her of her task just when it was getting interesting.

"Alidada. Nastro." he called out for measuring instruments. "Since you are so intrigued with Monsieur Lavasseur's cupboard, maybe you can assist him until they finish taking measure of the disturbance in your wall," he suggested. "It must be charted."

Kira smiled. "Grazie, Padrone."

"Quite something, eh?" Jean-Marc held out his arms to display his cabinet.

"Yes," she replied politely, scraping gingerly at the pumice around the wood.

"What do you suppose we'll find inside?" Dominic asked tentatively, almost afraid of her answer.

Kira turned to address Il Padrone, her pulse racing, but he was quickly distracted by the summons of another voice calling to him from the second floor of the villa. She breathed a sigh of relief and returned her attention to the Frenchman beside her.

"I don't expect we'll find many more cupboards like this," she suggested to Jean-Marc.

"Much of the furniture is damaged." He spoke slowly, trying to recover his lingual skills.

The ornamentation of the wood renewed Kira's respect for the artisans of the past, but she still trembled from the peculiar sensation she had experienced at the wall. "I need to take a break," she told Jean-Marc. He waved her off, completely absorbed in his task.

The weight of the debris clinging to Kira suddenly seemed enormous. She walked out into the garden below the ground. Climbing the staircase slowly, she looked up to Vesuvius. The sun was dropping opposite, sparking brilliant shades of purple on the horizon.

Back at the surface, she stretched and took several deep breaths. Pulling off her dust spattered glasses the mountain blurred into a kaleidoscope of colors.

"It is beautiful, is it not?" Hastily, Kira replaced her glasses in time to see Franco Fioretti wheeling out from the dining room. "Tell me, what are they finding below?"

She marveled again at how attractive Franco Fioretti was and found she could not fault Laura for her musings. His bright blue eyes sparkled like mountain lakes, his brown hair, slightly unkempt, gave him a slightly boyish quality. "Jean-Marc has exposed a cupboard."

"Has he?" He seemed to be studying her intently, ravaging her with his eyes. "And the contents?"

She felt uncomfortable under his scrutiny. Too handsome, too flirtatious. In the end, that was what made him unattractive. "Not yet." She was looking at his legs, wondering how long he had been without the use of them. Self-consciously, she ran a hand through her hair, the color of the dust blending with the mud brown strand that clung to her fingers. "If you'll excuse me," she said, realizing the state of her appearance. "I think I'll take the opportunity to get cleaned up."

The wheelchair moved backward as he made a courtly bow for her to pass.

Kira ran up to her room where she settled into the seat beside the window and pulled the leather book from the drawer of the desk. Making some casual notes in her journal, she found herself drawing the goblet. Startled, she closed the book and returned it to the drawer.

༄   ༄   ༄

Placing her hands on the excavation walls had felt like touching a TV after crossing a static-filled carpet.

Unable to sleep, she slipped out of bed and into a pair of jeans once more. Remembering a flashlight, she hurried from her room down to the courtyard below. Franco would just have to forgive her for breaking her promise.

She paced along the edge of the pit several times trying to decide if she should descend.

"Are you not afraid to be out here alone?" Franco's basso voice floated through the night air, interrupting her circles. "What calls to you Kira?" The lyrical sound of his words combined with the deficiency of sleep had a hypnotic effect.

"I'm sorry if I disturbed you," she murmured.

"I am not at all disturbed. It is very pleasant to meet a lovely woman walking in the garden on a moonlit night…" He wheeled up beside her and then stopped abruptly.

"Almost as if it were planned." Dominic's voice carried out across the courtyard, approaching from the opposite wing and breaking Franco's spell. He was taking giant strides from the casa.

"I couldn't sleep," Kira explained nervously, holding the bottom of her shirt around her waist. She hunched her shoulders, feeling the cooler night air cutting through the thin fabric.

"How convenient. And you, brother?"

"I am not allowed to move freely about my own home?" Franco teased with a subtly amatory undertone.

"So it is merely coincidence that you should meet out here in the middle of the night?" Dominic demanded, moving closer.

The blood was rushing into Kira's head. She felt like a child caught out after curfew.

Dominic turned to Franco. "La Amazzone, non c'e besigno." He insisted in Italian with an angry flourish of his hands.

"I know you don't need me," Kira translated, her voice taking on a rough edge. "I realize that I am here by your grace, but I have also paid for the privilege. Whatever reasons I choose to come to your little project, Signore Fioretti, I am supporting my right with the financial resources you have demanded of me."

"And what are your reasons, then?" he demanded, advancing, challenging. "Perhaps you feel pity for a poor cripple? Or have you come in search of buried treasure?"

"That's enough!" Franco's voice thundered, chasing itself around the courtyard. He pointed back to the villa. "Miss Ellison, you will return to your room. And you," he pointed to his brother, "you know I will not be a cripple forever and any woman who would chose me will know that also. I do not need a woman's pity." He spat out the last sentence, gripping his wheelchair tightly.

Dominic smirked with satisfaction. "Ah, yes. She chose you when you were still whole—while you were in England."

"My affairs are none of your business!" Franco shouted.

"I didn't choose anybody," Kira insisted at the same time, arms firmly planted on her hips. "And I certainly didn't expect this excavation to be a cover for ensnaring women!"

The three of them stood glaring at each other in the dark courtyard until Dominic finally broke the silence. "You would be safer in your room, Miss Ellison."

Unnerved by her own forthrightness and their lack of defense to her remark, Kira wheeled around and marched back to the villa without a backward glance.

❦ ❦ ❦

She pushed her way into her room, sitting down abruptly behind the desk absently fingering the journal that lay open. Her blood raged through her veins, her thoughts jumbled. Closing her eyes, she took deep, measured breaths to regulate her blood pressure.

When she felt more composed, she opened her eyes and looked at the pages beneath her hands.

She stiffened, realizing something wasn't right. The letter from Joe lay on the floor. Before she left her room, she remembered putting the journal in the drawer.

IT EXISTS. The words jumped off the page below her last entry making her drop the book and stand up staring at it. She retrieved the book and held it closer to be sure the words were really there.

She wanted to run from the room, but she didn't dare, afraid of who she might run into. But now she felt violated. This made twice someone had been in her room. Suddenly she felt trapped, and then she remembered the suite door.

"Laura," she called quietly. She walked across to the door and tapped lightly on it. "Laura." She listened tentatively, afraid that if she breathed she might not hear a response. Minutes passed and still there was no answer.

Kira fell back into the chair behind the desk and looked out across the sky. "There's no such thing as ghosts," she whispered a little less certainly.

CHAPTER 6

❁

*A*rtisans were restoring a section of Kira's mural when she arrived the following morning. Dominic Fioretti was moving around the site, issuing orders, supervising work. He gave her no sign of recognition as he continued to bark out orders in several different languages.

Abjectly taking a shovel, Kira gathered up some of the debris that lay on the floor and carried it out to the refuse container in the sunken garden. Several laborers were doing likewise, carrying shovels and pushing wheelbarrows.

It would be counterproductive to try to clean away the lava that filled the crevice in the wall while the other work was being done. Placing her hands at the base of her back, Kira threw her shoulders back to ease the protests of bones screaming against unnatural alignment.

She went back into the tablinum and looked over Jean-Marc's shoulder, giving him a reassuring pat at the progress he was making with his recovery. Maeve was working with him, carefully sifting through the contents of the small compartments.

"Ye could help us here," Maeve invited, nodding her acknowledgment of Kira's dilemma.

"How many archeologists does it take to change a light bulb?" Kira laughed, applying the joke to their present situation. "Where's Laura working? Maybe I could see what she's up to."

Maeve brushed off her clothes and rose to her feet, lifting her eyes toward the ceiling and giving a quick shake of her head. "She's up top. Il Padrone suggested a day off for her."

"Where is Il Padrone?" Kira asked haltingly, almost afraid of the answer. "I'm surprised he hasn't relieved me as well."

"I am sure he feels you have more to contribute," Jean-Marc suggested distractedly. "And if Maeve is no more helping, than you will help me?"

"I'm comin', ye bloody Frenchman," Maeve retorted, dropping back down on her haunches. "I'm sure ye can find someplace to make yerself useful," she told Kira.

"I'm probably best out of the way, like Laura," Kira said half to herself.

She couldn't blame Dominic for thinking the worst. It was no wonder that he chose to ignore her after the way Franco continued to insinuate himself.

She mounted the staircase back up to the Casa dejectedly, vowing to avoid Franco in the future as she made her way through the dining room toward the foyer.

Pushing her glasses back up her nose, she stopped in the hall. Hearing whiny protests in a voice that sounded very much like Laura's, Kira ducked behind one of the Doric pillars. The female voice was answered by a stern male, that brooked no opposition.

Holding onto the cold, smooth curve of the column, Kira watched Laura emerge from Franco's office, blond hair flying in her wake as she ran up the stairs.

"Signorina?" Anna came up from behind.

Startled, Kira jerked upright, her cheeks flushing bright red. "I-I didn't want to intrude," she explained, nodding toward the retreating young woman.

Anna furrowed her brow. "Intrude?" she repeated, shaking her head with lack of comprehension.

"Disturb?" Kira suggested.

Anna nodded, understanding. "Maybe better to intrude," she commented, continuing down the corridor.

"Miss Elleesone?" Franco called out as Kira passed the study.

She tightened her hands into fists and forced a congenial smile. "Signore?" she answered, turning to acknowledge him.

"Ah, yes," he remembered with an exaggerated nod of his head. "The artisan will be working on your wall. You will maybe assist me today?"

Kira felt her pulse quicken, searching for a plausible excuse. "I thought maybe I'd do some sightseeing, learn a little more about the region."

He wheeled deftly out of the study. "Yes, excellent idea." He looked up the stairway. "And perhaps you will take Miss Griffith with you. She is also unable to work today." He nodded as he considered his suggestion. "Yes. It is better not to go alone."

"I'll be sure to ask her, then."

Franco stared at her with a smile on his face, seeming poised to ask her a question but not speaking. Kira waited uneasily, courtesy keeping her from taking her leave but still he made no attempt to speak.

Kira motioned up the stairs with her hand and offered him a smile of dismissal, rising up to find her American companion while still half-expecting her host to speak.

Franco remained at the foot of the stairs, watching her. Kira looked away from him and saw a dark shadow retreat toward the dining room.

She opened her mouth to call out, certain that Dominic had caught them once again in a compromising, albeit innocent, exchange. Instead she closed her mouth, berating herself for caring.

What did it matter? In a few weeks she would be gone from here with little chance of ever crossing paths with Dominic Fioretti again.

His attention diverted away from her, Franco maneuvered backward into the foyer to see what had caught Kira's eye.

Kira took the opportunity to hurry up the remaining stairs unscrutinized and disappear into the safety of her room.

"Laura?" She knocked lightly on the adjoining door.

Laura turned the knob from the other side and then wheeled around and returned to her bed, sinking face down.

"I thought maybe you could go to Pompeii with me," Kira suggested. She stood in the doorway, trying to determine if Laura was ill or in need of comfort.

Laura sat up again, looking out her window to the mountain in the distance. Her voice was soft, subdued. "No, let's go to the volcano. Maybe I can throw myself in."

CHAPTER 7

❀

"I am so bored!" Laura complained while they rode the cable car up the volcano.

"Then why did you come here?" Kira asked.

"I had a professor that said it would be a good experience. The way he talked about it..." the young girl sighed and closed her eyes. "He made it sound so romantic. And then he introduced me to Franco." Laura looked at Kira guardedly. "I didn't really mind his being so much older, you know. And then I got here, and then I met the other one, and then there was the accident, and now everyone just treats me like I'm some sort of kid or something."

The other one? Kira felt an irrational wave of animosity toward her companion. "Why don't you leave, then?"

Laura sat silently, staring out at the mountain as the cable car came to a stop, dismissing its passengers to finish the trek to the summit on foot.

"Have you ever been in love, Kira?" Laura asked unexpectedly.

She forced her thoughts to Joe Cochran and sighed. "No," she finally answered. Then she looked curiously at Laura. "Do you mean to tell me you've fallen in love and that's what keeps you here?"

"Maybe."

Was she intimating that she had fallen in love with Dominic? "You're a long way from home. You said yourself that you find foreign men appealing. You're letting your imagination get the best of you. If you're so bored, you couldn't possibly be in love."

"But he's so…so…virile," Laura sighed dreamily. "He's the best lover I've ever had."

Kira attacked the hike up the steep path to the peak. "If he was so perfect, you wouldn't be so bored. Isn't the other face of the mountain a little less steep?"

"What's the matter, Teach, can't keep up?"

"I'm ahead of you," she retorted, "And if I can keep up with a bunch of junior-high girls on the basketball court, I can keep up with you." She frowned, hating the emotions that were clouding her reasoning.

"There's something peaceful about Vesuvius on a cloudy day," Laura sighed. "It's like walking up to heaven."

Kira raised her eyebrows, startled by the abrupt change in Laura. "Peaceful? We're walking into the face of death. Who knows when it could blow."

Laura burst into laughter, a breathy giggle that grated on Kira the way her junior high girls did when they were talking about boys. "It hasn't erupted since World War II, and that blast capped it off."

"The eruption that buried the cities in 79 blew the top off the mountain. It probably looked just this peaceful way back then before it threw up all over them." Kira pulled up short, aware that Laura had stopped behind her.

At the lower peak, Laura pointed across the fissure to the sealed volcano. "Just look at it, Kira." Her voice was little more than a reverent whisper.

The earth released steaming tendrils from the heated soil. "And somewhere below that quiet exterior the earth is seething, cooking up a liquid fire."

"He's evil, Kira."

Kira turned curiously to the young girl, waiting for her to elaborate, but Laura guarded her silence, staring into the crater below.

Something told her the volcano wasn't the only explosive beneath a calm exterior.

Looking across the vista Kira began to relax, feeling the tranquillity of the countryside. Below, the sea shimmered blues and greens and silvers. Unparalleled crops of grapes and olives marked out patchwork in the rich volcanic soil. Kira closed her eyes and raised her face to the sky, absorbing the serenity that the moment provided.

"It is like walking up to heaven," she sighed, bending down to grab a handful of the warm earth around her feet. "A hard climb through hell rewarded by peace and beauty."

"We're on a volcano, remember?" Laura chided. "It could turn back into hell again without even a moment's warning."

Like Dominic's temper, Kira thought, Laura's unparalleled lover.

With a sudden intake of air, Kira felt a flush creep over her body as if the mountain itself was embracing her. The heat from the earth radiated through her.

She shook herself to throw off the fantasy that threatened to take over, picking her footing carefully back down the trail.

"Did you hear anyone in my room last night?" Kira asked, eyes firmly planted on her feet to see that they remained on the ground.

"Why do you ask?"

"Someone was in my room."

"Lucky you."

Kira looked across at Laura, puzzled by her evasiveness. "I wasn't there at the time. Did you hear anything?"

"What should I have heard?"

"Was it you?"

"No." Laura inspected pieces of lava with her feet, looking anywhere but back at Kira. "I wasn't in my room last night, either." She turned her attention to the panorama, shielding her eyes against the falling sun. "I guess that means I didn't hear anything."

"Where were you?"

Laura looked directly at Kira now. "Who are you? My mother? Where were you?"

Kira blushed, newly upset by the accusations Dominic had made the night before. "Just making conversation."

"Well don't."

Kira laughed uneasily. "Look. I don't really care where you were or who your latest conquest is. I was just hoping you might know who was going through my things."

"Did they take anything?"

Kira told her about the rose and about the entry in her journal.

Laura waved a hand testily in the air. "Could have been anyone. They're all crooks, after all." She wrapped her arms around her shoulders and screwed her face up tight. "Can't trust any of them," she finished in subdued tones.

CHAPTER 8

❀

Dominic watched the medics carry the artisan out through the tunnel into the courtyard. He knew Jean-Marc was staring at him, waiting for him to reassure everyone that all was well.

But all was not well.

From where he stood, he could see the same shreds of hemp attached to the fallen beam, another piece of evidence tangled in the wheelbarrow. The same method had been used in both sabotage attempts.

"It is not safe," Jean-Marc complained. "Too many times the top falls down." He illustrated with his hands. "If Kira had been there today…"

"Then she should consider herself fortunate that she was not," he barked back. "We cannot expect that all of the lava is solid. There will be stress points."

Jean-Marc threw his trowel to the ground and kicked his bucket over his tools. "And my arm?"

"If it is so serious you should have gone to hospital with the artisan."

"What are you going to do, Padrone?"

Dominic looked up to the opening in the ceiling of the tablinum. "I am going to have the engineers see that this area is safe. You are in the field now, not in your precious museum. Is that not why you are here? To see how your displays come to you? There is always inherent danger. I would not subject you to undue risk, Monsieur. If you are uncomfortable, you may return to the safety of the Louvre."

Dominic walked over to the wall, feeling the crevice Kira had exposed with his fingers.

"And what of your ghost now?"

Dominic wheeled around and glared at Jean-Marc. "There is no ghost."

The Frenchman lowered his eyes. "It is not unlike the last time."

"This is my home," Dominic thundered. He turned his head away quickly and squeezed his eyes closed, struggling to regain his composure. He reached a hand out, resting it on Jean-Marc's shoulder. "I will not allow any harm to come to my students."

"And the artisan?" Jean-Marc reminded him sarcastically. Shaking his head, he walked away from Dominic, still nursing his arm.

"Lay down your tools," Dominic bellowed. Outside the tunnel he heard the command being repeated.

He looked to the ground, kicking at the damning piece of evidence partially hidden by the fallout from the ceiling. The large boulder had broken in two right in front of the doorway Kira was uncovering.

🍁   🍁   🍁

Kira watched Laura run up the stairs without even a backward glance.

"A letter for you, Signorina," Anna crossed the foyer holding out an envelope.

"Grazie." Kira carried the letter to the dining room and took a seat, slitting open the flap and removing the page of neatly scrawled words.

"Dear Kira,

I hope you don't mind my writing, Greg gave me the address. I don't understand what it is that takes you to Italy, but I hope you will be home soon.

I have an important question to ask you, and I would prefer to ask it face to face.

It's been very quiet without you. But then, I never was a very good bachelor.

I hope to hear from you, or better yet, come home soon.

Fondly,

Joe"

She tore the page in half and crumpled it in her hands. Her cheeks showed a deeper pink and her lips curled into a pout. "Fondly," she sputtered.

"Kira!" Dominic came striding into the room. She shrunk into the chair, her present opinion of men not fit for sharing. "Kira, I must speak with you." He pulled her to her feet and led her out of the dining room. Gently, he guided her through another doorway along the great corridor.

The salotto was elegantly decorated. Lace curtains lined the windows like a bridal veil. Kira dropped her letter unobtrusively into a waste can while Dominic walked across to a bar and picked up a glass of wine. Raising it, he asked the unspoken question.

"No, thank you," Kira responded.

He came back across the room until he stood directly in front of her, crossing the invisible boundary of personal space. Kira stood toe to toe, primed for a fight and not wanting to give him the satisfaction of backing her down.

"Tell me more about the disturbances you have had in your room," he prompted.

Kira stopped, startled. "How do you know…?"

"There is very little that happens in this house that I don't know about."

"But you couldn't possibly know—unless it was you?" She rolled her eyes, remembering Laura's words about her unparalleled lover, and then her resentment rose again. The suite door provided access. "Boy she doesn't waste any time."

Dominic turned his back, studying the glass of wine in his hand. He took a sip and directed his black eyes at Kira again. "I am responsible for the safety of my guests. Someone overheard you accusing Laura of going through your room. I went to ask her…"

"I didn't accuse her…" Kira blushed.

"I am sure you did not accuse her just as I am sure you do not have anything that one would be interested in searching out. In the interest of your safety, I want to know exactly what happened."

She stepped back, pretending to examine a pottery vase, clearly a souvenir recovered from the earth and carefully pieced back together. *In the interest of my safety*, she thought skeptically. More like he couldn't wait for her to get back. Or Laura was worried that she would be implicated by his actions. Anger made her look up at him again and then she rapidly blushed, envisioning the consummate lover Laura had described.

"There was another incident while you were out," he continued.

"In my room?" she cast an anxious eye toward the corridor.

"No," he reassured her, "but I would like to be sure they are not related."

She gathered her thoughts and turned to face him again. "There was a rose," she related, wondering if this was a test to see if she actually would tell him what he undoubtedly already knew. "The petals were scattered on the floor and the stem laid on my pillow. And then last night someone disturbed my journal."

"Disturbed how?"

Kira pulled back a lace curtain, touching the glass of the window tentatively as if looking for a way out. "Didn't Laura tell you?" Her tone was sarcastic.

He took a deep breath, his brow darkening. "I asked you."

Folding her arms across her chest, she faced Il Padrone. "It was taken out of the drawer. Some of my correspondence had fallen to the floor, which I would have noticed had I done it, and someone wrote in my journal."

He raised his eyebrows. "Wrote what?"

"It exists."

His eyes narrowed. "What?"

"Someone wrote 'it exists' in my journal." The look of surprise on his face disarmed her.

"What exists?" he prodded.

Her eyes diverted to the window again. "Ask the person who wrote it in my journal." Kira reached for a book laying beside her on a table, but Dominic reached out and stopped her from picking it up.

"This person will not have written it in your journal if they did not think it would mean something to you." He stood beside her, the forced calm of his voice sending it an octave lower. "What exists, Kira?"

Shaking free of the hand that still lingered on hers, she set her jaw firmly and took a deep breath. "I don't know, Padrone."

He turned suddenly, the glass of wine shattering in his hand. "Do not call me by that name!"

Her mouth relaxed, her eyes wide with wonder. "Padrone? That is your position among us, isn't it?"

He was drying his hands on a towel by the bar. "It would not have been written for you to see if you did not know it's meaning." He faced her again, demanding a response. "What exists?"

She considered for a moment before answering. He held her with his eyes from across the room, following a fleeting glance toward the door. He took a step in that direction to block any attempt at putting him off and folded his arms behind his back, ticking his fingers off against his thumb, one by one.

Kira shrugged her shoulders resolutely. "It's only a theory."

"A theory?"

She shrugged her shoulders. "I have heard your legend of St. Paul and I was considering the possibilities of religious artifacts."

The color drained from his face, his fingernails clicking faster against his thumb. "What makes you think this?"

"I told you it was only a theory."

"And then someone writes in your journal that it exists." He glowered at her and took a step back. "What would you do with this religious artifact?"

Kira stiffened at the volatility of his moods. "Everything we find belongs to you. *Padrone*."

"How well do you know Maeve Ryan?"

Kira blinked several times, his rapid change of subject catching her off guard. "I worked with her for a week in England."

He waved one hand in front of him. "And you became fast friends?"

"Yes…" she tilted her head to one side, waiting for him to make his point.

He nodded, waiting for her to continue. "But what do you know about her?"

"You probably know more about her than I do." Kira folded her arms across her chest and squinted back at him.

"That may be true, but I am curious to hear what you know."

Kira smirked. "Well I know she's Irish." She thought about how fondly Maeve referred to Dominic and Franco, as if they were her own sons. She raised a hand triumphantly, then, when she remembered another piece of information Maeve had given her. "She had two sons, but they're dead now."

"And do you know, perhaps, how they died?" he prodded, leaning forward.

Kira's shoulders fell and she took a step backward. "I didn't want to pry."

"They died in the war," he supplied.

"Which war?"

Dominic lowered his head, his fingers tapping out their cadence against his thumb, each one in turn. "If you have made a friend of her it may be best you do not know."

Kira crossed her arms again and stepped back up. She tilted her head and raised her eyes to the ceiling, her jaw firmly set as she considered releasing the mounting anger that was building inside her at his cat and mouse game.

The corners of Dominic's mouth twitched in amusement watching her struggle. He made a half bow by way of apology. "I don't suppose it would hurt to tell you she is Sinn Fein."

Grabbing hold of a chair another step in front of her, Kira leaned forward and unleashed her temper. "Shin feign? Is this another attempt to remind me that I don't have a sufficient grasp of Italian? Another reminder of how much more intelligent you are than I am and how I couldn't possibly know anything—being female? I am here to learn, Signore, but if you're afraid I might match your intelligence then you shouldn't be taking students at your site."

Dominic covered his mouth discreetly, turning his attention to the patterns of the carpet. "You have a masters' degree in history. Am I right?"

"Is that a problem?"

"You specialized in European history?"

"Do you suppose you could be more direct, Padrone?"

He cringed slightly and raised his eyes to look at her once more, his temporary good humor gone. "I respect your intelligence, Miss Ellison, and for that reason I will not embarrass you by telling you something I'm sure you already know. Sinn Fein is not Italian and once you've had a chance to think about it, I'm sure it will come to you."

She let go of the chair, uncertain again. Just when she thought he was pointing out her ignorance, he applauded her intelligence. It was true her thoughts were clouded by the unexpected confrontation. Dominic's glowering expression effectively pushed her temper back into check.

"You may go," he growled. "And Miss Ellison…" he waited until he was sure he had her attention, "she does not know I know. I would prefer it remained that way. As for the intrusions into your privacy, I would feel more comfortable if you would bring them to my attention in the future? I would be assured of your safety in my home."

Kira nodded once in acknowledgment and left the salotto. Outside the doorway, she closed her eyes and took a deep breath.

When she opened her eyes again, she looked into the dining room. Most of the workers had gone home. Maeve and Jean-Marc sat huddled in a corner, sharing a bottle of wine.

"Has he finished with ye, then?" Maeve called out, pulling out a chair.

"For now. What a temper." She accepted the invitation and took a seat at their table. "I don't know if I'm supposed to be afraid of him or be grateful for his concern."

"A little of both, I expect."

"So what happened here?"

Jean-Marc took a sip of his wine leveling his gaze at her. "A section of the roof fell in."

"Another cave-in?"

He sat up and leaned across the table. "No one knew the artist would come today. He was there instead of you."

"I don't understand."

"The artisan got a nasty boomp on the head," Maeve added.

Kira shivered, watching long shadows creep across the floor with the setting of the sun. "More from this infamous ghost, I expect." And then it hit her all at once.

Sinn Fein. The Irish nationalist movement active in Northern Ireland; they were rumored to control the Irish Republican Army.

"Have ye seen him, then?"

"Who?" Kira was looking through the arch to the excavation beyond, miles away from the conversation.

"The ghost?"

Jean-Marc and Maeve exchanged glances.

Kira turned her attention back to her friends at the table, looking first to one and then to the other. "I don't believe in ghosts," she insisted, squaring around to face off against her companions. "How can you dig up the past if you're always waiting for it to attack you?"

"You must be careful, *ma chere amie*."

"I'm beginnin' ta think it was maybe not such a good idea to bring ye here. I didna know what was happenin' here while we were in England."

Kira paused to gather her wits, wondering if the woman seated across from her could ever be a terrorist. "You didn't bring me here," she answered cautiously. "I chose to come."

"And the brothers?" Jean-Marc questioned. "They fight very much since you come. They fight for you."

Kira rose from the table, slamming her hands down on the surface. "One thinks he's Don Juan and the other's just plain rude. If I had ever met either one of them before, I might very well have thought twice about my decision to come to this godforsaken death trap. But I'm here now and for the next couple of weeks I intend to learn all I can about whatever Greek, Roman or Etruscan artifacts surface or about archeology in general. That's it, end of story. I don't want to get in anybody's way, no hidden agenda. Is everyone satisfied now?"

"We're all a little edgy," Maeve soothed. "Jean-Marc meant no harm. Share a glass of Lacrimae Christi with us, why don't ye."

Kira was looking at the small Irish woman in a different light. "I'm a little more than edgy. I think I'd rather be by myself right now."

❈   ❈   ❈

She burrowed deeper into the double bed, staring at the locked door with the chair wedged beneath the doorknob. Sleep would not come.

Through the open window came anguished cries. Somewhere outside words evaporated into the night air leaving only the mist of their intonations behind them. The resonance of the angry man was interspersed with the cries of the woman, sometimes angry, sometimes weeping. Kira lay motionless in the bed, listening to the sounds of the argument beyond.

After several minutes, she rose from the security of the bed to look out across the hills.

In the distance, the moon glinted off a woman's hair, the figure of a man leaving her in the shadowy night. A midnight tryst?

Kira thought of Laura and wondered if she was the abandoned woman. Had Dominic left her alone in the dark?

Kira's eyes strayed to the connecting door now imagining the lovers secreted on the other side.

Closing her eyes, Kira filled her lungs with the night air, letting the warm breeze caress her upturned face. And then the wind was Dominic. Her body betrayed her with a responding flush of heat. The wind seemed to murmur her name and she sighed, wrapping her arms around her shoulders. She opened her eyes and looked toward the door once more, not quite comfortable with her attraction to the man.

Dominic was dynamite. At thirty-two, her experience with men was limited. That a stranger could arouse these feelings frightened her.

Kira slid back between the covers of her bed. Reluctantly her mind gave in to the demands of her exhausted body and sleep laid its warm blanket over her troubled thoughts.

CHAPTER 9

The Sunday morning sun warmed Kira's face, calling her back from disturbed sleep. She awoke to the realization that the excavation was closed to observe the day of rest.

Rolling over, she stretched out arms and legs listening to the now familiar sounds of singing in the streets and church bells issuing the call to matins.

With the light of day came rational thought.

Maeve was no more a terrorist than her own mother. And her feelings for Dominic were nothing more than infatuation. He was a handsome man. He had complimented her intelligence. It would all fall into perspective given time.

And yet she couldn't forget the dark man—her conjugation with his mind. Remembering his pain at the loss of his father, she felt her own once more.

"I'm leaving you money," her father had told her, his emaciated body ravaged by cancer. "I want you to do something for yourself. Spend it foolishly."

She had hardly been able to look at him in those final months, a shadow of the man he once was. His talk of death made her angry, but she could not contradict what she knew to be inevitable. Instead she argued with him and swore she would give her inheritance to charity as if the idea would make him struggle to live just a little longer.

"Well this is certainly a foolish way to spend it," she said out loud.

Throwing her feet over the side of the bed, she got up and pulled on a pair of tan pants and a powder blue polo shirt, finishing her ensemble off with a fanny pack around her waist.

"I'll spend my money how I please," she muttered. "And today it's going to be souvenirs for Greg's family."

She stalked out of her room and down the staircase, slowing a little with each step toward the foyer. Stopping on the tiled floor, she looked up to the dome overhead, losing some of her resolve.

"Goin' out, are ye?" Maeve greeted, appearing at Kira's elbow.

How could this woman be a terrorist? "Aye," Kira responded in mock Irish. "And will ye be joining me then?"

"I'll be showin' ye where ta go, ya great Amazon, but not on an empty stomach. Come along then and we'll have some breakfast." She hooked her arm through Kira's and led her down the corridor.

"I overheard an argument last night, out beyond the garden."

"Sure an' that's to be expected. These Italians are a hot blooded lot, they are." She winked.

"Do you think I could ask one of you ladies to give my tired arms a rest?" Franco called good-naturedly from behind, turning the oversized wheels expertly.

Kira moved obediently behind the chair. "This is most kind of you, Miss Elleesone," he said. "Such a beautiful day to be out. Where are you going today?"

"I'm not sure. Maybe the Resina Quarter to do some shopping, although I'm afraid my Italian will need a little more work," she laughed.

"Oooh, I've just remembered," Maeve apologized. "I've promised to catalog those things from the cupboard for Il Padrone. Will ye be okay without me, Kirie?"

"Perhaps you would allow me to escort you," Franco offered.

"Maybe I'll go to Pompeii," Kira countered.

Maeve squeezed Kira's hand, giving her a reassuring smile before she retreated back down the corridor.

Franco reached a hand behind, resting it over Kira's, his warm skin hard and calloused. "Did you have a quiet night?"

"I slept very well, thank you."

"No more disturbances, then?"

Kira caught her breath. "No secrets in this house," she commented.

"Your safety is most important to us." He put his hand back down into his lap. "Perhaps it was nothing after all."

Kira stared at the back of his head, admiring the sheen of his smooth, chestnut hair. "You will forgive me if I'm being too bold by asking, but it must be very difficult for you…I mean not being able to be an active part of the excavation."

"That is why I have all those pictures," he laughed good naturedly. "I am still involved, and I will not be in this chair forever. The doctors are very pleased with my progress."

Kira blushed. "I didn't mean to pry."

"I am honored by your interest."

She moved out from behind him, taking a seat behind one of the dining room tables.

"You should go with someone," he cautioned. "It is not always safe to venture out alone."

"I'm sure I'll be fine."

"I wish I could go with you," he sighed. "But perhaps you will tell me how you enjoy it when you return. Will you have dinner with me this evening?"

"I'm sure I'd appreciate discussing what I've seen," she answered slowly, "but if you don't mind, I'd like to pass on dinner this time."

"I am at your disposal. I will remind you to be careful," Franco said reaching for her hand and patting it as if petting a dog.

Kira smiled shyly. "I suppose I should get going before the day gets away from me."

She rose from her seat, her appetite forgotten.

❧   ❧   ❧

He needed time away, to sort through his oppressive responsibilities at the Casa. Following the throng into Pompeii through the Porta Marina, the western wall of the city, Dominic walked through the arched tunnel down cobblestones and into the past. Tourists swarmed the ruins like ants on a discarded piece of cake.

Plaster casts of bodies made from impressions left in the volcanic ash writhed in their cases. These were the images of the people and animals who had not escaped the disaster, buried alive, their final agony preserved as a reminder of the cataclysm that erased the town from existence. He saw them differently now, since his father's death. Each one of them represented the injustice of a life taken too soon. The site tempered his anger, feeling a kinship for the survivors left behind to mourn.

Justice would be served. By trying to frighten Kira away, the murderer had tipped his hand. Dominic knew how to ensnare the guilty party. It was only a matter of time. Until that time, he needed to find peace.

The Pompeiian ruins were his church, the Pater Noster the altar. Already his spirits was lifting.

The blazing Italian sun radiated off the dry earth in waves of heat that seared through the soles of his leather shoes, a cloud of dust rising up and making him cough. He smiled as a guard waved to him, inviting him across to the cooler shelter of the Forum Baths.

Sightseers filled the Baths, necks craning upward to see stuccoed ceilings and frescoes. People bustled all around pointing to the niches in the walls where ancient bathers once kept their clothing.

"Signore Fioretti," the guard greeted effusively in Italian, quickly explaining his need for an interpreter.

Dominic bowed graciously, dark curls falling over his shoulders. "You have a question?" he asked the American tourists. They were an older group, none of them under fifty years old, he quickly surmised. One well-kept woman giggled coyly, putting a hand to her mouth.

"You speak English so well," she complimented, batting her eyelashes.

Reaching for her hand, Dominic played his role and placed a kiss gently on her knuckles, caressing the heel of her thumb momentarily before releasing it.

Her eyes shone with appreciation as Dominic tore his attention deliberately away from her to the rest of the group. "What can I do for you?" He bowed gallantly, keeping his eyes raised.

"Yeah, whaddoes it say?" a man asked, pointing to the graffiti on the walls of the bath, glaring at the younger gallant.

With a broad smile and a sweep of his hands, Dominic began to regale the tourists with stories his father had related to him of the bathers and the history that the graffiti bestowed to future generations of a civilization long past. He turned slowly, pointing out the niches in the walls for their clothes, giving them the full benefit of his knowledge with great flourishes and off-color humor gleaned from the former patrons of the establishment that delighted both men and women.

Dominic looked around briefly, and then again when he recognized Kira. She stood alone, staring at him with her mouth open.

He hesitated, seeing her as an angel with the brilliant sun glistening in her hair. He began speaking more quickly, finishing his speech while trying to signal Kira to wait for him.

Her eyes darted around her like a frightened rabbit while he tried to disentangle himself from the tour group. He managed to suppress a smile, noticing that she was dressed in similar clothes to his, tan cotton trousers and a light blue polo shirt. The older woman who had commanded his attention was already justifying his departure as a duty call. They looked like tour guides.

"Kira," he greeted, looking around for her escort. "Are you alone?"

"Yes."

"May I join you? A woman alone…"

"Yeah, I know," she stopped him, raising a hand. She looked back to the group of older tourists, shaking her head as if she had seen something beyond belief. "I don't want to take you away from your friends."

"The guard asked me to act as translator."

She tossed her head to invite his company. Dominic placed a hand firmly in the center of her back. "You are taking notes," he said, pointing to the notebook she held in her hand.

"There's so much I want to remember."

"They have some excellent books," he suggested.

"Yes, I know." She showed him the book she had tucked under her arm. "I thought I might make some notes for my classroom. Lessons."

"I'm impressed. Here let me show you around."

He pointed to the walls, still the guide. "These tiles are specially treated to permit the passage of hot air. The suspensurae on the floor provides the circulation. Much of the engineering here went unmatched until the twentieth century."

"Is that what you were telling those people?"

He gave a short laugh. "They were more interested in the romance of the ruins." He gestured toward the graffiti. "I was translating some of the colorful expressions that were left behind."

She gave way to a smile, catching his good humor. "Come. I will show you Pompeii." His voice took on a more casual tone, his English pronunciation giving way to Italian inflection. His steps were buoyant, almost like a child on a playground.

"You have seen the 'Cave Canem?'" he asked, finding her watching him guardedly. He laughed at her dubious expression, dancing around in front of her. "Oh come now. I won't bite!"

She smirked, nodding to the mosaic. "Beware of the dog," she translated.

He took both her arms, "Am I a dog, then?" He felt her tremble and saw the fear in her eyes. "Kira? What is it?"

Blushing prettily, she laid a hand on one his arms. "I'm not quite used to seeing you this way. Forgive me if I don't quite trust my eyes."

"You prefer my bad temper?"

She laughed in response, a sound that reminded him of water tripping across the stones of a waterfall. He fell back in step beside her, replacing a hand firmly in the middle of her back.

"Your tour, Signorina?" As she fell more comfortably into step beside him, he marveled at the advantages her height offered him. His arm rested naturally on her back without having to stoop.

With his free arm, he pointed out where the ruins had been reinforced with modern materials to keep from crumbling.

"I've seen this statue before," Kira recalled, stopping to see the half man/half faun.

"The original is in the Museo in Napoli. This is the House of the Faun."

She reached out for the statue, stopping just short and instead scribbling onto the piece of paper in her hand.

"Perhaps you prefer Cupids?" He suggested seductively, leading her into the Vettii House. With a sweep of his arm, he showed her the varied depictions of cupid that covered the walls. "Does it stir your imagination?"

Kira put the notebook back in her pocket, mesmerized. Her imagination was more than stirred, it was smoldering. She looked up at a fresco of a conquering hero, standing over his lady love with one hand on the woman's breast.

"Here Cupid looks on Mars and Venus," Dominic told her in a deep, quiet voice that felt like the light touch of a finger on her spine. "Returning from war to the woman he loves." He stood a step behind Kira, watching.

"Stuck by one of Cupid's arrows," Kira observed somewhat breathlessly. "One quick sting and boom, you're in love." She looked nervously over her shoulder at Dominic, suddenly self-conscious. "Not quite so simple as that, is it?"

"No," he agreed, watching her circumspectly.

There was an obvious sensuality in the artwork that did not go unnoticed by the lovely American woman, but it also did not incite her to the same inviting manner he recognized in the older tourist.

She followed him out to the Peristyle garden, where engraved ivy branches entwined two central columns topped by two-faced busts. With some amusement, he watched her comparing him to the statues. "You would like my head on a platter?" he suggested.

The smile his remark invoked reassured him that she wasn't quite so ill at ease as he imagined. "I was just noticing how classic your nose is. It almost looks chiseled," her voice faded so that he could barely hear her last words, "as if someone breathed life into a statue."

He grasped her hand to his heart. "I assure you, I am not made of stone." From behind her glasses, her hazel eyes took on a muddy green hue, alive with feeling. Without thinking, he wrapped a hand behind her neck and touched a kiss to her lips.

Without skipping a beat, he fell back in step beside her, continuing to regale her with the stories of gods and goddesses communicated on the walls of homes destroyed long ago. He could sense her uneasiness by the stiffening that crept into her shoulders beneath his protective arm. He continued talking, hoping to take her mind from his impulsive reaction to her.

At length, Dominic slowed his tour, sensing she might once more be more receptive to less general conversation. "But I have been doing all the talking. Tell me, what do you think of our Pompeii?"

"It's magnificent," she answered firmly, her tone of voice reassuring him that he had not misread her interest.

"I am glad you find it so." He smiled and pushed her forward gently along the cobbles. "Kira. It is a Greek name?"

"For Cyrus, the sun god." She smiled. "Is there anything of Cyrus here at Pompeii?"

Her answer stunned him for a moment. The sun. His hand fell from her back, fingers taking up a cadence against his thumb in his agitation. "Perhaps it is Latin?" he suggested, "Kyrie. Even the last name fits," he thought out loud. "Kyrie Eleison."

"Lord have mercy. My father..." she lowered her head and began rubbing the backs of her fingers.

"You are very close?"

She nodded and he watched the muscles of her throat as she swallowed twice before continuing. "It was a great joke of my father's."

"You were a difficult child?"

"On the contrary. I was very conscious of not calling attention to myself."

He nodded in sympathy. "I became very good at hiding," he confessed. "Franco cast quite a shadow but they were always looking for the other one, the quiet one." He looked back at Kira with a sheepish grin that gave him a boyish quality.

"Not very easy to hide when you're six foot tall, is it?"

"It would be harder for you," he agreed. "You're hair...it reminds me of straw; almost brown but shining golden in the sun." He reached involuntarily to touch it and then checked himself. Instead, he pressed forward in the direction the crowd was flowing.

Stopping, he stood before the Cryptogram of the Pater Noster. Kira genuflected reflexively, recognizing the icon, and reached for her notebook again to copy the letters arranged into a cross.

This was what he had come to see. Instead he had found an angel to answer his prayer. "It is quite awe-inspiring, no? To see the advent of Christianity in a hedonistic community." Dominic's voice rumbled in quiet reverence, his eyes resting on Kira's halo of golden hair.

"Are there other artifacts?" she asked excitedly. "Other evidence of Christ?"

He shook his head. "They would be hidden away, probably destroyed. Persecution was beginning." The struggle was building within him, recognizing his weakness standing before him. With a sweep of his arm, he invited her to continue the tour into another building.

"Do you see this?" he said, holding an arm out to the artistry of another of the beautiful murals that once graced Pompeii. "This is how they expressed themselves. Their love of nature, their devotion to their gods." Hercules looked down from the wall, his son beside him. "These are their gods."

With his back to her, he could feel her curious stare. "Surely you've seen this dozens, more likely hundreds of times," she suggested quietly. "And yet it seems you're just seeing it for the first time."

He smiled, finding his excuse. "It is my passion, archeology." It was the right answer. Turning to face her once more, he found understanding in her eyes. His passion was further inflamed, but it had little to do with ancient rocks and paint.

"It is fascinating, isn't it?" she agreed, looking around the ancient villa. "This is why I became a history teacher." She twirled slowly, absorbing everything, reveling in the experience of Pompeii.

"Come," he invited. "There is more." Passing through into another room, a cloud came across Dominic's face. "There used to be…." Looking around the room, frustration becoming more evident. "I do not understand. They do not understand. To take these things as souvenirs, it is like taking the statue of the Madonna out of the church." He looked around the streets crowded with tourists and then looked back to his companion.

His expression softened and he put a hand to Kira's shoulder, redirecting her through the rutted streets of half walls growing with grass. She fell in step beside him, moving easily into his protective embrace.

"What was it like growing up on an archeological site?" Kira asked.

His broad shoulders tensed visibly. Memories of his mother intruded, screaming at his father for his "ridiculous digging." He remembered her long, flowing black hair, flying in her wake with every loudly announced escape from the "tomb" Enzio had made of her home. Excuses, he reminded himself, that eventually led to her pregnancy with Paolo and her final removal from their home. "I imagine it was no different than growing up anywhere," he stated flatly.

"I understand you lost your father not long ago."

"I do not wish to talk about my father," he answered quickly, his English accent suddenly perfect again. He moved a step away from her, once more dropping his arm to his side.

"My father died last spring," she continued. "It's because of him that I'm here, because of his bequest."

"My father was murdered," Dominic told her matter-of-factly.

"Is that why they say he haunts the excavation?"

He sputtered his distaste for the idea. "Have you seen any ghosts?"

Kira hesitated, remembering her experience alone in the dark.

Aware of her pause, he stepped before her, his black eyes in a squint trying to read her silence. "What have you seen, Kira?" He took hold of her shoulders, demanding her attention.

"I didn't see anything." But she wasn't looking at him, she was remembering something that kept her from reading his insistent stare.

"You were alone, in the dark," he reminded her.

"Fertile ground for an overactive imagination."

"What did you imagine? I must know."

She laughed timorously. "It was the most unusual thing. I heard a rock slide and then I could swear I heard someone say 'il sole.'"

Dominic paled, releasing her shoulders. "Are you quite certain that's what you heard? Those exact words?"

"I remember thinking how odd that I should be thinking of the sun in the middle of the night." She nodded her head. "I'm sure. Isn't a ghost supposed to say boo or something?"

Dominic didn't answer, her attempt at levity lost. Instead he continued in silence through the next building along the cobbled road. "We should be getting back," he suggested quietly. "May I drive you?"

"Do you spend a lot of time in Pompeii?" she asked quickly, changing the subject.

"There is a tranquillity here." He looked across to Vesuvius, standing silently against the sky. "When I see the Pater Noster…" one of his hands rolled in front of him while he groped for the words to express his feelings.

"I understand."

Kira rubbed her thighs. "We must have been walking for hours. Is it far to the car?"

Heads turned as they passed back out of the ruins. "Do people always stare at you?"

"I suppose it's because I'm so tall."

"Is that what you believe?" He laughed.

"What then?" She checked her clothing and smoothed her hair.

He did touch her hair then, admiring the many colors he found there to create the golden tones. "The women," he purred, "they envy you. The men," he paused finding her eyes with his, "they envy me."

Her hand pushed gently against his chest, pushing him away. "I didn't come for…" she insisted quietly.

"I know that."

Her eyes had gone to that shade of muddy green again, he noticed with some satisfaction.

"It couldn't turn out well," she insisted. "I'll only be here a few weeks…"

"Not so easy as being stung by an arrow," he reminded her.

The color in her eyes shifted back toward hazel. "And I don't believe in jumping into bed with every attractive man I meet."

"I was not suggesting…" he stammered, surprised by her forthrightness.

"I can take the train back."

He shook his head, still reeling with her implication. "I will see you safely to the casa. He directed her to a black Fiat, unlocking the passenger door and holding it open for Kira. She hesitated, finally taking the offered seat while he closed the door securely behind her.

※ ※ ※

"Thank you for the tour." She felt a need to acknowledge his kindness, noticing that he was growing visibly more rigid with each mile that passed.

He nodded silently, his fingers flexing around the steering wheel.

"What led your father to begin the excavation at the Casa?" she prodded, trying to draw him back out.

"Our intuition, our instincts lead us to the great treasures of lost civilizations," he began. "These instincts can be enhanced by modern technology, but my father believed the true archeologist can find the greatest treasures simply by following his own feelings." He paused, taking a deep breath. "My father had such a dream."

"There is a tradition in my family…" He stopped and shook his head, reconsidering. He turned to look at the young woman beside him, his dark eyes shining. "But you could not understand such things."

"Why couldn't I?"

"What could you know about upholding a family name, keeping a lineage alive generation after generation? What could you know about protecting what has been in your family for centuries even from relatives who have no heart for it?"

"Why haven't you married then? And Franco, if you need to continue your family name."

He sputtered out a half-laugh. "I expect that Franco is interviewing prospective wives now—now that he is disabled."

"And you?"

His hands continued to massage the steering wheel, his head turning away to look out his window to hide an expression that mirrored pain. "To marry unwisely would be worse than not marrying at all." He glanced over at Kira then. "You have never married?"

"I don't have to worry about carrying on a family name." She teased. "And I would have to agree with you about marrying unwisely. I haven't met anyone yet that I couldn't live without."

"Maybe you have and you just don't know it."

"Well I know who it isn't." She looked out her window at the passing countryside.

"And who isn't it?"

Kira smirked at the man beside her. "You, of course, being a man *and* Italian, could never understand."

"I spent some time in America. We are not so different." He kept his eyes carefully trained on the road.

"Oh, no," she replied sarcastically. "You would probably want your wife to be subservient, available at your beck and call to fulfill the whim of the moment." Her jaw set into resentment as thoughts of Joe crowded into her mind. "Not too intelligent. I suppose you would tolerate some spirit in your woman, Italians seem to enjoy their arguments."

"And this type of life does not appeal to you?"

"The man I marry must be willing to share my life, not rule it."

"That does not seem an unreasonable request." He turned to smile at her. "You see, you have been wrong about me."

"Wrong?"

He tightened his fingers around the steering wheel. "You said I could not understand."

They were reentering the city. Familiar streets heralded their impending arrival at the Casa.

"There is one question I want to ask you," Kira broached, harking back to their conversation of the day before.

Dominic nodded, his hands flexing and relaxing around the steering wheel.

"Maeve's sons. Were they Provisionals?"

"I told you it would come to you," he said triumphantly, giving her a satisfied smile.

"Just answer the question."

"Yes."

"But the Sinn Fein is more political, less terrorist. Am I right?"

"On the surface."

"Maeve told me she looks on you and Franco as she would her own sons, and there you sit calling her a revolutionary." Kira backed against the passenger door, looking directly at her chauffeur.

"I did not call her a revolutionary."

"Not directly."

He threw her another cautious look. "I am merely advising you to be careful."

"Fine. Then tell me what the IRA is doing in the South of Italy? Tell me what possible connection there could be between Herculaneum and the unification of Ireland? She's been here five years."

"Why are you here?"

"Haven't we had this conversation?"

Dominic's hands tightened around the wheel. "I make it my business to know the things people won't tell me," he began slowly. "I heard what you didn't tell me yesterday more plainly than what you did say."

"And what do you imagine it is that I'm hiding?"

The car passed the Herculaneum gate and drove down a dark, unfamiliar street. "There is something I have to pick up," he stalled, decelerating. "I hope you don't mind." He said it the same way he said things at the Casa, without waiting for a response and not caring if there was an objection.

Kira cringed at the imperious sound of his voice and turned her attention away from the man beside her.

He parked the car along the street. "You will wait here." He jumped out the door, leaving her sitting in the car on a street overcrowded with buildings that tried to block out the sky.

Kira looked out the window at two old men playing cards on a table set up in the street. They stopped their game to stare at her, making her turn away self-consciously. On the other side of the street a woman sat weaving a basket, her eyes watching Kira while hands moved knowledgeably through the rows in her lap.

Huddled against another building three young man were looking speculatively at the Fiat. When they saw the unescorted woman looking their way, they began to gesture, leaving little doubt about what they had in mind.

Kira watched the doorway where Dominic disappeared. She stared at the building until she saw his dark head pop out again carrying a package wrapped in white paper and tied with string.

He did not acknowledge her as he approached the car, fixing his attention elsewhere until he tossed the package into the back seat and took his place behind the wheel.

"Aren't you the guy who keeps telling me it isn't safe for a woman to be alone?" Kira shot at him.

His eyebrows lifted, the only expression on his face. "Alone?"

She crossed her arms. "I don't know where I am."

"You are with me. No one would harm you."

"What if they didn't know I was with you? What if they didn't care?" she demanded angrily.

"I would not put you in danger," he spoke quietly. "It is part of our obligation to protect you while you are at our Casa."

"Right. From an Irish terrorist who's about as frightening as my mother and from who else? What's Jean-Marc's secret?"

Dominic stopped the car and leaned across the seat, taking hold of her arms roughly. "I would like to remind you that in spite of your foolishness I have protected you."

"Where? At Pompeii? I was in a crowd there, not on some dark back street."

His hands tightened around her arms leaving white indentations where his fingers pressed. "Safety in numbers does not apply in Italy. Are you so blind?"

"You're hurting me," she cried out. Immediately he released her and turned back to the wheel.

When his eyes locked on hers again, his expression was steely. The transformation was complete. With the return of his insolent manner came Kira's indignance. Rubbing her arms where he had taken hold of her, she pushed open the door of the car and got out.

She looked down the street, taking her bearings. Setting her stride, she moved ahead purposefully.

"Get back in the car," Dominic called out.

"I'll take my chances walking."

"This is not America."

She turned to face the car, arms held out in exasperation. "I'm perfectly capable…" She shook her head and set her stride away from him once more.

"Get back in the car."

"I'll be fine."

Dominic drove the car slowly behind her, keeping her in sight. "You've had a long day," he argued. "You're not used to this kind of exertion."

She threw her head back and picked up the pace. "I'm fine."

"Let me take you back."

"I'd rather walk right now, thank you," she called back to him acidly.

"Kira…" his voice sounded strangely vulnerable, almost pleading for an instant.

Kira slowed in response to the unfamiliar tone, but then she reached the corner. The locanda loomed ahead. Without turning to acknowledge him, she stepped up her pace again, her destination now in sight.

The car veered away and Kira stopped, rubbing her thighs apologetically.

She allowed herself to limp into the Casa, walking straight to Anna's office. "Is there a library?—biblioteca?"

Anna looked at her curiously.

"I lost my reference materials," Kira explained in defeat. "I was hoping to find more information on what's been found in and around Pompeii and Herculaneum."

Anna smiled and motioned for her to follow, taking Kira down the other corridor of the Casa. The first room lay open without the barrier of the doors that lined the hallway Kira had become familiar with.

"Le Signores they live at the back." Anna pointed further down the corridor. "These are private rooms."

Kira nodded, understanding her implication and forged into the library. Bookshelves lined the walls filled with volumes. Counters were built in at regular intervals. Eagerly, Kira fingered through a section of Italian books. Stopping on an English title, she pulled the book from the shelf. "I don't believe it," she whispered to herself, opening a nonfiction version of the Arthurian legends in her hands.

She skimmed through, looking for references to the Holy Grail, alternately looking around the room to make sure she was alone. Sticking a finger inside the book she looked to the shelves for more information. A quick perusal showed more foreign titles.

Kira took the English book, pulling a big leather chair around to face the only lamp in the library. She sat down and leaned forward to bring more light to the pages. Notations were made in the margins: *Atti 22-28.* She reached into her pocket for her notebook, but it was gone.

She looked around the floor of the library and began retracing her steps, stopping when the voices of the brothers signaled their approach. She returned hastily to the chair curling herself into it and bending her head over the book.

The footsteps on the carpeting signaled which brother entered the library. Tucking her aching legs up, Kira tried to disappear into the upholstery.

A bronzed arm reached out for the bookshelf beside her, sending a ripple through the solid muscles. She closed her eyes and inhaled the natural musky fragrance of the man who stood only inches away.

As surely as she had not come for a summer romance, she was certain this day would be a memory to last a lifetime. The scent that pervaded her senses now would remain in her olfactory memory every time she thought back to her tour of Pompeii.

Soft, dark curls crowned the top of his head as he moved in front of her, the solid definition of his torso like granite straining beneath the thin cotton. She would not soon forget the beauty of Dominic Fioretti. She closed her eyes to quell the hunger that called out to her but found her thoughts focused squarely on the man standing only inches away from her.

Kira tightened into the cocoon of the chair watching Dominic trace a line of text with long fingers, dirt permanently ground into his knuckles.

Dominic looked up absently, his book nearly falling from his hands at the shock of finding her so near. His bronze skin took on a ruddy look. "Miss Ellison."

"Signore," she greeted uneasily.

He straightened, throwing his shoulders back while he recovered his book. His expression quickly masked what lay behind his black eyes. "I am afraid we do not have much in English for you to look at."

Kira unfolded from the chair. "On the contrary." She stood tall, smoothing her clothing.

He reached out a large hand, inquiring into what she had discovered. "May I?" Reluctantly, she handed over the Arthurian work, pulling back quickly as if avoiding the touch of a hot stove.

He raised his eyebrows. "That's right, you were in England, at Cadbury Castle," he recalled. "Where you met my brother." He stared at her, waiting for a deviation from the story she had already given him.

"I didn't meet your brother until I arrived here," she snapped.

"So you've said." He looked over the book at the young woman standing before him. Her complexion was flushed from the heat of the sun, her eyes shaded to green. Dominic hesitated a moment to admire the polish that brought out her natural beauty. "You are interested in King Arthur?"

"You might say that."

He handed the book back to her, staring at her with dark eyes and scraping the stubble that was surfacing on his chin.

"I suppose there are thousands of archeologists who hope to find the Holy Grail," she baited.

Dominic leaned back against the bookshelves, a slow smile spreading behind the hand on his chin. "I suppose. Is that why you went to England?"

Kira pushed her glasses back up her nose, afraid to answer for fear of sounding foolish.

His dark eyes sparkled with amusement. "And did you find it?"

"No."

"If you are looking for the Holy Grail, why did you come here?" He sat on his hands leaning on the shelf behind him.

"I have always been fascinated by Pompeii and its sister cities. Maeve captured my imagination."

His eyes narrowed and he replaced the book in his hand to its niche in the wall. "You are a treasure hunter just like the rest."

"I didn't know anything about any treasure when I made my application here."

"Why do you seek the grail?"

She put her fist under her chin and considered his question. "Historical significance. Curiosity, I suppose."

"And what would you use it for?"

"Use it for?" She laughed. "You mean like a magic wand?"

He turned a hand in front of him, inviting her to comment further.

"I don't really believe it exists, for starters. And in the second place, even if it did, and how could you prove it if you found it, I don't believe in magic wands."

"And still you are here."

"I have heard there is a legend," she coaxed, yearning for the patient teacher he had been a few hours earlier.

He motioned for Kira to sit down again. She quickly obliged, leaning forward to catch every word.

Bowing his head and grabbing his wrists behind his back, his fingers began clicking one by one against his thumb. "You know that the villa below is my ancestral home," he began. "In the year A.D. 61 the Apostle Paul was taken to Rome for a hearing with the Emperor Nero." He looked directly at Kira to make sure she was listening. "It is said he left a treasure with my ancestors during his passage from Puteoli. Puteoli was the main port then. This is where Pozzuoli is today."

"But surely, traveling as a criminal, he wouldn't have been carrying anything of value. What is this treasure said to be?"

He raised an eyebrow casually with a cock of his head and turned away.

She laughed again. "So you're digging up this treasure, but you wouldn't recognize it if you found it. Is that about it?"

When he faced her again, his expression was carefully veiled. "I think the question, Miss Ellison, is will you?"

She laughed. "Certainly not."

"I would like to ask a personal favor," he proposed.

Kira stiffened, her heart missing a beat. "You can ask," she invited, "but I can't promise anything."

He hesitated, his color deepening. He studied the toes of his brown loafers. "You may have noticed that people have been trying to pair us together."

Her heart rapidly made up for the lost beat and hammered several additional tattoos.

The top of his black head lifted only momentarily to make sure she was listening. "I do not wish to make you uncomfortable, and I do not know what arrangement you have with my brother…"

"I have no arrangement with your brother."

He raised his eyes to look at her. "You have made some unusual friends since you have been here."

"What other friends don't you want me to play with?" she asked sarcastically. "Are you going to tell me Jean-Marc's deep dark secret next?"

"Has he frightened you?"

"Of course not."

"He is helping you? Perhaps a little more than you are comfortable with?"

"No, he has been helpful but unobtrusive. What…?"

"Jean-Marc is a deeply religious man," Dominic stated firmly. "That is the most important thing you need to know about him."

"So…?"

He paced across the room, reaching for a book from the shelves. "It would be to my advantage if certain people believed me to be distracted from my duties." He turned to face Kira and took a deep breath. "Those who have started the rumors are hoping a relationship with you would draw my attention away from what they are doing. If they believed it were true, they might grow careless."

Disjointed thoughts were spinning through Kira's head. "I have been fairly vocal in my opinions of summer romance," she cautioned, while at the same time thrilling at the prospect.

He raised his eyebrows. "They have been encouraging you?"

With a nod of her head, Kira looked away. "I came here to work, Padrone."

Dominic's head was bobbing in agreement. "Your commitment has not gone unnoticed. No one could accuse you of less, unlike others we currently entertain…"

Like Laura, she thought, feeling an unreasonable pang of jealousy. Of the whirlwind jumbling through Kira's mind one thing stopped at the forefront in bold letters: DANGER. Whether he intended it as a charade or not, *she* certainly would be distracted. The result could only be detrimental to them both.

"Kira." Franco wheeled into the library. "Anna told me you were looking for some reference material. Are you finding everything you require?"

She was still watching Dominic. "I'm afraid I didn't think about the books being written in Italian."

"Perhaps I can be of assistance." Franco looked from Kira to his brother, assessing the situation. "Or perhaps my brother has already been assisting you as a translator."

"I think Miss Ellison knows much more than we give her credit for." Dominic bent his head slightly. "Perhaps I have made an error in judgment," he suggested coolly. "If you'll excuse me?"

Kira watched Dominic's exit frustrated. "Your brother was just telling me about the legend surrounding your mysterious treasure."

Franco laughed easily. "Just a legend. St. Paul is said to have visited our ancestors before Vesuvio buried their cities. A child's fairy tale, a bedtime story. That is all."

"What do you suppose the treasure to be?" she pressed.

"I have never heard it referred to as anything other than 'the treasure.'"

"Tell me about England," she encouraged. "You went to see some artifacts?"

"Yes."

"Greco-Roman?"

He nodded. "You will know about the Roman invasion of Jerusalem, causing the Jews to scatter. Some of the artifacts I went to see are said to have come from as far away as Solomon's temple—from Jerusalem."

She focused on a point on the floor across the room trying to see Solomon's temple in her mind's eye. "So the treasure? Perhaps something from Solomon's temple?"

He shrugged his shoulders. "It is only a story."

"May I borrow this book?"

He waved through the air. "Of course. Take it."

"Wouldn't it be something if the legend were true?" Kira laughed, starting back toward the corridor.

Franco caught her hand as she passed, taking it into both of his. "What is it that you expect to find?"

She looked down at his hands, hard from the callouses that had built up from managing his wheelchair. "History," she replied simply.

Franco held her eyes with his, bringing her hand to his lips. She flushed crimson, resting a hand on his shoulder before pulling gently away.

❦ ❦ ❦

In the dark corridor outside the library, Dominic's dark outline almost blended into the shadows of a pillar. He watched while Kira put a hand to Franco's shoulder in parting before she left the library.

A casual gesture, but one which she initiated.

She couldn't know about the grail.

And yet she seemed to know.

How many times had his father told him that it would be a woman who would find the grail? A woman he always referred to as the sun: il sole.

Superstitious nonsense.

That she had seen him standing in the shadow of the column he was certain. Transfixed, he watched her leave the library. She moved so gracefully, so fluidly.

Dominic looked back to Franco. His brother was showing remarkable restraint. Perhaps it was because Franco was so practiced.

There was something about her.

He thought of the way she moved through the broken streets of Pompeii, her long legs taking elegant strides.

She had seemed to absorb every detail of everything that she saw. Whatever else she was, her enthusiasm was real.

Dominic moved silently behind the tower of limestone, blending into the shadows. The other American woman was coming down now, her diaphanous nightgown leaving little to the imagination.

He watched for a moment while Laura teased Franco, playing with the buttons on his shirt while her bosom overflowed the constraints of the negligee inches away from Franco's face. Dominic watched while Franco cupped the rounded curves she offered.

He turned to walk away, but then he saw something that alarmed him. Franco got up out of the wheelchair. He was going to fall. Dominic moved out from behind the pillar to help his brother and then stopped, realizing that Franco was in complete control of his movements.

Franco was holding Laura, bracing himself against the shelves while he stood on still unsteady legs. It was clearly evident that he had no fear of falling.

Dominic did not understand his brother's insatiable appetite for women. The man had no common sense. How could he pursue Kira while entertaining Laura?

Let him fall.

Dominic walked out to the foyer and looked up the staircase at the closed door.

His father's last words to Dominic echoed in his memory: "It is a woman who will find the grail, a woman who is the sun." Enzio Fioretti had always told his younger son that one day the sun would come to Dominic. But even more unsettling were the origin of Kira's name and the color of her hair.

It must be a coincidence, he decided.

He was already far too distracted. Dominic reached out and punched his fist into a column, hoping to drive away his attraction to her with the pain.

His hand was throbbing, but he was thinking of her still, her beautiful eyes, the way they changed to green when she was aroused, the perfect structure of the bones in her face—a face that could have belonged to Aphrodite. And her hair—the way it shone in the sun like a halo.

"Signore, I am leaving," Anna called, crossing through the foyer. She stopped before the man holding one fist in the other. "You are bleeding," she observed.

He nodded brusquely and turned away from her. "I'm fine," he growled.

"You are hurt," she reproved. "You do not fool me, Padrone." There was a mocking tone in her voice. "I have been with your father too long." She looked up at him cautiously, worried about the effect of her careless words.

Anna set down her handbag and walked back into her office, returning to her employer with a gauze bandage and some tape to hold it in place.

She wrapped his hand tenderly, not wanting to upset him further. "Forgive me, Signore," she apologized.

Dominic flexed his hand beneath the bandage. "Thank you, Anna."

"Signore," she began hesitantly, "is it true what they say about your father?"

"What? You mean the ghost?"

She nodded uncertainly. "They say he has not finished what he started and that he cannot rest until the Treasure has been found."

"Again the Treasure." His black eyes flashed angrily. "There is no Treasure, Anna, and my father is dead. He knew he would not find the treasure. He told me this himself."

"Then why..."

"Carlo is a superstitious old fool." His voice cracked, his eyes glistening in the light that filtered down from the dome. "He should not have died, but I will not believe his spirit is not at rest." He held his hand, wincing with the pain.

"There was a package in my office," she continued, changing the subject. "A handbag with books in it. It was wrapped in white paper and tied with string."

"They belong to Miss Ellison. They were taken from her at the Stazione Central when she arrived. Will you see that she gets them back, please?"

Anna could not conceal a sly smile of amusement. "Wouldn't you rather do that?"

Dominic looked at her sharply. "I do not believe the lady trusts me."

"Maybe if you spent more time with her," the older woman suggested. "She is here to learn. You are the teacher."

"Her interests lie elsewhere."

Anna walked toward the door, following Dominic's line of vision to the closed door along the passageway overhead. "Good night, Signore."

Dominic set his stride to the private rooms without pausing to look into the library. He didn't stop until he reached the door to the courtyard and then he slid back into the shadows.

Right where Dominic knew he would be, the knight was kneeling reverently beside an olive tree facing the excavation. His white cassock gleamed eerily in the bright moonlight, the golden glint of his sword pointing down to the earth.

It was Franco who had assembled them all together. Dominic knew about Maeve; he knew about Jean-Marc. There had never been a question about Paolo. Years of careful planning were now coming to a head. His father's murder was only the beginning.

What a fool Franco was, gathering sticks of dynamite. He had already been caught in the cross fire. How would he be able to control them after the fuse was lit? And where did Kira fit in with the plan?

CHAPTER 10

Having foregone breakfast, Kira was one of the first into the cool site in the morning. The ground lay quiet, the air still and quiet as a tomb.

She approached the mural, hidden beneath the artisan's covering where restored images peered through. Kira brushed the crack along the edge of the images gingerly, feeling along the grooves with her fingers. Changing to a trowel, she began scraping a section of the hardened shell on the wall and continued the tedious process of opening the crevice.

Stepping back, she arched her back producing several loud cracks. Wiping the sweat from her brow, and wrinkling her nose at the dank smell that surrounded her, she looked to the painted wall again. Cupid supervised an orgy of bodies led by the satyr taking pleasure with a young woman. Mesmerized, the figures seemed to dance before her straining vision. She reached a hand out to touch the black-haired satyr, gently brushing back particles of dust. "He probably has no more use for women than you do," she told the picture.

But Dominic's body was broader than the satyr's. Powerful muscles strained against the fabric of his shirts, his torso tapering only slightly at his waist. He was nearing forty, but only the scowl spoke to his age. Kira wondered if the length of his hair was his personal protest against the years. The dark curls provided a buoyant effect, framing his Roman features and softening the starkness of his black eyes.

Kira exhaled, trying to blow the image from her mind. She removed her glasses and wiped at her eyes with grungy fingers.

"It is beautiful, is it not?"

Kira's glasses fell from her hands. The timbre of his voice rolled through the chamber like a cat purring.

She dropped to her knees to retrieve her glasses, but Dominic was faster. He held them out to her, his face inches away from hers. No tail, no points on his ears, Kira reminded herself. Only a man. She took her glasses, watching him cautiously.

Dominic reached up with a hand and smoothed the hair off of her forehead. His touch was gentle, lingering while the back of his hand brushed across her cheek.

He smelled of soap. His thick hair was neatly combed and his face was smooth from having just been shaved. The warmth of his hand on her face seared like the lighting of the Olympic torch.

"Padrone!" a voice called out from an adjoining room. He didn't move immediately, his eyes following while his fingers continued to trace the contours of her face, but then he rose abruptly and disappeared.

A stream of Italian issued by one of the laborers signaled his arrival. Released from his spell, Kira crouched down to catch her breath.

"Kira?" Jean-Marc strode into the chamber to resume his restoration of the cupboard against the wall.

"Talk about your demons catching you alone," she sighed. "Air's a little thick in here." She took another deep breath, trying to inhale all the fresh air before it was impaired further by the cloud that the workers would inevitably stir up. Rising to her feet, she turned her attention back to the fissure in the wall.

Using a trowel in one hand, she brushed at the crevice with the other. "Ow!" she cried out, sucking on one of her fingers and then quickly spitting it back out with the taste of dirt.

"Ca va?" Jean-Marc called across distractedly.

"I cut my finger on a piece of rock," she answered, shaking the offended digit. A peripheral flash of light called her attention back to the wall. Turning full face to her project, Kira reached out to trace the crack, angrily shaking back the bleeding finger and dropping her trowel to use the other hand. A puff of air blew dust from the other side. Impulsively, she pushed. The wall shivered behind the pressure but remained stubbornly set. Kira shined a flashlight into the void, peering through the break.

Her breath caught in her throat, one of her hands clutching her chest. Turning to face Jean-Marc, her mouth refused to utter the words that her lips were trying to form.

"*Qu'est ce que c'est?*" he whispered across the chamber, seeing her trembling and pale.

Her mouth continued to move, but no words could find their way out. She motioned to the wall. "A room," she finally whispered.

"Padrone," Jean-Marc called tentatively, watching Kira closely. He moved toward her, reaching his arms out just as she began to drop, her legs wobbling like a new colt. Jean-Marc eased her to the floor against the wall.

Hugging her legs to her chest, Kira watched the flurry of people coming to finish what she had started. Dominic choreographed the workers to document and measure. His hands moved about expressively, one bandaged with thick gauze. He helped to find the hinges on the door, expertly cleaning them, preparing to breach.

Jean-Marc put a reassuring arm across Kira's shoulder. "He has the hands of a surgeon," he pointed out. "Like a birth, is it not?"

❦   ❦   ❦

The new room had been a lararium once but the altar built to the Lares served a different god. Kira continued to work industriously to clear the endless succession of mire that preserved the past from the present. She chipped and brushed and scraped intently, pouring water to loosen the fossilized debris.

Dominic remained close at hand, watching her, not wanting to frighten her.

The cupboard stood against a wall, a wedge of pyroclastic mud blocking the lower section. The top section was nothing more than a shell from laying unpreserved through the centuries. The room had been almost completely sealed off, the lava flow merely seeping in through the small cracks of the concealed doorway.

Vaguely aware of the exodus for lunch Kira continued pulling at the debris. She was obviously not aware of the increased danger that surrounded her. Until he could bring the murderer out into the open, he would have to make sure she remained safe.

He called in other members of the team to work behind her, documenting, charting. The cleanup crew did their work unobtrusively, sweeping up the refuse to be sifted through for more minute artifacts.

Every time she moved, twisting to find a more comfortable position, he felt the tension in his own shoulders that came with restraint. He wanted to massage her shoulders for her, to work beside her.

Kira refused to relent. She chiseled away, insulated from the others by the muralled wall and by her narrow focus.

Two short beeps from his wristwatch signaled the end of the day. Dominic walked out of the antechamber and shouted out into the open courtyard: "Lay down your tools." Satisfied with the echo that followed, he returned to guard Kira's progress.

An awareness of the gathering darkness finally pushed Kira upright. Still kneeling in the small chamber, she stretched the complaining muscles in her back. Dominic watched the forward thrust of her breasts, silently committing the feminine outline to memory.

She remained still for a minute, her senses reaching out to fill in all that she had barricaded herself against for the past several hours. The vertebrae in her neck popped loudly as she turned her head to confirm his presence.

"Lay down your tools," he relayed quietly, calling an end to the day's work.

The surrounding silence was deafening. "Am I the last one out?"

He nodded slowly, not moving. Kira rose to her feet, brushing dust off her blue jeans. Still he didn't move, his black eyes watching her intently. The movements of her arms pulled her shirt up enough to give him a glimpse of her trim waistline.

"Have you found anything?" The words barely spoken rumbled off the walls of the small cell. He stepped up onto a shelf of lava inside the room, looking all around before fixing his intense stare on Kira again.

"There is only what you see," she replied, holding out her arms.

Dominic turned away, closing his eyes to fight his growing need for her. "What do you know of the Treasure?"

"Educate me," she replied, shaking dust out of her hair.

"Surely you must realize what you are up against."

She looked around her defiantly. "So where's the bomb? Who's out to get me?"

With a huff of exasperation, he disappeared through the tunnel. Certain that she was following him out, he climbed the steps two at a time back to the Casa above.

❦   ❦   ❦

The dinner crowd was subdued. Without searching them out Kira recognized that one or both of the brothers was present.

Still sifting remnants from the day's work from her clothes and hair, she passed through the dining room along the long corridor that led to the front of the Casa, staring at the floor and lost in her own thoughts. She was jarred momentarily when a man brushed by her as she approached the foyer. Looking up, her brow furrowed trying to recall where she had seen the man before, but he was gone before she could place him. Shrugging, she continued to the foyer and up the staircase.

Kira stopped by her room only long enough to retrieve a towel and a change of clothes. Continuing around the bend in the upstairs corridor, she made her way to the shower before the others finished their meals.

Ten minutes later and without her glasses, she retraced her steps to her room, her hair wrapped in a towel over her head. Squinting, she watched a man emerging from one of the doors down the hall near her room. Taking longer strides, she saw that it was Laura's door closing in Dominic Fioretti's wake.

"Gigolo. It is an Italian word, no?" she said sarcastically to herself. Safely inside her room, Kira yanked her clothes on, but the welcome silence of her room was perforated by sobs coming from the direction of Laura's room.

"Are you all right?" Kira called through the adjoining door. Footsteps were marked by the sound of the bolt being pulled back from its lock on Laura's side. Uncertainly, Kira opened the door.

Laura sat on the bed, her blond hair sheltering the face she held in her hands. Kira moved beside her. Laura's blue eyes were pools of water. Below one eye a narrow purple line marked the crease of her cheekbone. She brushed back the tears but the bruise remained.

Kira's eyes widened in surprise. "Do you have a black eye?"

She turned away, sniffling to keep back the tears. "He didn't mean it," she whispered.

Kira looked to the door remembering Dominic's broad back retreating down the stairs. "Why did he do it?" she asked, smoothing Laura's hair back off her face.

Laura shook her head. "We had a fight…I didn't want to…" She dissolved into sobs again.

"There's no excuse…" Kira fumed, "there's never sufficient justification for a man to hit a woman. Only a coward would use physical advantage…" She shook her head angrily. "Just wait 'til I…No, I won't wait." She got up from the bed, storming out of the room. She flew down the staircase, throwing open the door to the study below.

The brothers were behind the desk together, Dominic leaning over his brother's wheelchair, examining the day's finds. Franco looked up, startled. "Miss Elleesone. We were just discussing your chamber."

"How dare you!" she accused Dominic. "What have you done to Laura?" She advanced to the edge of the desk and leaned over, demanding an answer.

He stood back folding his arms behind his back. "What do you mean?"

"I saw you coming from her room. Do you realize she has a black eye?"

"What is all this about?" Franco cleared a spot on the desk before him, and placed his hands on the blotter.

Dominic's fingernails began their clicking, each nail striking the thumb in turn. His expression now was carefully veiled. "And you think I did it?"

"I sent my brother to invite Miss Griffith down," Franco interjected. "There is a matter we need to discuss. There would be no reason for violence. And since you are here, perhaps you might join us. This matter concerns you as well."

Kira didn't move. Facing Dominic, she refused to be distracted.

"Has she accused me?"

"She didn't have to."

With a sweep of his hand, Dominic dismissed Kira. "Leave us."

"I will take care of this, Miss Elleesone." Franco's soothing voice cut through the manacles that bound her to the desk.

Kira straightened, her fists clenching at her sides, eyes still fixed on Il Padrone. "What kind of a business are you two running here?" Turning her head slowly, she addressed the older brother before retreating.

"Santa Maria, Madre de Dio. I cannot bear it," Dominic complained to his brother while the door closed. Through the barrier, Kira heard the sound of Franco answering Dominic's grievance with quiet words.

❦   ❦   ❦

After being summarily dismissed, Kira stood uncertainly in the foyer until the rumbling of her stomach raised complaints about neglect.

Maeve was still in the dining room, seated at a corner table looking through a newspaper. "Where is Jean-Marc?" Kira asked.

"He's gone home for the weekend, hasn't he." She replied, inviting Kira to sit. "Have a drink with me."

"Is it Friday already?" Kira sighed, pulling up a chair at the table.

Emerald green eyes peered over the top of the newspaper. "Aye, and the site'll be closed this weekend." She reached out and poured another glass of wine.

"But there's so much to do." Kira lifted the glass to her lips, staring to the site outside the dining room.

"An excitin' day, to be sure. But we'll be needin' the rest."

"The new room…"

"It'll still be there, dearie." She patted Kira's hand. "Tell me about the room. Il Padrone has been keeping it quite a secret."

"A secret? There have been people in and out all day."

"'Tisn't normal to be havin' an amateur opening such a place," she explained quietly. "And 'tis only you that has been workin' in there."

"There's nothing to see, really." Kira fingered her glass, staring into the clear golden wine. "It's only a small chamber."

"Aye?"

Kira gulped another sip of the wine. "I'm sure he'll bring others in when there's something worth looking at. There's nothing in there," her voice trailed off, "only the cupboard."

"If i'twere one o' the others, they'd be dismissed for workin' alone." She leaned forward and lowered her voice. "Are ye here ta find the treasure then?"

"There's nothing in there," she repeated. "Just the shell of an old cupboard." Kira stared at the older woman across the table, angry at the seeds of doubt that Dominic had planted about her friend.

Maeve leaned back, giving way to a broad smile. "The workers are takin' wagers on ye."

"The workers?"

"Aye. Which of the brothers will it be then?"

Kira choked on a mouthful of the wine. "Excuse me?" Her suspicions grew hearkening back to Dominic's suggestion that "they" were hoping to divide his attention.

"They're saying you'll be the new Signora Fioretti, but they can't decide which brother ye'll be choosin'."

Kira's cheeks flamed crimson. "I'm sure that's quite absurd. I'm only here for a few weeks. Even if I were interested in one of them, I'm quite sure that neither of them would possibly contemplate marrying me." She waved a hand carelessly in the air. "Why does this feel more like the dating game than an excavation?"

"One could hardly ignore they're both fine lookin' men," she suggested, leaning toward Kira in hopes of getting an inclination toward one or the other.

"Oh, come on!" the younger woman protested, growing increasingly uncomfortable.

"Do ye not notice the way they fight over ye, then?"

"They're brothers. I'm sure they have many more things to fight over than one insignificant history teacher."

Maeve smiled and put her hand on Kira's again. "I've been here five years, Kirie. I've seen the women come and go, an' I'll tell ye plain, before yer time has finished here one of them will be askin' ye to stay."

"They're both extremely attractive," Kira conceded, squirming in her chair, "but that's not enough to make me even consider the possibilities you suggest." She winced and reached for her glass, taking another healthy gulp of wine. "Really! To marry a man I hardly know! As if the thought would even occur to him!"

Maeve tucked the paper under her arm and stood up. "Il Padrone is guardin' over ye like some great watch dog, and Franco, he always seems to know where yer at."

"It's their job to protect us. It's part of the package. Isn't that what Il Padrone told me?"

"Aye," she answered with a knowing smile, but she was looking past Kira at the arched entrance. The sound of wheels on the tiled floor heralded the arrival of Franco Fioretti. "I'll be seein' ya later, Kirie."

Kira poured another glass from the bottle Maeve left on the table, quickly taking another drink. She put a hand to her head and stared at one of the columns, trying to make it stand straight through blurred eyes.

"My brother is in a very agitated state," Franco said, rolling up to the table beside her. Franco reached out, wrapping his hands around the delicate stem where Kira fingered her glass.

As she lifted the glass to her lips once more, Kira looked over the crystal into Franco's beautiful blue eyes. "There is something very familiar about you, Signore."

"Perhaps you remember me from England," he suggested.

"You were there."

"You are not an easy person to forget, Kira."

She stared at him, trying to remember some meeting that she had misplaced in her recent memories. Surely she wouldn't forget such an aggressive man, but then there may have been other interests for him there.

He offered a rakish smile. "We were not introduced," he reassured her almost as if he read her thoughts. With the sound of more footsteps, Franco turned his attention away from Kira to the new arrivals in the dining room.

"It has come to our attention that you have not been informed about the fundraising ball," he continued loudly.

Laura and Dominic approached the table. Kira rose to her feet unsettling the chair. Irrational tears stung the corners of her eyes at the sight of the couple standing side by side.

Laura smoothed out her miniskirt and planted herself in a chair behind the table, stretching out long, tapered spindles and shaking her blond tresses behind her. She poured a glass of the wine and, doing her best Blanche DuBois, reclined coquettishly flashing her eyelashes and waiting.

Kira wiped her hands on her jeans, stepping backwards in an attempt to disappear into the shadows of a Doric column. The setting sun shone through from the courtyard, illuminating her hair and refusing to let her blend with the growing darkness.

"You will be our guests, of course," Franco continued.

"I did not expect to be attending any social functions," Kira protested. "I'm afraid I don't have anything appropriate to wear. I had only planned to visit England."

"Of course you will not know anyone," Franco continued, "so my brother and I will escort you. Our guests will want to meet some of the people who are working here. They will want to hear of our progress."

"I don't speak Italian very well. I wouldn't do you much good."

"Many of our guests speak as much English as you speak Italian. I'm sure there would be no problem understanding each other," Dominic said.

Kira's eyes darted to the dark satyr. Every other man in her life tried to downplay her intelligence, yet there stood Dominic, depending on it and expecting her to show it. The curls that fell to his square shoulders fascinated her distorted reason. She shook her head in an attempt to stay with the conversation.

"I have trouble following the dialect," she protested weakly.

"I think it sounds like fun," Laura said.

"I'd prefer not to attend, if you don't mind," Kira replied quickly.

Dominic's eyes seemed to be glowing, his face set firmly into the familiar scowl. "I would be honored if you would accompany me," he invited Kira reluctantly. "We will find you a suitable dress."

"I'll take you shopping tomorrow," Laura pressed. "I know just the place. It'll be fun."

"Thank you, but I'd rather not."

"Would it kill you to wear a dress for an evening?" Laura argued.

"Who's side are you on?" she fumed, her speech slurring slightly. She pulled her shoulders back, standing tall. "I wouldn't want you do something so distasteful as to escort an Amazon that you didn't want here in the first place," she told Dominic angrily, rediscovering some of the rage that kept her attraction at bay. Her eyes were shining with tears threatening perilously close to the surface. "What difference could it possibly make if I wasn't there?"

Franco looked from one woman to the other in a state of confusion. "Perhaps you would accompany me then?"

"We give you your choice, Signorina," Dominic finished, proffering a mock bow.

Kira laughed. "You can't be serious." Dominic stepped back into the gathering darkness. She imagined pointed ears hiding beneath strategically brushed twists of his hair. Her cheeks still showed a faint flush of color, her mind going back to the early hours of the morning when he had found her alone in the excavation ahead of the workers. She was remembering how surprisingly soft his hands had felt on her cheeks. Then she looked at Laura and saw the extra make up that covered the discoloration around her eye.

She took a deep breath to mount a new protest. "Sure. And where am I supposed to just find a formal dress?"

"Does a ball not appeal to you at all?" Dominic asked, his deep voice silky, seductive. He glided out of the shadows, standing just behind her.

Without realizing she had moved, Kira leaned toward him as if being pulled by a magnet. She closed her eyes and reached for the table and her glass of wine.

"You must come," Franco urged.

"I'm sure I won't be able to find a dress on such short notice," she wavered.

"But you will try?"

"Oh Kira, it'll be fun," Laura coaxed. "It'll be like going to the prom."

"I never went to the prom."

She laughed. "Then pretend you're Cinderella for a night."

Kira took another swallow of the cool wine.

"Oh, Kira," Laura sighed. "You've just got to go. Maeve won't talk to me and no one else speaks English well enough to spend the evening with."

She moved an unsteady hand to set her empty glass down on the table, reaching out for support. "Is there anything left from dinner, I'm afraid I haven't had anything to eat all day."

Dominic reached for her, bracing her languid body against his. She closed her eyes and became instantly aware of him, his body solid against hers stabilizing the uncertainty of her equilibrium.

She looked up at him, feeling the responding fever rush through her like mercury in a thermometer.

"You will save me the first dance?" He whispered into her ear, his deep voice sending a shiver through her.

"Yes."

Dominic's mouth twisted into a smirk. "Perhaps its time you said good night," he suggested.

"Yes." She melted into the strength of his arms, sinking against his shoulder while he supported her gently, leading her through the corridor and up the stairs.

She took a deep breath, inhaling the essence of the man. He still carried an earthy scent from being in the ground mingled with the freshness of a gentle breeze, but beneath that was the essence of the man himself—strong and virile. There was nothing artificial about Dominic Fioretti.

"You don't drink much, do you?" he asked, his voice suppressing the amusement he was taking at her expense.

"I told you I haven't eaten all day."

Outside her room, Dominic turned the knob, pushing open the door. "Good night, Miss Ellison." His hand went under her chin, placing a light kiss on her lips.

"Don't go..." She circled his waist with her arms, opening her mouth against his for a deeper kiss.

His response was immediate, matching her inflamed passion. With his tongue he could still taste the wine that had released her from her reservations, and that was what stopped him.

He pushed her away, hungering for more. Instead, he stood in the doorway for several minutes massaging his bandaged fist. He squeezed his eyes shut with deep felt frustration. "You would be wise to avoid drinking our Lacrimae Christi on an empty stomach," he advised. "It might cause you to do something you would later regret." The door closed quietly against his hasty exit.

Holding her head, Kira fell backward onto the bed. Muddled thoughts crashed into each other, spinning on the stationary bed while she passed into the realm of sleep.

They glided across the crowded dance floor like Cinderella and Prince Charming, spinning, spinning. The clock struck twelve. The beautiful dress turned into a sweater and jeans, the glass slippers into gym shoes. Terrified, Kira flew out of the palazzo and into the night air. The whole world was turning.

She rose out of bed and ran to the toilet, resisting the need to regurgitate along the way.

Projecting her misery into the commode, Kira hugged the porcelain for balance. "There is no Prince Charming," she muttered to herself. "There is no happily ever after."

She squeezed her eyes tight to suppress the pain, images of the dream dancing in her head. His face whirled in front of her with each revolution. She threw up again, hoping to send Dominic's reflection from her mind with the discomfort from her belly.

CHAPTER 11

The private tour of nine men stopped in a remote chamber of the dark catacombs carved deep beneath the city of Rome. The tenth man, the guide, appeared from the shadows after locking the final barrier of iron bars that would ensure the privacy of their meeting.

Each of the men donned a white soutane emblazoned with a red cross, a hood of chain mail covering their heads. In silent ritual, the men formed a circle, each unsheathing a sword from his belt and pointing it toward the floor in the center of the ring.

"Soldiers of God," they said in unison when the last sword completed the circle. Then each man fell to one knee, heads bowed in reverence, their vow echoing ominously through the chamber illuminated only by torchlight.

Jean-Marc smiled, indulging himself in a moment of sinful pride. The strength that ebbed through the brethren when they were together gave him the courage of a gang member ready to threaten any outsider walking mistakenly across his turf. The image faded quickly with a silent reprimand from his conscience.

The men relaxed into comfortable camaraderie. Each sheathed his golden sword, lifting it shoulder high to reinsert it into its sheath around his belt.

"Brothers," called out the Master, Ambrose. "I would ask for your reassurance of secrecy." He addressed each man individually, by name.

Jean-Marc routinely gave his oath with no second thoughts. The history of the Knights Templar had long been engrained into his heart. One of the knights who had burned at the stake in Paris when the order had been interdicted was one of his ancestors. He understood the need for secrecy all too well.

They were armed monks, soldiers of God. Since their abolishment, they had been considered outlaws—a renegade gang.

Still the order continued, their ideal intact in spite of being renounced by the Pope seven centuries ago. Forced underground, they maintained their trophies jealously from the days of the Crusades. After losing the True Cross to the infidels, the Knights closed ranks, channeling the power of the treasures of Jesus into their sacred cause. The loss of the shroud of Turin had weakened their brotherhood a second time. After that, the order became even more clandestine.

The imminent recovery of the Holy Grail would restore the order to full strength. Only the Knights Templar definitively knew the location of the sacred relic. It had been in danger of discovery once before, during the second World War when Hitler had tortured one of the Knights into revealing its hidden location. Together with Mussolini, the two devils began an excavation of Herculaneum in search of holy power to fuel their selfish ambitions. The volcano had erupted to protect the treasure yet another time, calling an end to their search.

At the Casa del Fioretti, Jean-Marc felt confident that he would recover the artifact before anyone else knew it existed. His was a noble quest; he and the nine other men in the dark tomb were the only ones to know of its location. There was only a momentary attack of conscience from the museum intellectual depriving his precious archives of the priceless find. Jean-Marc knew it would be better guarded by the brethren.

"I will bring you the grail," he promised Master Ambrose, kneeling in the presence of the future Pope.

"Tell me about Maeve Ryan," Brother Ambrose prodded, seeing the threat in the other archeologist that Jean-Marc refused to acknowledge.

"She will never see it," Jean-Marc dismissed.

Ambrose shook his head, not as easily swayed. "You should not dismiss her so lightly."

Jean-Marc felt his heart skip a beat. While he couldn't quite picture his colleague shooting at a Protestant in the streets of Derry, he knew her well enough to recognize how deeply her convictions ran.

"No," Jean-Marc agreed. "Certainly I will be more attentive." He looked to Ambrose with an instant's fear. "Is it possible she would know?"

Ambrose shrugged his shoulders. "There have been many secrets to leave our ranks through the years. It is always possible."

Jean-Marc nodded reluctantly.

"And the others? There is a new group of students, is there not?"

Again Jean-Marc nodded. "There is one, she is very close to it, but she does not know what lays hidden. If she should stumble onto it, she is under my supervision. It will come to me."

"Danger is always where you least expect it."

Jean-Marc saw Maeve in his mind, and closed his eyes sadly. "I will return the grail to the Brothers," he promised.

"It will restore the order," Ambrose reminded him. "It will return the knights to power and the Pope to his position of undisputed authority."

The battle for unification in Ireland startled Jean-Marc with the first disturbing thoughts since he had answered the call to the Knights.

They fought a war, Irish nationals against the English, Catholics against Protestants. But wasn't it all one God?

"Jean-Marc?" Ambrose interrupted his thoughts.

The war was never meant to be Christian against Christian. What had once seemed remote and unimportant suddenly seemed foremost and critical.

"Brother?" Ambrose said again, taking Jean-Marc's arm.

Jean-Marc nodded hastily. "I will return the grail," he promised again.

"And Signore Fioretti? Will we invite him to join our ranks?"

Jean-Marc smirked, thinking of the new teacher who had joined the excavation. "I think *that* time has passed. He has other distractions now."

Ambrose nodded sagely. "A woman?"

"A well-timed diversion to divide his attention away from the task at hand."

"A pity. I was rather looking forward to meeting the formidable Dominic Fioretti. His power, his strength of character…"

His money, Jean-Marc completed the thought. He looked suddenly to his master, afraid that Ambrose could read his thoughts. Disloyalty to the Knights had never entered his mind before; why now?

"Everyone must have a crisis of faith," Ambrose continued almost clairvoyantly. "It is a pity we did not approach the Signore sooner." He nodded reflectively. "Still, there may be another time." The Master eyed his brother suspiciously. "Something troubles you."

Shaking his head, the Frenchman formulated a question. "If Maeve were to recover the artifact, would she be able to reunite Ireland with it?"

"You have just reassured me that she will not find it. You need not dwell on that question." Ambrose thumped Jean-Marc soundly across his back. "When I am Pope there will be no more war in Ireland. The Knights will once again come forth to restore order and bestow our benevolence."

For the first time in his life, Jean-Marc doubted Ambrose's vision.

CHAPTER 12

"Come on, Kira, wake up." Laura was knocking on the door between the rooms.

The sun shone brightly through her bedroom window. Holding her head, Kira squeezed her eyes closed and sat up on the edge of her bed before shuffling across to throw back the latch.

"You look like you're in pain," Laura giggled. Kira frowned. "We're going to Capri today to find you something to wear."

"I don't need anything to wear."

"Would you wear jeans to the ball?"

Kira squinted to keep out the glare of the sun. "I was hoping it was just a bad dream."

"Nope. Let's get going, sleepyhead. Better get moving or you'll miss breakfast, too." She bounded back into her room, leaving Kira to assemble the pieces of shattered sleep.

Holding her head, Kira reached for her glasses. Bleary eyes stared back at her from the mirror over the dresser where fresh clothes lay waiting.

She groaned unsure of how much she had dreamt and how much of the previous night had actually happened. Had she really invited Dominic into her bedroom? Had he really declined?

She pulled open the dresser, reaching into her backpack for a bottle of aspirin. Shaking out two little white pills, she popped them into her mouth, chewing them.

"I'm going down," she called through the door to Laura's room.

The aroma of coffee wafted through the corridor from the dining room.

Kira followed the scents, taking a seat at a table with a glass of orange juice and a roll. With the first sip of juice, she returned to the sideboard to pour another glass of juice in addition to refilling the one in her hand.

"Why do you suppose they picked us?" Laura wondered out loud, walking through the arch.

"Because we're the only ones here."

"You have to stop feeding my ego that way. C'mon. Let's go find you a dress, Cinderella."

Kira cringed at her inopportune reference.

❦   ❦   ❦

The hydrofoil traveled quickly across the Bay of Naples toward the Isle of Capri. "They say a man should never take his lover there," Laura sighed, the wind whipping through her beautiful blond hair. Putting one hand on her heart and reaching out across the water with another, she recited: "For on Capri a man cannot escape the bonds of true love and his lover becomes his wife."

Kira looked over the top of her sunglasses. "Does it say all that in the travelogue?"

Laura's faced glowed with a radiant smile. "Don't you believe in romance?"

"There is no happily ever after." Kira continued to rub her temples. "You can't find true love over a few short weeks on holiday."

"A girl can dream. Tell me, Kira, what man would you take to Capri?"

Kira saw the image of the dark man, howling with grief in her dream. She cringed in sympathy, feeling fresh tears in her own eyes. In that moment it all came clear to her. She understood his grief, more painful than her own because of the circumstances and because they would not let Enzio Fioretti's spirit rest.

"I knew it!" Laura proclaimed.

"Knew what?"

"There is someone! Is it someone back home?"

Kira felt a wave of alcohol induced nausea. She hadn't thought of Joe Cochran in more than a week. Laura's words brought him right back to the forefront. "I'm going to vomit," Kira groaned.

When the hydrofoil came into the Marina Grande, Laura stepped off as if she had lived there all her life. "Are you going to be all right?"

"Let's just get this over with."

"Come on. Dominic says the funivia will take us to the town. We're supposed to head for the Via Vittoria Emanuele."

"Dominic says," Kira mimicked, annoyed.

"Lighten up, already."

"I suppose you'd bring your perfect lover here?" She hoped her voice didn't betray the contempt she felt for her companion.

Laura's lower lip disappeared between her teeth, a shadow of doubt clouding her beautiful face.

"Something wrong between you and Prince Charming?" she prodded.

Laura shrugged her shoulders, casually throwing off Kira's ridicule.

Kira followed her, past whitewashed villas built one on top of another into the mountains, and into the center of commerce. Well-dressed tourists walked the streets, darting in and out of the high-priced shop fronts.

Kira stopped to look at a sweater hanging in a window, but Laura pulled her away to a store boasting finery.

"I feel like a man in a lingerie store," Kira whispered.

"You're not a man, and this is not a lingerie store," she replied quietly. "Now, what size do you need?"

"We're in Italy. How should I know?"

"Signorina?" The saleswoman was immaculately attired, thick auburn hair tied in a bun at the nape of her neck.

"We need a dress," Laura spoke slowly in English.

"Very pretty dresses?"

"Si."

The woman crooked her finger and led them to a display of elegant attire. "For the Signorina?" she inquired, nodding to Laura.

"For the Signorina," Laura answered, nodding to her companion.

The woman snorted. "Como grande!"

"I don't need this," Kira whined, trying to turn away.

"You're not going to spoil the only moment of fun I'm going to have on this dig," Laura insisted pulling Kira's arm.

"But going to a ball? Laura, I came here to work, not to play dress up with those two Italian gigolos."

The shopkeeper held up a dress. "Perfect," Laura squealed.

The emerald green dress flowed with velvet, black beads sparkling into a yoke covered by a bolero jacket. "It'll be too short," Kira protested.

"Try it on."

"Really, Laura. Nothing fits me off the rack. I'm too tall."

"Let's go." Laura ushered her to the back of the store and handed her the dress.

Reluctantly Kira moved behind a curtain and removed the dress from the hanger, slipping out of her comfortable jeans and sweater.

"How does it look?"

"It fits," came the meek reply.

Laura pushed aside the curtain. Her eyes grew wide. "It more than fits. Quanto costa?" She put the back of her hand to the side of her face and whispered confidentially to Kira, "A bargain at any price." Laura began pulling lira out of a belt purse to pay the woman.

"Why are you paying for it?"

"Courtesy of le fratelli."

"Oh no," Kira denied, waving her hands emphatically. "Absolutely not. This is my dress, I will not have those men paying for it. I do not want to owe them anything."

"But they do owe you."

"No." Kira raised her hand to the saleslady. "*Io saldando*."

"Now, shoes. Black velvet, I think, and a bag to go with." She waited for Kira to finish the transaction, watching the woman wrap the dress carefully.

"What are you going to wear?" Kira asked.

"I bought a dress in Paris. Can't cross the ocean and miss Paris."

"It's not exactly around the corner."

"Closer than Cleveland."

Laura continued to pull Kira through the cramped shops, their packages multiplying. Laura shopped like a seasoned veteran, fingering accessories and passing by the merchandise she labeled as "not up to the occasion."

When they left the shopping district, they were burdened with packages.

Laura stopped before a large white villa on the way back to the porta. "Just imagine, Kira, if we married them—we could live here forever."

"Is it worth what you have to give up?"

"Don't you ever dream?" Her cheeks flushed with excitement.

"It doesn't happen in real life. There is no happily ever after. Only bad choices that eventually lead to disappointment."

"You don't know what you're missing."

"Disappointment? Rejection? A black eye, perhaps?"

From across the road came the now familiar kissing sound of men expressing their appreciation for a beautiful woman.

Shaking her head, Laura hooked her arm through Kira's and led the way back to the marina. "Maybe you'll feel better after you put on some real clothes. Might even want to show off that fancy underwear we found you."

Kira laughed good naturedly. "I'm not showing anyone my fancy underwear."

"You'd be surprised how sexy lingerie makes you feel—like you want to show it off. Like you can't wait for him to take it off."

"I can't think of any hims I would want to show it to," Kira insisted. Before the words were out of her mouth, she was thinking of Dominic again.

Her breath caught in her throat, remembering the touch of his hands on her face.

"Maybe you'll meet someone at the ball," Laura was saying.

"You're a bad influence," Kira scolded huskily.

CHAPTER 13

Laura ran across the room in her slip, giggling and carrying cosmetics. "This color will bring out your eyes," she instructed, "and the perfume came from Paris. Can't come this close and not visit Paris. Who knows when I'll get to come abroad again. Isn't Europe the most fun? Take a drive, see a new country."

Kira dried her palms on the towel laid across the dresser for the fourth time, listening to the younger woman chatter nonstop. She concentrated on drawing a straight line across her eyelid, her hands trembling. Satisfied with the effort, she let out a deep breath and laid the make-up back down on the dresser. "One more thing that women have to do and men don't."

"What's that?"

Kira waved her hand across the cosmetics laid out before her. "What's wrong with the way I look? Maybe I don't want red lips. Maybe my eyes look better without liner."

Laura stopped to consider, a mascara applicator poised in front of her face. "Maybe you can get away with it," she commented, looking at Kira without moving in the mirror and then stroking her eyelashes out with the miniature brush. "I, for one, want them to remember that I was there. A little extra color makes me that much more desirable."

She dropped her hand to the dresser beneath the mirror. "Every woman wants to be desired, Kira." She turned to look full at the taller woman. "At least one night in every girl's life has to be special, and on that night, everything has to be perfect, especially the way she looks."

Kira touched her eyelids with light brown shadow. "Seems like a lot of trouble. I always feel so foolish—like a clown—all painted up."

Laura brushed away the excess blush that colored Kira's cheeks, inspecting her handiwork. "They won't be able to keep their hands off you," she sighed. She pulled Kira's dress down from a hook against the wall. "You're gonna give me some real competition, I can tell. Will you make sure somebody dances with me?"

Kira smirked and took the dress from the hanger, sliding into the smooth velvet. "I'll send them all your way." She stared at her unfamiliar reflection. "I feel so...so..."

"Beautiful." Laura stood behind her, a reassuring hand on Kira's shoulder.

"I was thinking more along the lines of gaudy, overdressed, theatrical...."

"You are none of those. You shouldn't hide your femininity, Kira. You're quite a stunner when you try."

"Guess I don't have much occasion to try." She smiled shyly, looking at Laura for the first time since they'd been primping.

Laura was adorned in a dress decorated with shimmering blue sequins the same color as her eyes. "Now *you* look beautiful."

"Help me with the zipper?" Laura turned her back to Kira, smoothing away the strands of hair that escaped from a french knot secured to the back of her head.

"God, I'm nervous." Kira shivered.

"Live a little," Laura encouraged. "It'll be fun."

"The skirt. It's not long enough."

"Yours is longer than mine. This length is the new fashion." Laura took Kira's hands, looking up at her. "It's because you're so tall."

Suddenly, Kira burst into a fit of giggles. "I just got this weird picture in my head. I have a friend back home, a man. I suddenly had a vision of him sitting in front of a television holding a beer can and wearing a stained T-shirt, and me dressed for the ball." She stopped to catch her breath as she continued to fight the nervousness. "Could you imagine anything worse?"

"If that's what you've got to choose from, it's no wonder you're not married."

Kira shook her head to clear it and then declared: "I think I'm ready."

Laura stopped in front of the mirror once more. "Just a minute." She smoothed her hair one last time. "O.K." Together, they left the sanctuary of their suite.

"I do feel like Cinderella," Kira whispered.

"It's the Casa."

❦   ❦   ❦

The house was lit with a thousand lights refracting off sparkling chandeliers that were only lit for special occasions. Dominic surveyed the corridors with satisfaction, noting that every corner sparkled. Anna had indeed worked wonders preparing for the ball. It was no easy task to remove all the dust and grime that was carried back and forth from the excavation.

He came to a stop in the foyer, bowing to greet more of his guests and laughing at the joke the fat Signora Gelato was telling, even though his face hurt already with the smile he had pasted on.

Deep breath, he reminded himself. Charming. Each of these people represented a shovel full of earth. Dominic adjusted his tie, moving slowly against the grain through the room of tuxedoes and jeweled necks that swelled toward the main hall at the end of the corridor. Levato's son took his hand now, shaking it firmly and congratulating him on the recent donations to the museum in Naples. What was his first name?

Without realizing he had been waiting for her, he looked up and saw her coming down the stair. A scent of lemons came from the highly polished wood of the banister where he laid his hand in expectation.

The lights glistened off her hair. Black sequins shimmered subtly below her breast before her dress cascaded into a sea of green velvet. Unable to take his eyes from her, Dominic buttoned his coat discreetly.

Franco rolled across the floor beside his brother, taking Kira's hand as she finished her graceful descent. "You are magnificent," he praised, pressing her hand to his lips.

Not even jealousy could dampen his admiration for the beauty who stood before him. No man could ignore such a vision. Maybe Franco had brought her here to seduce his brother. The way she looked tonight it would be difficult for any man to resist her.

Unexpectedly, it made him remember another time—another woman. Dominic remembered a string of emeralds gracing another pale white neck—Julia's—but that green dress had shimmered like metal casing, it was not the soft, inviting velvet that Kira wore.

Julia had been so sure of herself. He thought he loved her, but always he hesitated. The more he postponed intimacy with her, the more determined she became to get him into her bed. The more obsessed she became with making love, the less interested he was.

He hadn't thought about her in years and even now the vindication for his hesitance only mildly annoyed him.

How many times had she waited in his bed, so sure that he wouldn't be able to resist her? It wasn't really so surprising when he came in from classes one day to find his roommate taking advantage of the secret pleasures he had denied. For her, it was a way of taking possession of her man.

She had cried and begged and pleaded for forgiveness but by that time he just didn't care anymore.

But Kira stood before him now, her conservative dress doing more than anything Julia had contrived to do to his libido. He wondered as he stared at her now if it had been Kira instead of Julia, could he have resisted so easily?

Franco pulled her down to whisper in her ear giving Dominic a view of her lovely, rounded breasts.

"Thank you for your most gracious invitation," she was saying somewhat haltingly.

"Some vino?" Dominic suggested casually, pulling glasses off a passing tray. Surely she knew her effect on men. Dominic held a glass out to Kira, and then pulled it back. "You will take care in drinking this?"

"I have eaten well today. Grazie Padrone." She said the words as easily as if she would throw a glass of ice water in his lap. His teeth clenched at the thought and he let his coat fall open again.

Music began to float down the corridor from the dining room which had been converted once again into the ballroom that it was meant to be.

Dominic bowed deeply before the women and extended an arm to Kira. "I believe the first dance is mine."

She started to defer, looking to Laura for support, but Laura placed Kira's hand on Dominic's arm and pushed her gently away.

She walked beside him down the corridor somewhat timidly, he thought. Was that part of her scheme—to play the frail female? She would never be that. Kira was much too self-sufficient.

They walked into the ballroom, already filled with couples moving elegantly across the marble floor. Dominic turned to take Kira's waist, leading her through the waltz.

They moved well together—her movements fluid and graceful. She was staring at the floor but he could not take his eyes from her face.

As she began to relax, she looked up at him and offered a resigned smile. The room seemed brighter and he found the steps easier. He pulled her closer and together they established a silent understanding.

She wasn't like the other women Franco had brought home. Had he misjudged her?

The waltz ended and Dominic was still staring into her eyes. "I am reminded of a custom of my father's," he told her. "He said one should always kiss his dancing partner as a way of saying thank you." He put his hands gently on either side of her face, feeling the soft flesh of her cheeks.

He had meant it to be only a peck, a glancing pass across her lips, but when they joined he found he could not break away from her so easily. It was like fighting the pull of a magnet.

She flushed and pulled away first, her eyes a vivid green. "Maybe I should sit the next one out."

With a courtly bow, he took her hand, kissing her knuckles. "I am yours to command," he offered.

He stood riveted to his spot on the dance floor, unable to follow after the swishing green velvet. He was duty-bound to attend to his guests. He turned around, purposely looking away from Kira. Seeing her in that dress only made him want her that much more.

The seven-piece orchestra was playing again. Dominic smiled politely, nodding to his guests as he moved off the dance floor. Against the wall he found the elder Signora Levato waiting for her husband and moved gallantly in her direction.

🍁   🍁   🍁

"Don't you just love a man in a tux?" Laura bubbled. "And every one of them a romantic Italian." She leaned closer to Kira and whispered loudly to be heard above the music. "You and Dominic move well together. Bet you'd be very compatible in bed."

Kira gave her a look of shocked indignation. "Excuse me?"

"Actually, I don't think you'd be able to find anyone to prove that." The women turned together at the sound of the man's voice behind them. His eyes sparkled aquamarine as he lifted a glass of champagne in greeting.

"I am Giovanni del Ponte," he introduced himself, "and you must be the archeology students?"

"Laura Griffith." She placed her hand in his and curtsied deeply. Kira noticed a slight movement of her fingers against his palm and looked away, disgusted with the open invitation Laura extended to every handsome man she met.

"Kira Ellison. Please forgive Laura for her lack of tact." She shot her companion a look of reproach which Laura answered with a sweet smile.

"Dominic has been my friend for many years," he explained. "When he was younger he thought to be a priest. Some men, when a woman breaks their heart, find it necessary to love many women to compensate for their loss. Some men turn to God." He pointed to Dominic now dancing with an elderly matron in the center of the room.

"But he's *not* a priest," Laura pointed out.

"No," Giovanni admitted, "but I fear he may be somewhat inexperienced."

"I doubt that," Laura answered.

"I don't think this is quite an appropriate conversation," Kira interrupted. "Whatever Il Padrone does with his personal life is of little concern to me."

"I thought when I saw you dancing…" Giovanni began, his arms moving around expressively, "and then when I heard Signorina Griffith's comment…"

"Signorina Griffith spoke out of turn."

"You do look well together," he continued. "And I do not believe I have seen him quite so taken with a woman for many years."

"I'm sure you're mistaken."

He nodded his head apologetically. "Forgive me if I, too, speak out of turn. You see I am responsible for his suffering. I stole away the woman he loved. I thought maybe there was something between my friend Dominic and you. It would give me some measure of absolution to know he had finally found another worthy of his attentions."

Kira felt a thrill of excitement believing, even if only for a moment, that a man like Dominic Fioretti could be that interested in her.

Giovanni set his glass on a passing tray. "Maybe you would dance with me then, Signorina Ellison?"

Kira hesitated, looking at Laura and then to her host politely taking his turn with one of the attending matrons. "I'd be delighted," she accepted.

"How long have you been in Italy?" Giovanni pursued, leading her into the dance.

"Two weeks."

"You are enjoying it?"

"The excavations are very interesting. It's quite a different experience."

A sly smile spread across his face. "And my friends are treating you well?"

"They have been most accommodating."

"Are you allowed free time? Perhaps we could take a ride into the countryside one afternoon."

Giovanni stopped, turning to acknowledge a tap on his shoulder. Dominic stood beside him, his generous dark hair tied back with a black ribbon.

"And where is your beautiful wife this evening?" Dominic asked. "I would hate to see you lose her to another man."

Giovanni bowed, offering Kira's hand to Dominic.

"What happened to the woman you were dancing with?" Kira asked.

"Her husband cut in." He rolled his eyes and put a hand to his heart, fainting at the knees. "Jilted again."

Kira laughed at his theatrics and he smiled, not the wooden, obligatory smile, but a warm, relaxed expression.

He was alarmingly handsome in his tuxedo, his bearing reminding her of the engaging guide he had been at Pompeii. He pulled her close against him, his movement smooth and sure. Leaning her head against his shoulder, Kira closed her eyes, letting him pull her gracefully around the dance floor.

The song ended and Kira drew shyly away, dropping her eyes to the floor. Once more his mouth closed over hers and in an instant she was in his arms again, not seeing anyone but the man in front of her.

"Such beautiful students you attract!" An older gentlemen shook Dominic's hand, breaking her free from his embrace. "If I did not know you better I would think you invited them here on purpose!"

Kira felt a stab of discomfort, irritated at letting herself be drawn into the idiotic game that the brothers continued to play. She would not be treated like a prize to be won.

Dominic bowed. "Signore Levato, may I introduce Kira Ellison?"

Signore Levato bowed to the lady, taking her hand and kissing it with characteristic Italian style. "What could such a lovely lady know about archaeology?"

And then Dominic disarmed her once more with his response. "Quite a lot, actually. Kira comes from America. She spent some time in England before she came here and has a feel for the earth."

Kira's mouth dropped open and quickly closed again. Praise from Il Padrone was rare and usually given grudgingly, yet he handed it to her easily once more.

"You are earning your degree?" Signore Levato was asking.

"I'm a history teacher," Kira told him. "I wanted to see some history first hand."

The music was beginning again. "Will you dance with me?"

She looked to Dominic for affirmation. He placed her hand gently into Signore Levato's care.

"It is good to see Dominic so happy," the older man was saying as they danced into the crowd. "It has been very hard for him since his father died. Tell me, what are you finding in the villa below?"

"My work is very insignificant, of course, but I have seen many wonderful things. A cupboard has been recovered in the room near where I'm working. They are still cataloguing its contents."

"And what are you doing that is so insignificant?"

"The room I'm in has a shrine," she told him, "but the contents are badly damaged by the surge."

"You are as intelligent as you are beautiful. Perhaps you would dance with my son? He should meet more women like you." He nodded to a younger man leaning against a column, flirting with Laura. His black hair was greased back and he was grinning like the Cheshire cat.

"He seems to be doing all right."

The older man shook his head. "I have met that one. She is one of Franco's. My son needs a more reliable girl."

The dance ended and Signore Levato reached up to plant a kiss on Kira's cheek. "I cannot kiss you like Il Padrone," he teased. "I am a married man."

Kira blushed crimson as Signore Levato bowed and took his leave.

"You are enjoying yourself?" Franco positioned himself beside her.

"Your guests are very charming."

"You are breathtaking. I would dance with you myself if only for the excuse to kiss you."

"I don't think you'd wait for an excuse," Kira replied.

Franco laughed. "True." He was watching the parade of couples, now dancing a tarantella. "Even he cannot disguise his desire for you." She followed Franco's finger to where Dominic stood in a crowd of guests, watching Franco warily.

"Maybe he's a better actor than you imagine."

There was something unhealthy in the way Franco laughed. "Not even my brother can act that well."

Kira moved behind Franco's wheelchair, suspicious of the direction he was taking the conversation. "Then again this atmosphere is most conducive to people to be on their best behavior. The beautiful music, people all dressed to the nines…"

"Shall I prove it to you, Kira? Would you like to see the reaction of a jealous man?" He turned his head, looking over his shoulder and pulling her down by her hand. "Kiss me, Kira."

She pulled away. "You're quite a tease, Signore."

He was laughing again. "You are very wise. A jealous man is not a pretty thing to see." He turned the wheels of his chair with formal white gloves, still laughing while he crossed to a table of guests. "Come greet some more of our guests."

Kira followed Franco uneasily. He spoke rapidly. She nodded at an introduction, straining to catch his words. The dialect he used was beyond her comprehension.

"Does it not bother you to get so dirty?" a woman asked in stilted English. She looked to be about Kira's age, but she was heavily made up to assume the beauty that nature had not given her.

"It is a necessary part of finding the keys to the past," Kira replied in Italian.

The other people at the table wore smirks, staring at Kira and leaving her to wonder if she had misspoken her Italian or if Franco had said something untoward.

"Kira?" Dominic summoned from a small clique with a beckoning finger.

Now feeling like a display, she held her head up and forced a smile for the next round of questioning.

Dominic was entertaining two couples, speaking Italian slowly, deliberately so that she could understand. He was watching to make sure she could follow the gist of the conversation almost in direct contrast to his brother's attitude.

A silver-haired matron smiled warmly at her. She was elegantly dressed in blue chiffon with a chain of diamonds wrapped around her neck. Beside her stood a stately gentlemen with salt-and-pepper hair and a small mustache, the lines in his face marking the years.

The other couple consisted of a younger woman holding the arm of an older gentleman dotingly. She had long brown hair fashioned into ringlets that fell over one shoulder.

"It is a slow process," Dominic was telling his guests. "Sometimes we find only the traces of what *was* rather than the artifacts themselves."

"Many things were displaced by the surge," Kira added. She motioned with a sweeping gesture of her hands. "Moved from here to there. Only impressions are left."

"It must be hard to decide where to dig and where to leave it alone," the younger woman commented.

Dominic nodded his approval, smiling. "Sometimes we learn more by not disturbing the lava than by scraping it away."

The orchestra had begun again, making conversation more difficult. Dominic bowed before his guests and, with a hand to Kira's back, guided her back to the dance floor.

Kira was smiling now, basking in the glow of Il Padrone's approval.

"I don't believe I've told you how beautiful you look tonight."

"You are very kind to say so."

He smelled faintly of champagne his chest buzzing against her ear as he began to hum to the tune the musicians were playing. Dominic's humming turned to quiet singing, his tenor voice blending with the musicians. Kira laid her head in the crook of his neck, mesmerized by the effect.

Against the wall, Franco and Giovanni laughed loudly. "How quick they are to believe," Dominic scorned, his voice deep and low.

"Hmm?" she sighed dreamily.

A large hand cupped her face. There was a trace smile on Dominic's handsome face. "I could almost believe it myself, you looking so lovely, the night so perfect…"

The warm fuzzy aura that Kira had drawn around her like a cloak turned suddenly cold. She shuddered with the resultant chill, stiffening in Il Padrone's arms. "You shouldn't let your guard down," she warned him icily. "It would be too easy to be carried away with the game."

"I don't want to play games any more, Kira." The music continued, but they stopped dancing.

Misreading his words, Kira stepped back. "I knew I didn't want to attend this party."

He blinked with the force of her words hitting him like a slap in the face. "Did he say something to you?"

"Who?"

"I saw you speaking with him a moment ago. What were you talking about?"

"You wouldn't be interested."

"You don't think so?" He moved her back into the dance, his steps more mechanical.

"He was talking about you, telling me some of the same things Giovanni said."

"And what was that?" Dominic's embrace tightened reflexively.

"They were teasing you."

His hand was squeezing hers until tears welled in the corners of her eyes. "They meant no harm," she winced.

"Then what was it that they said? Surely you don't think I would be upset at a little fun—taken at my expense?" He was staring at her, his dark eyes now menacing.

"Laura was saying how handsome all the men looked," she began. "How handsome you look." Tears welled in her eyes. "Giovanni only said he thought something must have met with your approval as you seemed to be enjoying yourself. Franco said the same." She took a deep breath, afraid to let the tear escape for fear it would streak her face with the makeup she was so unaccustomed to wearing. "Your act worked. Now please, you're hurting me."

Dominic released her, standing still on the dance floor once more. "Giovanni has been my friend for many years, but I would warn you. He is a married man although he often does not act like one."

"And your point?"

"He has invited you for a ride in the country. I would advise against it."

Kira shook free of him, standing toe to toe. "I am perfectly capable of taking care of myself."

Dominic's jaw tightened, the color rising in his ruddy complexion. "Forgive me. Maybe these things come more easily to you. I merely meant to advise you. Of course you may do as you like."

Kira's fists were shaking at her sides, fighting to control the anger he provoked. "I assure you, Padrone, I am no more experienced in these things—as you call them—than you are."

The blood seemed to drain from his face, his skin taking on an ashy color. "What do you mean?"

Several surrounding couples were watching the discourse with curiosity, the puzzled looks showing that they could not quite translate the English discussion.

"I am saying that Giovanni told me that you have never...that your experience with women..." she flushed a deeper red, looking at the sea of faces swimming around them before bowing her head to one side. "I do not wish to embarrass you in front of your guests."

Dominic took her arm and led her out of the ballroom and into the corridor. "Would you care to tell me what it is that my friend said to you?" he hissed, a frightening mask of calm on his face.

She looked into his eyes. Goose flesh jumped up along her arms.

"That is not something he would know," Dominic whispered, saving her from having to repeat what she had been told. Although his expression remained carefully composed, his voice betrayed his animosity.

Kira strained to leave. Inside the ballroom, the music stopped. She stepped away from him, guarding against any further invitations to dance.

"Dominic!" A beautiful woman came up beside him and wrapped her arms around him. She kissed his cheek and prattled in singsong dialect something about how long it had been since their last meeting. Seizing the opportunity, Kira slipped away and into the salotto down the hall.

❦ ❦ ❦

"You're not dancing with me," Stella accused.

Dominic smiled, giving his partner a reassuring squeeze. "Then who is the vision of loveliness in my arms?"

"I know you too well, Dominic Fioretti," she teased, nodding her head in the direction of the recently departed woman in green velvet. "She's very lovely."

"Damn my temper," he sighed.

"You should go to her," she encouraged.

Dominic looked into Stella's beautiful eyes, as blue as the ocean and ran a hand gently across her soft brown hair. "How did I ever let you escape?"

"You were only too happy to let me go," she scoffed. "As I remember it, you were quite finished with me."

Dominic laughed and held her close. "Don't tell Giovanni. He takes much more pleasure in believing he stole you away from me."

A mood of melancholy quieted her. "I fear it's not quite so interesting once the conquest has been made."

"He loves you. Have no doubt on that account," Dominic reassured her.

"Oh, that much I know." She looked up at him, wistful over remembrances of lost youth. "You would never have strayed from my bed, Dominic."

"There were many times that I didn't," he reminded her affectionately.

She slapped him playfully across the back as he turned her around the dance floor, bending her low in a dip. "You know what I mean."

She smiled sadly and shook her head. "I must admit there will always be a soft spot in my heart for you." The music stopped and Stella nodded toward the corridor. "And it would seem you have an apology to make?"

Dominic followed her direction and saw Kira, her eyes glistening brightly as she watched him. "Thank you, Stella," he called without looking back at his dancing partner.

Giovanni was stepping up beside Kira, staring lecherously at her exposed flesh and insinuating himself into her vulnerability. Dominic recognized the expression from another time when it hadn't mattered quite so much.

"…maybe you would like to take a walk," Dominic heard him suggest, watching the arm slip around her narrow waist.

Kira's eyes were fixed on Dominic's, seeing his approach. She turned to escape Giovanni's grasp and ran down the corridor. Dominic moved faster, almost running to catch up.

CHAPTER 14

She changed out of the velvet dress and slipped back into jeans like a school girl returning home from a date. She sat on the side of the bed with one hand over her mouth, embarrassed that she could believe in fairy tales.

She closed her eyes, but he flooded her senses. Holding the dress to her face, she could still smell him—the scent that was Dominic. Her skin tingled reaching out for his touch.

She laughed a frightened laugh, tears falling freely down her face once more. From below came the sounds of guests leaving, voices rising from the foyer. Music no longer floated through the Casa del Fioretti. Kira looked at the clock and was surprised to see that it was well past midnight.

She moved across to the window, closing her eyes to welcome the breeze that pulled its fingers through her hair, cooling her burning cheeks. She listened to the peaceful whispers of the olive trees below.

"I've been waiting forever," Laura's voice carried.

The man's reply was lost in the intermittent breeze. Kira leaned out to locate where the voices came from and saw the top of Laura's blond head. Her companion was hidden in shadows, tall and dark, pulling Laura in like a vampire cloaking its victim.

Turning away from the window, Kira wiped at her eyes. Laura was much more experienced than she was. Naturally he would turn to her after being rejected by Kira.

Her breath caught in her throat as she tried to control her pain. Frustrated, she began filling her journal with insensible words. Suppressed emotions flowed through the pen and into the book.

She tapped the pen against her jaw and took a deep breath, deliberately moving her thoughts away from the dark man.

She thought of the cupboard below, bare against the wall of the shrine. Her archeological vacation had turned into an extraordinary quest. Or had it turned into a Miss America pageant?

"And what if I find it?" she asked herself out loud. Back home, her thoughts answered. Back to the classroom. Back to Joe Cochran.

A tear slipped down her cheek considering how easy her life had been before she left home. If she had been satisfied with what she had, she wouldn't now be fighting her feelings for the mysterious dark man. She could have lived a contented, uneventful life.

She knew well the opinion of European men toward American women: easy conquest. A wall of anger began laying bricks inside of her, bristling at her breakdown of willpower. Piece by piece she began reconstructing the evening, seeing every event in a different light.

It had all been a plot, she decided. The little innuendoes his friend and brother planted in her ear, the contrived closeness; if Dominic Fioretti was a virgin, she was Queen Elizabeth.

She was jarred from her thoughts by a knock on the door.

Kira put a hand to the doorknob and turned her ear to the door. "Who is it?"

"So here ye are," came the gentle lilt of Maeve's Irish voice.

She opened the door guardedly. "Is something wrong?"

"Well I saw ye leave with 'im…"

Kira put her hands on her hips, "and you thought you'd make sure the Great Padrone had me safely preoccupied. Come to look through my room?"

"Nay, Kira." She held an arm out to stay Kira from closing the door. "May I come in?"

Kira threw her arms up in defeat, allowing the older woman entrance to her solitude.

"Ye looked fine tagether," Maeve continued, "just grand. Himself as dark as the devil and yer hair shining like an angel's halo. Twas like watching the forces of dark and light coming together, it was."

Kira's back was turned, but Maeve reached up her hands, placing them on Kira's shoulders. "'Tis been a hard time for Dominic since his da's gone. That he cares for ye is plain. Ye canna' break his heart, Kirie."

"No, I canna' break his heart if he has no' got one." Her voice broke and fresh tears stabbed the corners of her eyes.

"He's a proud man, Kira."

"And then there's Laura's black eye. He's not quite the casual flirt his brother is, now is he?"

"Has he harmed ye, then?"

"The ball is over. No offense committed, none taken."

"They've been like me own sons," Maeve told her slowly.

"I'm just another American tourist, and he's just another Italian gigolo. Well the game's over. I have no intention of indulging in a vacation romance to pine about for the rest of my life."

"Yer wrong," Maeve insisted.

"And he's like a son to you. Where do your loyalties lie?" She leveled a steady eye on Maeve, searching for any sign of hidden rage. Then, with a weary sigh, she closed her eyes and shook her head. It's late," Kira suggested. "It's time we were all in bed. Asleep."

Maeve hung her head and turned to leave. "Don't judge him too harshly, Kira."

Closing the door behind Maeve, she wondered how many other people were talking about the woman Dominic had taken to that ball.

Kira slid between the sheets of her bed, laying in the dark and staring at the ceiling.

"*Kee-ra,*" the wind seemed to call her name, an androgynous whisper in the night air, gently caressing her troubled mind while she held close the memories of his touch.

❦   ❦   ❦

He paced like a caged lion. How she had bewitched him!

He tore at his shirt, throwing it carelessly onto the floor and sat on the edge of the bed. Leaning over, he cradled his head in his hands, and then he was on his feet again.

Pulling back the curtain, he looked out at the garden beside the casa. He took measured breaths, and closed his eyes, his fingers unconsciously ticking off against his thumb one by one.

Dominic sat on the edge of the bed again and pulled off his suit pants, laying them down neatly before reaching for a pair of comfortable cotton trousers. Barechested and barefoot, he left the room, moving outside toward the chasm below his home.

"Signore," the guard greeted, doffing his hat.

"Antonio," Dominic grunted, easing down the staircase.

He moved swiftly through the ruins to the atrium, circling in the dark, knowing each step and yet not able to see inside the tunnels of the buried house.

"Papa," he moaned quietly. "Papa, if you are truly here you must come to me." He touched the walls, still warm from the heat of the day, feeling them for the life he searched out. "You spoke to her," he cried, "you must speak to me. I need to know. Is she the sun that you told me of? She burns my soul, Papa, with such a heat I cannot bear."

❦   ❦   ❦

She dreamed of her father, thin and ravaged by cancer, standing on the edge of the world, pointing into the chasm beneath the Casa del Fioretti. "Papa," she cried out in her sleep, crying and running toward him.

"You must help him," her father said, his form a wavering shadow.

A cloud seemed to rise from the floor of the excavation, showing her Dominic Fioretti.

Her back arched, taking on the mantel of images that filled Il Padrone's head. The emptiness of his despair overwhelmed her. She watched through his eyes as he searched blindly for his father, falling to his knees where the atrium had not been cleared. Her own heart bore the weight of his unhappiness.

Every muscle in her body was pushing her down, deeper into the mattress. Opening her eyes, Kira relaxed, taking deep breaths to regulate her pulse.

She kicked her feet over the side of the bed and reached for a pair of jeans. In spite of her resolve not to fall into an emotional trap, she knew that her heart had already committed itself. If she ever believed she could settle for marriage to Joe Cochran, she knew it was out of the question now.

Cautiously Kira unlocked her door, pulling open the heavy wood so as not to make a sound. Supporting herself against the portal, Kira closed her eyes, wondering what she would do if she found him where her vision predicted.

If it was only a dream, she had nothing to fear. But how could she help him if it wasn't? With every meeting she found herself less in control of her own emotions.

With another deep breath, she moved her head around the door and peeked into the hallway.

Starlight shone down through the skylight on the empty foyer below. The only sound was the clock, patiently marking the minutes.

Her eyes filled with tears, feeling the intensity of his grief. Kira's own father had lingered with his illness, providing her ample time to say her good byes. Dominic's father had been torn away from him without warning.

She recognized the difference as she found herself tiptoeing down the staircase, shoving her flashlight in the back pocket of her pants.

The corridor swallowed her into an envelope of darkness ending in the wide expanse of the cleared dining room that still seemed to echo with the sounds of the ball.

Images assaulted her, reminding her of the feel of Dominic's arms holding her as they danced, the touch of his lips on hers. Her knees felt weak and a wave of guilt washed over her. He had been reaching out for comfort.

She stopped when she passed through to the courtyard, finding her bearings in the dark.

"Who is there?" the sentry called out in Italian. Kira took a step closer to the staircase that led down into the earth.

"Signorina," he greeted, smiling and doffing his cap.

"Antonio," she returned with a nod of her head.

He gave her a wink and waved her past with a flourish.

Kira breathed deeply the dusty smell of scraped stone mingled with the sharp tang of fresh wood supporting crumbling walls. Shivering in the contrasting coolness of night, she wrapped her arms around herself, continuing across the familiar marble floor.

The eerie chambers embraced her, frescoes and mosaics dancing in the spotlight of the beam she held. She moved slowly, reaching out to touch the faded images of the tablinum wall. Her fingers traced the curves of the unclad bodies, all of them engaged in intimate encounters, some intertwined in the act of love. The wall retained the summer heat, its inhabitants alive with their passions.

❈ ❈ ❈

The moon glinted in her golden hair, giving her a halo effect. As if in answer to a prayer, she stood just within his reach, the delicate sandalwood scent of her perfume radiating from her warm skin and swelling his desire for her. Could she possibly be real?

The flashlight dimmed and then flickered out, leaving Kira standing in the darkness. She tapped the cylinder into the palm of her hand, getting little more than a flicker in response.

She jumped at the touch of his hands, giving out a cry of alarm. "Didn't Franco tell you it wasn't safe to come down alone?" His voice wavered slightly, still afraid she would disappear.

Kira fumbled with the switch on the flashlight which stubbornly refused to produce the desired illumination. "I didn't see you." She banged the casing against her hand once more.

"Why would you come down alone? Have you not been warned against the dangers?" He could almost taste the skin on the back of her neck, breathing deeply the heady scent that was much too close.

Her body shivered in response where his finger trailed along her shoulder and down her arm, pulling gently at her wrist so that she faced him.

"I had a dream," she whispered.

"You were dreaming of a lover?" he suggested in a deep, rumbling voice, "one who jumped from the painting on the wall?"

"I dreamt of a cry for help," she replied breathlessly.

"Did you?" His words disappeared into her mouth, his hungry mouth closing over hers. His hands slid down her arms to where her shirt ended, coming up again to find her waist beneath.

Kira struggled for balance. Her head fell back while his lips caressed her neck. The scent of her perfume intensified with the heat of her passion.

"If you are a dream," he whispered in Italian, unable to concentrate beyond the awakening of each sense that she filled, "I pray God that I do not wake up."

"*Bellissima,*" he sighed. "*Molto bella.*"

Above them, the moon shone through the collapsed ceiling of the tablinum. Beads of perspiration gave her skin a surreal silvery glow and he felt sure that she would disappear at any moment.

Her eyes glistened brightly, not moving from his face, watching him like a deer assessing a hunter. "This isn't why I came down here," she told him in a husky voice. Even as she spoke, she touched his bared shoulders her hands closing around him contradicting her words.

"I cannot stop what must be between us," he hissed in pained Italian, covering her with hungry kisses.

"Stop?" she asked with minimum comprehension.

"You blind me like the sun. I can see nothing else when you are with me."

He wrapped his hands behind her head, pulling her face to his as he leaned into her. Feeling the unevenness of the wall behind her back he tried to place his hands to ease her discomfort.

He moved slowly, afraid to bruise her against the coarse surface. The sounds of the night seemed magnified, crickets singing a ballad to his desire until he was sure he would explode. With a concerted effort, he pulled away from her.

"What are you doing?" she asked breathlessly while her body answered, inherent knowledge responding to the light touch of his kisses.

The walls came alive with echoes as old as time ringing in Dominic's ears as he felt the long withheld emotions gathering like steam before a volcanic eruption. Gritting his teeth, he held Kira tightly against him, absolving himself of all his pain in the arms of this beautiful woman.

He felt the deafening pounding of his heart in his ears. The humidity enveloped them both, inviting a host of new sensations with the thin layer of moisture that fused their bodies together. Dizzy with desire for her, his muscles began to tense instinctively in response to another almost inaudible sound.

They were not alone.

"What is it?" Kira whispered, sending a chill down his spine.

He took a deep breath, wanting to stay in this dream forever, to absolve all his pain in the comfort of this woman who had come to him in his refuge. "Wait here," he cautioned, resolutely disengaging himself from her embrace.

Spots of light began jumping around the wall. Dominic pushed Kira back into the shadows, placing a quieting finger over her lips.

From his vantage point he caught a glimpse of his brother and the rage returned. He grabbed his head with both hands, squeezing his eyes closed to fight off the flood that threatened to destroy him.

"So this is why you came down here," he accused, his voice barely a whisper. He turned to face her, his hands clenched into fists.

"I told you why I came down here," she contested, still flushed from their encounter.

She sat in the corner, eyes wide with genuine fear. He felt a wave of regret over his own lack of self control. He could not punish her for his own weakness.

Looking into her face, he called out to the searching man in the Neopolitan dialect he knew she did not comprehend.

"Dominic?" came the expected answer, followed by an equally unintelligible stream seeking him out.

He lingered a moment longer, watching while she struggled for composure. He had embarrassed her once before; he could not do it again.

Bowing his head, he moved away quickly, silently toward the beam of light.

CHAPTER 15

She shivered alone in the dark for what seemed like hours, afraid to move. Voices echoed from above, carrying through the empty tomb like the whispers of civilization long dead.

"*You must help him.*" The voice spoke to her in Italian this time, separate from the chorus of whispers that seemed to surround her.

She turned slowly toward the atrium. "Signore Fioretti?" she called out timorously.

A cool breeze lifted her outgrowth of hair up, carrying with it the voices of the men receding from the excavation. Kira moved slowly through the dark tunnel, searching out every shadow.

"What do you want from me?" she cried out, turning slowly in the darkness. And then her breath caught in her throat—a pale face seemed to take shape against the black atrium.

The image disappeared as quickly as it had materialized, leaving Kira standing alone with her mouth hanging open. Fear overcame her curiosity, sending her sprawling through the dark site and up the wooden ladder to the courtyard above.

Stopping to catch her breath before reentering the Casa, she froze at the sight of a red glow beneath a lemon tree. She backed away nervously until she recognized the smell of a cigarette.

Jean-Marc stepped out from the shadows, exhaling smoke heavenward. "You have been below?"

She nodded dumbly, taking a deep breath to compose her rampant imagination.

"How do you go by the guard at the night?" He cocked his head toward Antonio, stalwartly maintaining his post.

"He didn't try to stop me."

The tip of the cigarette glowed brightly while Jean-Marc pulled in his last taste of smoked tobacco. "He does not let me pass." He threw the stub to the ground and stepped on it, extinguishing the remaining fire.

It had not occurred to Kira that she should have been stopped from going into the excavation, but then Antonio knew Dominic was there. "I wasn't alone," she whispered.

Jean-Marc nodded, then held out an arm, inviting her to walk with him.

"I thought you'd gone home for the weekend," she sighed.

"Only to Roma. I am anxious to return and my friend brings me back tonight."

She watched her feet, walking carefully through the dark grass that led away from the Casa del Fioretti.

"So what's your secret, Jean-Marc?"

The lanky Frenchman stopped walking, his pale skin and gaunt face making him look like a ghost under the dim light of a crescent moon. "Pardonnez-moi?"

Kira pulled a leaf from a nearby olive tree and tore at it to keep her trembling hands busy. "Everyone I've met here has a reason to be here other than the excavation. I was just wondering about you."

He gave her a nervous laugh in response. "It is part of my job. I am here to learn—like you."

"But even I came in hopes of finding something," she admitted. "What are you looking for, Jean-Marc?"

He shook out another cigarette and paused to light it, bending toward the flame in his cupped hand. "Peut etre la meme chose," he exhaled.

"I don't have much French."

He raised his eyes to look at her, resuming his stride. "The same thing, perhaps?" he translated.

"And that would be what?"

He pulled a long draw from his smoke, holding it a second and then exhaling slowly. "The Treasure. You say religious artifacts." He nodded. "This is what I wish to find."

Dominic's words came flooding back to her: The most important thing she should know about Jean-Marc is that he was deeply religious. The thought should have brought her comfort. Instead, she found herself doubting her French companion.

Sensing her discomfort, Jean-Marc reached for her, laying a hand on her shoulder. "The possibility is small, but if there is a piece here, our Lord will have touched it." He walked around in front of her, showing her an intensity she had not seen in him before.

"Kira, if you find something, I am ask only one favor." He let the cigarette fall to the ground and took both her hands, turning his foot over the butt as he spoke.

"He," he looked toward the sky when he said the word, "have touch it. I want only the opportunity to touch it also, before it goes to the museum." He held out his hands to the sky. "To find something of our Lord, buried for all time until now." He took hold of her arm again. "Promise me, if you find something, *un petite quelque chose*, you will show it to me?"

Her anxiety increased with his fervor. "What would it hurt?" She began walking backward in the direction of the Casa, turning when she felt sure he wasn't going to accompany her return.

Behind the closed doors of her apartment, Kira fell into the hard wooden chair behind the desk and looked out across the horizon. She wrapped herself into a ball, caressing her arms with her hands. She shivered, unnerved by the myriad events of the evening.

The moon crept across the sky, illuminating the room. A sparkle of light called her attention to the bed. Pulling the flashlight from her desk she directed the light to the object glistening on the pillow. Propelled to her feet, she began backing up to the window, gasping for air.

"Kira?" Laura's voice called through the common door. "Kira, what is it?" She pushed open the unlocked door and seemed surprised to see Kira standing by the window.

Kira pointed to the bed.

Laura turned the lamp on at the desk and produced an ear piercing shriek.

"Kirrrra!" Dominic's voice boomed from below, followed by his footsteps bounding up the staircase. With one great tackle, the door flew open behind the stress of his shoulder. He looked from the two women huddled next to the window to where their eyes were trained on the bed.

Dominic pulled the dagger from the pillow, taking a piece of paper from the end of it. He closed his eyes with a sigh. "Love notes?"

"Bastard," she spat out, tears welling in her eyes.

Maintaining his distance from her, he offered her the note, extending an arm to the furthest point he could reach.

"The Treasure is mine," she read out loud. She stared indignantly at the note in her hand and let out a long, slow breath. The paper crumpled slowly in her hand before she threw it to the floor.

"If I were you I'd give it to him," Laura suggested.

"First of all the Treasure is only supposed to be a legend. Second of all, even if I knew anything about it, and why should I, why would I give it to someone who leaves knives in my pillow?"

"*Kee-ra.*" The voice floated through the window, but it wasn't the wind this time.

Laura clutched at Kira's arm.

"It isn't going to work!" Kira shouted out the window. "I don't believe in ghosts." Removing Laura's fingers from her arm, Kira rested her hands on her hips. "And I don't have the stupid treasure."

"I don't want you sleeping alone tonight," Dominic dictated.

"You take one more step in my direction and you'll be singing soprano into your next girlfriend's ear," she warned in a husky voice, a renegade tear falling down her cheek. Even as she spoke the words she wanted nothing more than for him to hold her in his arms.

Laura began to giggle, losing herself into a near hysterical fit of laughter as the nervous tension took its release.

"Dominic!" The call came from the open doorway, Franco's voice carrying up from the foyer below.

The younger brother retreated, walking out to the railing overlooking the marble entrance. "All is well," he reassured Franco.

Kira followed as the proof, standing close behind Dominic in the narrow hallway with her arms folded.

"We have kept you here too long," Franco said apologetically, holding Kira with his blue eyes. "Much to my displeasure, it may be better if you left us."

Dominic dropped his head and let out a slow exhalation. "I think maybe Franco is right."

Kira's mouth dropped open, her hands set firmly on her hips as she looked from the upturned face below to the back of Dominic's dark mane.

CHAPTER 16

She slouched in the chair in Laura's room, watching out the window for the sun to rise. When the first rays finally lit up the mountain, she crossed back to the adjoining door in search of fresh clothing.

Dominic sat slumped across her desk, his broad back rising and falling with the rhythm of each breath. Kira hesitated in the doorway.

His hair fell in dark curls around the folded arms that cradled his head. His wide mouth was slightly parted in sleep, the black eyes that could be so forbidding were hidden behind the deep recesses of closed eyelids. On his cheeks and chin a fresh black film of coarse hair mounted its daily forestation attempt.

She rubbed her own cheeks, recalling the sandpaper feel against her face. Closing her eyes and swallowing hard, she reached for a fresh change of clothes and retreated to the relative safety of Laura's room.

Kira tiptoed down the staircase, continuing to look back up like a teenager sneaking out after curfew.

"Signorina?" Anna Giannini's voice echoed in the corridor, her head peering around the wall of her office. "*Attend*...will you wait a moment?"

Busted, Kira thought. She stood still, staring at the toes of her dust covered sneakers.

Anna appeared minutes later with the wrapped parcel Dominic had recovered on the return trip from Pompeii. "Il Padrone asked me to give this to you. He said it was taken from you in Napoli."

Kira accepted the package curiously. The events of her arrival in Naples had been overshadowed by the discovery of the dark man. Her memories prior to meeting Dominic seemed oddly missing.

"I hope you do not mind, I opened the package before I was told what it was," Anna apologized.

"What is it?"

"Books."

"Books?" Kira looked at the package in her hands, turning it over and seeing the almost new purse of books that had been taken from her at the train station. "My books!"

Anna smiled. "They are yours, no?"

"Yes!" Kira pulled the purse out anxiously, spilling the books on the ceramic tiles at her feet.

Both women dropped to their knees, reaching for the scattered tomes. As Kira gathered in an opened volume, she paused to examine what lay before her.

Atti. She read the word again, trying to remember where she had seen it before.

"Anna, this book…"

Anna turned the cover up and looked at the text opened before Kira. "La Biblia, si?"

"Bible," Kira repeated half to herself, fitting pieces of the puzzle together. "Atti. What does it mean?"

"Atti?" Anna looked at her quizzically. "It is a…how do you say? A small part." She began counting on her fingers to illustrate: "Matteo, Marco, Luca, Giovanni, Atti…"

"Acts! Kira leapt to her feet when the realization hit her. "The library," she whispered. Kira closed her eyes to visualize the reference she had seen in the margin of the Arthurian book she had pulled off the shelf in the library. Acts 21. She began flipping through the pages of Acts.

"Anna, what is this passage?" She thrust the Italian Bible in front of the older woman, searching her face for enlightenment.

Anna accepted the book and began reading the requested excerpt in Italian before stopping the translate. "He was blinded by the great light. He spoke to Jesus. The story, it speaks of Paolo's travel to Rome, his arrival at Puteoli, the miracles he performed at Malta."

"The blinding light. Miracles," Kira gasped incredulously. "It's really here."

"Signorina?" Anna's face mirrored the growing concern in her voice.

Taking a deep breath, Kira pulled herself together. "I am making arrangements to leave," she began. "It seems le fratelli are concerned that it is no longer safe for me to stay here. Would you check on flights for me?"

Bewildered, Anna nodded her head and returned to her office.

Overhead, her bedroom door burst open, hitting the wall inside her room with a loud bang. Dominic grabbed for the railing in front of him, shouting in rapid Italian. His hair flew wildly around his face, his open shirt flying behind him like a wind sock in a tornado.

Franco emerged from the study, looking up to the wild animal hanging onto the railing. "What is it?"

Dominic's eyes fell on Kira and he immediately straightened, muscles quivering with the release that accompanies relief. He pulled his shirt closed across his chest fastening each button as he advanced down the staircase, daring her to move with his eyes.

"I do not want you going ANYWHERE without someone else," he barked at Kira, pushing past his brother.

"And do you intend to spend the night in my chair for the remainder of my stay?" she answered calmly.

He took the last step more slowly than the previous, setting his face into icy diffidence. "We will talk." He grabbed her arm roughly and led her toward the study.

"I am not much in the mood for talking just now," Kira argued. "Please let me go." She shook free of his grip. "I do not appreciate being manhandled, Padrone. I will not be treated this way." She looked at him defiantly, meeting his black stare.

Along the railing overhead, the boarding archeology students lined up to witness the spectacle that Il Padrone invited. Dominic cocked his head and forced a conciliatory smile for the gallery of people overhead.

"It was not my intention to manhandle you," he replied quietly through gritted teeth. "But I do whatever is necessary to protect you while you are still in our care."

"I am perfectly capable of taking care of myself."

Dominic bowed for his audience and took Kira firmly by the arm, leading her under protest into the study where Franco blocked the door open for him.

As Franco shut the door safely behind them, Dominic paced around the desk, attempting to walk himself out of his blind rage.

"I would leave you," Franco told Kira with a smile, "but I do not trust my brother just now. Have I told you how beautiful you were last night?" His eyes twinkled with amusement.

"You are not safe here," Dominic blurted out, slamming his hands on the desk.

"I have asked Anna to check into making my return arrangements," Kira answered quietly.

Dominic exhaled dramatically and dropped into the chair behind the desk, pulling his dark hair back behind his head.

"May I have permission to go below?" Kira asked timidly.

"You may not," Dominic roared. "The site is closed for the weekend. It is not safe…"

"I see no reason why not," Franco interrupted. "It may be the safest place for you."

"She will not go below," Dominic insisted fiercely.

"Let her go."

Dominic began expostulating in angry Italian dialect, waving his arms furiously at his brother and pushing himself back to his feet.

Franco answered him calmly, pushing Kira protectively back toward the door. "Go," he encouraged gently. "There can be no reasoning with him until he has had a few moments of peace. You have my permission to go below as long as you keep contact with the guard."

Kira nodded and left quickly before Dominic could pose further objection. The sounds of the brothers shouting at each other followed her through the corridor and into the courtyard.

CHAPTER 17

Kira scraped the residue from the floor, shoveling her way to what remained of the cupboard and sweeping aside the refuse that her efforts created.

Her hair hung down straight, weighted down by the oppressive heat and humidity that accompanied the daylight.

Antonio made his rounds at regular intervals offering to bring coffee on each security check as well as delivering the summons to lunch, all of which Kira ignored.

She kept finding her attention drawn back to the hard floor of the tablinum, rubbing a tender spot on her back where she had lain on a rock. Each time her concentration wavered, she fought back her feelings with anger aimed directly at Dominic. And then she was angry with herself for allowing it to happen.

Damp clothes clung to her skin. Wiping at her face, Kira sat back on her knees, flexing the muscles in her overtaxed back. With the sound of falling dirt, she turned quickly, setting off a series of pops along her spine.

"Antonio?" she called out, expecting the watchman to reappear. When there was no response, she rose to her feet and leaned out of the chamber, looking around the tablinum. "Is somebody there?" she tried again.

Petrified lava cut into her hands as she supported her weight against the hot walls. She pulled back, clutching her injured hands to her chest, and walked toward the atrium. Her heart pounded as she began to recall all the warnings that she had chosen to ignore and the face she had seen in the dark.

Kira stood frozen before the alcove she had first seen in a dream on the train from Rome. A wooden sieve lay exactly where the dark man had left it.

"You must help him. You are the sun."

The whispered words carried the impact of a physical blow, jarring Kira. "Who is there?" she demanded in Italian.

In the shadows she saw the image of a man, all but hidden except for a generous shock of white hair.

"Is there someone with you?"

Kira wheeled around, startled by the solid, deep reverberations of Dominic's voice behind her.

"Kira?" Dominic asked again. "What is it?"

Her head turned from Dominic to the shadows and back again before she pointed to the vacated corner of the half-excavated room. "I saw a man."

Dominic leapt past her and into the shadows, disappearing into the void beyond.

"There is no one here," came his voice, muffled behind the walls of the atrium.

"I saw him!" she insisted.

Dominic reappeared a moment later, a riotous frenzy of black curls tightening with the increased humidity. "What did he look like?"

Backing out of the chamber, Kira returned to the tablinum forcing slow, even breaths.

"Who was it?" Dominic repeated.

"I think it was your father."

CHAPTER 18

❈

"My father is dead."

"Then his spirit lives," she replied, walking straight for the shrine she struggled to free from the earth's embrace.

"Who are you?" Dominic demanded.

Kira turned to face him, the angry wall she had been building replacing her fear. "Who are *you*?" she fired back. "You who would protect me. How did you know where to find my books? Maybe it was you who arranged to have my purse stolen at the station. Disappointed by the contents so you decided to give it back?"

Dominic's eyes narrowed as he watched her building up steam. He stood silently, legs spread wide apart, hands behind his back ticking out a cadence as each finger struck his thumb.

"And how *did* you know about the rose, and my journal? And is it a coincidence that you returned to the house before me, giving you just enough time to leave a knife in my pillow?" She took a step toward him, hands on her hips as she continued to fling accusations at him with each angry bob of her head.

She began pacing around the murky room, waving at the encrusted walls. "You could have just sent me back home in the first place. Or isn't that how it works? You and Franco draw lots to see which one gets to screw all the women first?"

"Why are you here?" he demanded, drawn out Italian syllables replacing the practiced American accent. His arms whipped around in front of him, his hands opening and closing to orchestrate the tirade of Italian that followed.

Kira stared at him in amazement, seeing the fires of hell reflected in his angry black eyes. She understood none of what he said but was more than aware by his tone that none of it was very complimentary.

She fought the dangerous urge to giggle, his outburst bringing to mind an irate Ricky Ricardo from an old I Love Lucy rerun.

Inflamed further by her reaction, he advanced toward her, backing her against the wall of hard lava. His gestures became more pronounced, using his whole arms to throw out strings of insults until his words changed abruptly back to heavily accented English. "What is the first thing you say to me when you try to knock me over at the train station?" His face came within inches of hers so that she had no choice but to meet his black mood. "You ask about my father. Tell me how you would know about him? Maeve did not tell you. It happened while she was away. I ask myself, who else could have tell you?" He reached an arm out and pinned her shoulder to the wall. "Could it have been my brother, Franco? Why does he bring you here?"

"To find the damn treasure. Isn't that what you keep telling me?" she taunted.

He wheeled around on his heel, raising an arm toward the heavens and muttering another Italian epithet. Just as she took a sigh of relief, he was on her again, backing her to the wall, standing an inch away. "Why do you say you see my father?" He could not mask the pain in his voice. "Why he would show himself to you, a stranger, and not to me, his own son?"

All his strength seemed to ebb away in that moment. His eyes closed and a strangled breath escaped through his open mouth. He hung his head and backed away.

Kira knew his grief. Her heart ached for him and yet she knew if she spoke he would not, could not, believe her. "Tell me about *il sole*. What does it mean?"

"The sun. The sun," he repeated shortly.

"That much I know."

Dominic threw his arms up again. "He told nobody about *il sole* but me. How do you know about *il sole*?"

She proceeded cautiously. "The same way I know about your father."

"Then tell me who killed him."

Tears threatened very near the surface, but Kira continued. Was this how she was supposed to help him? "You were there. He spoke to you. The man who killed your father spoke to you."

Dominic paced about the room like a cat, his eyes darting to the ceiling and then back to the floor searching for further signs of sabotage.

"I don't know who it is," Kira continued, "But you do."

"We must leave now. It isn't safe."

"You're beginning to sound like a broken record."

"You are in danger," he repeated.

"Why did you let me come down then?"

"As if I could stop you." He was pacing, like a lion in a cage. "They would have killed you once already. Or perhaps that is what they would have me believe."

She shivered in response. "What do they want?" A trickle of perspiration sneaked a path down her neck and between her breasts.

"It was buried by the hand of God two thousand years ago. If you are the one He has sent to find it, then you will find what you search for."

"What makes you so sure?" Her voice echoed ominously through the tunnel.

He nodded to the shrine. "You have come this far."

"Look at it." She crossed to the splintered cupboard. "Destroyed by the surge and by time. There may be nothing inside that cupboard, Padrone. Maybe the treasure has been stolen already. Maybe it was never there."

"You look for something all your life and then when you find it you wish you never had." Her voice caught in her throat, tears filling her eyes.

He was beside her before she realized he had moved. "We are not talking about the treasure anymore, are we?" he suggested.

"Look," she tried to laugh, "it's been a real kick, but I don't think I can stand much more fun." Her voice dropped to a whisper as she turned away from him. "I don't know the rules of this game very well. I don't think I want to play anymore."

Dominic stepped back to the entrance of the lararium, laying a hand on the wall and bowing his head. "I have committed a great many sins since you have arrived here. I find I must apologize for my behavior. I assure you it will not happen again."

His head came up again. Kira turned to thank him and stopped. His eyes were shining in a most uncharacteristic way. "You will leave the excavation now and, yes, I will be forceful if you resist me," he commanded huskily. "I will not have you down here alone, guard or none." He folded his arms across his chest, his Adam's apple bobbing in his throat. Dominic took a step back from the entrance and waved Kira through.

Kira's passage back to the surface and into the casa was all a blur, the tears spilling out of her eyes as she made her way through the dining room and down the darkening corridor.

"Miss Elleesone," Franco called from the study. Kira brushed her sodden clothing with her hands and her eyes with dirty sleeves.

"Is anything wrong?" Franco wheeled into the foyer bringing with him a wave of overused cologne.

Kira shook her head, trying to regain her composure.

He maneuvered beside her and Kira sat down on the great staircase. Franco leaned across his chair, inviting Kira into his arms and patting her back like a child.

"I don't want to leave," she sobbed. The tears continued to fall.

Franco buried her face against his crisp cotton shirt. "You may stay with us as long as you wish," he offered. The older brother looked up to see the shadow of a figure coming to a halt in the corridor, the dark curls of a satyr flying with the turn of a head before it disappeared. Patting the back of Kira's head, Franco indulged himself in a satisfied smile.

CHAPTER 19

The suite was dark, not even the moon was shining into the bedroom. He looked at the blond angel sleeping beside him, her hair shimmering on the pillow. She was getting tiresome.

Things were not going as he had planned.

He sat up on the edge of the bed and reached for the packet of cigarettes on the night stand. The match light glowed momentarily as he found the end of a smoke, pulling it in until the tip shone red in the dark room. The dark hairs on his hands seemed exaggerated in length by the irregular dancing of the flame before he extinguished it with a short puff of breath.

The excavation should have been closed after Enzio Fioretti's death, but his brother was a stubborn man. Repeated efforts had failed to bring the desired effect. It was time to take a more direct approach.

Drawing in the smoke from the cigarette, he blamed Enzio Fioretti one more time—blamed him for not fathering him. Certainly Enzio knew how many children he had sired, and yet he did not deny parentage.

The Italian man caught sight of his reflection in the mirror across the room, still searching for the family resemblance that would vindicate him. Instead, he looked more like a pirate in the shadows.

He had the dark hair, not unlike one of his so called brothers, but his features were much softer than the others. His face was square, his mouth wide. He didn't even resemble his mother. She had given him the Fioretti name, but there was no Fioretti blood in his veins.

A more direct approach.

The tip of the cigarette glowed with the idea forming in his mind. He stared at the closed door of the adjoining room.

It was fairly obvious that Kira wasn't quite so easily impressed with foreign men. He gave a contemptuous look to the woman sleeping quietly unaware beside him. She had been too easy. Maybe if he had tried harder with Kira…she knew where the treasure was. Then he could be free. Away from the suffocation of the Casa del Fioretti. Away from his self-righteous brothers. Away from the ghost.

The cigarette fell unexpectedly from his hands. He jumped to his feet and stomped it out with bare feet, gulping back the guilt that attended Enzio Fioretti's death. He muttered an Italian epithet and grabbed his foot, hopping on one to ease the burn on the other.

"What are you doing?" Laura asked sleepily from her bed.

"It is time I go," he answered softly, running his fingers through his greased back hair.

"You won't try to hurt her anymore, will you?"

"Sleep now. Dream of palazzos and gondolas. Very soon we will have the treasure."

CHAPTER 20

She located the book easily, pulling it from the shelf before it slipped from her hands and fell to the floor. Kira crouched down to retrieve it and then froze, the sound of approaching footsteps ringing out across the tiles of the foyer.

Watching Dominic's long legs enter the library, she clutched the book tightly to her and crouched into a niche in the built-in shelving.

From where she hid, she watched him unbutton his shirt. He strode across the room to the solitary chair with a book in his hand, hiking his pants up to take a seat in the large leather chair.

"Padrone?" Laura's voice cut through the silence, quietly seductive.

Kira closed her eyes, wishing to be invisible.

Dominic rose from the chair to meet her. "Trouble sleeping?" she asked intimately, putting a hand to his bared chest. "Perhaps I can help."

"You've done enough," he replied, removing her hand. "Go back to your room." He looked past her, alert to a subtle change in the shadows of the room.

Laura played with the buttons of her short nightgown, unfastening another one to display more of her cleavage. "Maybe you'd like to come with me," she suggested, stroking one of her long legs.

"Go!" he growled at her, pushing her out to the corridor.

Kira held her breath, watching Laura pass close beside her and muttering while she disappeared toward the foyer.

Dominic stood in the corridor, squinting to see in the darkness. He turned his head to look from the foyer to the dimly lit private rooms before returning to the library and picking up his book again.

Kira sat down on the floor, her legs crossed. She studied the satyr unnoticed, shivering beneath the shelf as memories of the flesh reached out for him.

The ground rocked gently, a sensation similar to that of a passing truck. Kira swayed uncertainly. But Dominic was staring into the corridor, pale and unmoving, clearly alarmed. He turned off the lamp and moved quickly through the passage to his rooms.

Unfolding from her hiding place, Kira stared down the dark hallway after Dominic, certain that if she followed he would send her away the same way he had sent Laura away.

Kira ran up the steps two at a time until she arrived in her room, bolting the door behind her.

She stretched out on the bed with a book in her hands. Throwing her head back, she took off her glasses and rubbed at tired eyes.

When she opened her eyes again, the purple shades of dawn were replacing the night. Not knowing how much longer she would be a guest, Kira felt a sense of urgency. She would have to move quickly if she hoped to discover what lay hidden within the shrine.

She pulled on her tool belt and flew down the staircase ahead of the other workers.

Antonio slept against a tree in the garden, not seeing her dart past and down the wooden ladder.

The lights in the tablinum were on, preparing to meet the team that would be arriving soon. Kira ducked through the opening into the lararium.

The cupboard stood before her. She hesitated, knowing the work that needed to be done before opening the doors had not been completed.

Kneeling before the cupboard, Kira stopped to cross herself. "Please let it be all right," she whispered as she reached out and pulled on the bronze handles of the bottom doors.

"No," she cried, horrified as the handles broke off in her hands. She reached into her tool belt and pulled out her trowel, delicately sliding it against the ancient catch to spring the latch.

Gold turtledoves shone brightly from within the cabinet. Kira reached in, removing the solitary bowl.

The earth began to tremble throwing her off balance. Hastily, she packed the relic into her tool belt and regained her footing to get out of the tomb running full force into Franco. She gasped and stepped back.

He stood eye to eye with her. "Have you found it?"

She stared at him, dumbfounded. Nervously, she looked back to the desecrated cupboard, aching for it to be whole. Inside came the glimmer of more gold. Kira's mouth fell open. A moment earlier she was certain that she had emptied the cupboard.

Franco took her into his arms but she struggled to be free. Confused, she stepped back against the wall as the earthquake seemed to build in strength. "We have to get out of here," she cried out.

"Just a tremor. They happen frequently," his voice had the texture of silk.

"We'll be buried alive."

"You have brought me my treasure." He reached out for her again, but she sidestepped him. He laughed—a sound that echoed eerily through the tunnel.

"We have to go." Frightened, she ducked through the hole in the wall grabbing for the sides of the tunnel to propel herself into the courtyard.

"Kira!" His voice thundered from behind, becoming Dominic's shouting for her at the top of the wooden staircase which was now shaking violently.

Kira stretched for the courtyard. The tunnel seemed to go on forever. And then she was trapped, coughing as the rising dust filled her nose and throat, the gritty taste forcing her to close her mouth. She fell to her knees and covered her head while a landslide of debris rushed to bury her.

CHAPTER 21

She opened her eyes in a strange room, thinking for a moment that she was dreaming again. She saw white curtains hanging in a window that danced as if someone pulled them with a string.

Squeezing her eyes tightly closed, she tried to open them again, hoping to sharpen her focus.

Turning her head she discovered a small woman slumped in a chair beside the bed. She squinted, gradually bringing Maeve into focus.

The Irish woman straightened in her chair and smiled at Kira. "Yer all right then?"

Kira stared at her dreamily and then sat bolt upright in the bed, her eyes popping open as remembrance flooded over her. "The earthquake. What about the volcano?"

Maeve reached forward to steady her. "We're in Naples, Kirie. In hospital. Do ye remember anythin'?"

Kira reached for her waist. "My pack. Where is it?"

"Il Padrone took it when he lifted ye out of the dig. 'Tis certain he'll have it. Don't ye be worryin' about yer tools just now. Ye've come through fine."

"I want to go home," she whispered.

"It seems ye havna' been seriously injured."

"That's a matter of opinion."

Maeve gave her a puzzled look. "They said i'twas more shock and breathing all that dust in. Ye should be well enough tomorrow, and Dominic will be by ta take ye home."

Kira shook her head defiantly. "I can't go back there—with the two of them. I need my tool pack. Will you bring it to me?"

"He's closed the site," Maeve told her. "We've all been relocated." She scrutinized Kira's frightened expression. "And as for Franco, he's in a bad way, is he."

Kira swallowed hard, remembering the man blocking her way out of the quaking villa. "He was standing there," she remember out loud.

"He will not be standin' again."

"He shouldn't have been there. He couldn't get out."

"Aye, and the same should be said for you. Why were ye there?"

She looked up through bleary eyes. "They were sending me home."

"For yer protection, as I understand."

"I suppose." She closed her eyes to block out the memories that still filled her senses.

"Ye'll be missing Dominic?"

Kira turned away, afraid of exposing her feelings.

"But ye care for him still?" Maeve guessed.

"Oh course I care for him. The man's lost his father and now his livelihood. I feel sorry for him."

"Aye, and a wee bit more maybe?" Maeve cocked an eyebrow inviting confidence.

"You can stop matchmaking now. They asked me to leave. I'm going home."

"The airthquake has done quite a bit of damage. We were lucky to get to Napoli. It will be some days before ye can travel."

Kira sat up again, her head swimming with the effort. "Where am I going to stay? I can't go back there."

"With me," she answered simply. "The locandas are full with people who cannot leave. Ye best accept what hospitality ye can find."

"Where?"

Maeve turned her face to look out the window. "Capri." Her voice took on a dreamlike quality. "What did ye find, Kirie?"

"Nothing." Exhaling a loud sigh, Kira fell back against her pillow. "I don't know."

Maeve's back straightened, her chin raised a little higher in profile at the window. "Something?"

Kira watched the almost undetectable ripple of each muscle in Maeve's back as the thrill of a possible discovery betrayed her. "If it was anything, it's buried again now."

Maeve turned slowly, her eyes bright with excitement. "But ye found something? Was it the treasure, do ye think?"

It seemed as if Il Padrone was right about Maeve Ryan after all. "I lost it as quickly as I found it."

CHAPTER 22

❀

The villa on Capri was white, almost to sterility and although fresh picked flowers broke the monotony, Kira felt stifled by her new surroundings.

It had been three days since she had last seen Il Padrone—three days since he had carried her, so she'd been told, unconscious from the site.

She fanned herself with a magazine while she paced around her sparsely furnished room, frustrated by the interminable delay in leaving Italy. Nothing mattered anymore but getting home. Maeve had confined her to quarters, insisting that she should rest after the ordeal in the excavation.

For the first time in her life, solitude did not agree with her.

Even as she vowed that she wanted nothing more to do with the Fiorettis, her head reeled with the thought that she might never see Dominic again.

The manner in which he acknowledged her intelligence was something she was unaccustomed to from a man. His insistent protectiveness, though at times primitive, had given her the strength to be angry rather than frightened. She found she missed the battle.

Now she was afraid.

Three days ago she had found the grail—had held it in her hands. And Maeve knew it. Maeve continued to question her about what she found in the site. Without the tangible evidence, Kira wasn't sure anymore if it hadn't all been a dream.

"Yer things have arrived from the Casa," Maeve called out to her, interrupting her thoughts.

"I expect he's glad to be rid of me," Kira sighed, taking her back pack and her tool belt from the older woman.

Maeve smiled, secretly amused. "But he's not rid of ye yet. You will see him before ye go, will ye not?"

Kira dropped her head, shaking it slowly. "There isn't any reason." She curled her fingers around her tool pack and felt the curve of the cup still concealed inside. Her heart skipped a beat. He had not taken it.

"Ye may wish to thank him for his hospitality," Maeve pointed out.

The possibilities of the treasure she held hidden in her hands assaulted her rational mind. "What?" she asked absently.

"He has opened his home to ye."

"Right. I'll send him a card. Maeve, is Franco still unconscious?"

"Aye…"

"Will he live?"

"Yer playin' with dynamite, Kira. Ye do know how it is with Dominic, do ye not?"

Kira waved a hand impatiently. "It's only a game to them, who can get the girl. It's only his pride that's hurt. Does that mean I shouldn't help his brother if it's within my power to do so?"

"And when did you become a doctor?"

"I have to try, don't I? He went down there because he thought I knew where the treasure was."

"Do ye?" she asked simply, crossing her arms across her chest.

Kira leveled her eyes at her friend. "Of course I do. And I saw the ghost, too."

Maeve waved an arm in disbelief. "Go on with ye."

"Maeve, I want you to know how much I appreciate your taking me in like this. You've done so much for me."

"But I've done nothin', Kirie, and too soon you'll be on a flight back across the ocean."

"Maybe I'll check on the international flights again while I'm in Naples."

"No," Maeve answered quickly. "I'm sure they're doin' their best to get the tourists back home. Sure and they'll be calling us soon to tell you ye have a seat."

"I have to see Franco."

"Shall I go with ye to Naples then?"

Kira took a deep breath. "I have to do this on my own."

Maeve shot a nervous look over her shoulder and then shrugged. "Are ye sure yer feeling well enough?"

Kira laughed. "If I don't get out of this room, I'm going to go crazy." She watched Maeve's reaction to her statement. Was she a prisoner or a guest?

"A spot of air may be just what ye need."

The sigh of relief couldn't be contained. Kira reached out and hugged Maeve to her. "Thank you."

From somewhere else in the villa, two sharp rings sounded from a telephone.

"Saints preserve us," Maeve cried out, clapping her hands. "It's the telephone. I've been trying to ring home since the airthquake."

Kira watched the small Irish woman run toward the salotto while she picked up her backpack.

Eavesdropping wasn't her intention when she walked by the room a few minutes later, but the hushed tones of Maeve's voice and the seed of doubt Dominic had planted made it inevitable.

"'Tis certain that she has found something," Maeve said in a low voice. "I think she is going to tell Franco. It may be after she sees how he fairs that she will tell me."

Kira hazarded a look into the salotto. Maeve's back was turned toward her, shaking her head and turning slightly in disagreement to what she was hearing. "'Twill not be necessary. The lass has no need for it. I need only to keep her from Il Padrone until after she's told me what she knows."

Kira wrapped the shoulder straps of the backpack around her wrists, holding tight to the small package inside.

※　　　※　　　※

She walked at a brisk pace, clutching her prize close.

Slowing, Kira found herself in front of the Duomo, the home of the Cathedral of St. Gennaro. Twice a year the dead saint's blood came to a boil, a local miracle that occurred without fail.

Kira stepped inside, eager to believe that miracles did happen—they seemed a part of everyday life in southern Italy. And yet…

Her insides wrenched at the thought of Dominic Fioretti, the man she might never see again. She had fought the attraction from the start, had known it could only end poorly. Summer romances were always lopsided. One person always read more into it than the other and she wasn't going to give him the satisfaction of seeing her wounded heart.

She bent over, taking deep breaths to keep the tears from falling again. Once she was back home, near her family, the pain would go away. Greg would tell her what to do and she would get on with her life.

Clutching at the hard cup in her backpack—stolen goods—she felt an electric current rush through her.

"Can I help you?" A priest addressed her in English, catching her off guard.

Tingling with the odd sensation, Kira raised her head in confusion. "I—I came to pray for a friend."

"He is very ill? Perhaps you light a candle?"

She stared at the old priest in the black soutane before her. "How did you know I spoke English?"

"English?" he replied as if he didn't understand. "I don't speak English."

"But you just…"

The lines in the old priest's brow creased, a frown scoring his benign features. "I live all my life here in Napoli," he said. "I do not speak English."

She began backing away, frightened by the sensation that continued to emanate through the canvas of her bag. "I have to go."

She ran from the cathedral all the way to the hospital.

Arriving out of breath, Kira darted into an elevator and leaned against the wall, closing her eyes.

She hugged her pack tightly, fighting to relax while the lift carried her to her destination.

When at last the doors opened, she slipped silently down the corridor and into Franco's private room.

She gasped at the sight of him. A series of tubes and beeps transformed the man into an alien life form.

She fingered the relic through the canvas. "Do your stuff," she whispered.

A nurse's hand grabbed onto Kira's shoulder, pushing her out of the room and administering Italian remonstrations while escorting Kira back to the elevator.

"I'm a friend," Kira protested in English, eliciting more irate ranting from Franco's warden. "I only wanted to help," she explained, her voice dying away.

The nurse, a stout woman who was almost a foot shorter than Kira, rested her hands on her hips and waited for Kira to get back into the lift, not moving until the doors had closed and Kira was safely away.

Back on the ground floor, Kira searched the lobby while her mind sorted through other options. Her parcel lay dormant.

And then she spotted the chapel.

The small room seemed little more than a confessional beside the ornamentation of the churches and cathedrals Italy had to offer.

Kira knelt down behind a pew still clutching her bag, afraid to let it go. Before her, a gilded cross dominated the front of the chapel.

"You could not leave him after all?" Dominic's voice was quiet, the deep resonance raising the hairs on the back of her neck.

"Leave him?" she repeated without turning to acknowledge him.

"To have come all this way—and then this."

She began to shiver, feeling him close behind her.

"You were with him when it happened. I should have seen how it is between you."

She squeezed her eyes closed, not wanting to face him and unable to ignore him. "How is it?"

Her fists clenched around the bag, tightening the canvas around the cup inside.

His breath was warm on her neck. "You went to meet him the night of the ball," he continued, his English impeccable. "But you found me instead. Tell me, did you make love to my brother in the home of my ancestors?"

She wheeled around angrily to face him. "No."

"Would you lie in the presence of God?" he whispered. "Did you come to make a fool of me? To be with him? Why are you here, Kira? What do you want?"

"I didn't know he was there, and he was standing," she motioned with her hands to illustrate, "and then the earth started to shake, and then…and then…" she stuttered, trying to control herself. She felt the contraband in her backpack, hard against her fist. It seemed to tremble beneath the pressure she exerted.

"Signore Fioretti!" A man came into the chapel, summoning Dominic in urgent, hushed tones. He pulled Dominic from the pew, his rapid dialect beyond Kira's comprehension. When the man finished, Dominic glared at her.

"Were you in his room?"

"Yes."

His dark eyes accused her once more before he turned abruptly and left the chapel with the other man.

"What is it?" she called, following after him.

The elevator chimed its arrival. "He is awake."

The color drained from her face. Her backpack fell to the floor and she began to sway uncertainly.

"You've dropped your bag." She cast wide eyes on the face of an older man in a black suit with a white collar. He had picked up her pack and was handing it back to her. She continued to stare at him. "Are you an American?" he continued.

"Are you speaking English?"

He laughed. "It is nice to hear one's own language in a foreign country, isn't it?"

"Sometimes."

"You look quite pale. Is everything all right?" He took Kira's arm, leading her back into the chapel. "We are visiting, my wife and I. With the earthquake and all, well, my wife broke her arm. I had some time to myself so…" he looked up at the cross at the front of the nave. "Professional curiosity, you know." He winked. "You have a sick friend?"

Kira nodded.

"You are very pale. Do you want me to call a doctor?"

She shook her head vehemently. "Let me ask you something…Father? No, you're not a priest, you have a wife."

"Wouldn't be much of a priest with a wife, now would I?" he laughed. "John Thompson."

"Pastor Thompson," she repeated. "Do you believe in the Holy Grail?"

His eyes became saucers followed by another chuckle. "The Holy Grail? Dear me. That's a can of worms." He motioned for Kira to take a seat beside him in one of the pews. "There are those that worship the grail," he began, eyeing her suspiciously, then shaking his head. "Do I believe in it?" He rubbed his chin thoughtfully. "Don't suppose I ever gave much mind to it before."

"I've been thinking about it a lot lately." Kira faced him on the hard wooden bench. "May I tell you a story?"

"I'd be glad to listen." He folded his arms in his lap and sat back, studying her.

"I've been reading some. Suppose for a minute that Paul, when he was on that road to Damascus, was given the grail by Jesus." She held up a finger, asking for his patience. "He was blinded by the pure light of Jesus, but his sight was restored when he reached Ananias."

"I know the story. I'm with you so far," Pastor Thompson said.

"Suppose Ananias healed him with the power of the grail."

"I'd have to disagree with you there," Pastor Thompson interjected. "The grail could have no power on its own."

Kira nodded in agreement. "Yes, but suppose one's faith is magnified when they are in possession of the grail. Suppose that's where the power comes from. Some might call it channeling."

"Interesting idea," the Pastor agreed. He eyed her suspiciously. "Are you in possession of something you believe to be the grail?"

"What about eternal life? Isn't the grail supposed to grant eternal life to the bearer?" she continued, the color returning to her face.

"Are you a Christian, child?"

"Yes."

"Then you already have that gift. No symbol can supply or deny you that."

She paused, pushing her glasses back up her nose. "What powers would you project on the grail?"

"IF a grail exists," he started, narrowing his eyes, "I do not believe it could have power. As an amplifier, as you have suggested," he paused, rubbing his chin again, "Interesting idea."

"When Paul was taken to Rome, before he died, he performed miracles. He told the crew about the shipwreck, he healed the sick," she pointed out. "Could it have been the power of the grail—no, the power of God channeled through the grail: the faith of Paul, amplified?"

"This is how a legend begins," he replied, smiling.

"If you had the grail today, here, do you think you could heal your wife's broken arm?"

"No," he answered immediately. "Things happen for a reason. If God wanted my wife's arm to be broken, then it would have to be broken. If she were ill and I wished her well with the power you suggest, it would depend on what God's purposes were. If she did return to health, it would be the will of God and not the power of the grail." He leaned forward conspiratorially. "Do you have the grail?"

She shook her head, not wanting to voice the lie but afraid to answer. "How could I prove it if I had?" she laughed nervously. And then she caught her breath, remembering her experience at the Duomo. "Could the grail have a Pentecostal effect? Become a translation tool?"

"I would very much like to see what has sparked your curiosity."

The chapel door opened allowing admittance to some other people in search of solace.

Kira shrugged noncommittally. "I get these inane ideas when I'm upset. It helps keep my mind from dwelling on the worst. I must sound like a mad woman." She smiled, reaching out to shake his hand. "I think you'll find Naples fascinating in spite of the earthquakes."

"What is your name?" he asked, trapping her hand.

"Kyrie Eleison," she replied. Then catching herself, "No, it's Kira Ellison."

"Church has that effect on people," he joked.

"Kira!" Dominic was returning to the chapel.

Pastor Thompson jerked away from her much like a lover caught in forbidden embrace.

"Franco wants to see you," Dominic commanded gruffly, casting a suspicious eye on the clergyman.

The Pastor leaned over and whispered, "We will talk again."

Kira smiled gratefully, moving reluctantly toward Dominic.

"Another accomplice?" Dominic asked, pushing the elevator button that would take them back upstairs.

"An American tourist. There's a certain amount of comfort in speaking to one's countryman."

He raised his eyebrows. "Perhaps you don't find my English satisfactory?"

"Your English is perfect, Padrone."

CHAPTER 23

Franco was sitting up in his bed. The corners of his mouth lifted into a smile. He began to laugh until he choked. The nurse gave Kira an irate stare.

Kira held her arms out in supplication.

"So you have not gone." Franco's voice was raspy, almost indistinguishable.

"It is not a simple matter after the earthquake," she explained.

"Much of what we have found has been destroyed," Dominic added.

"So you are unable to leave?" He shot a frightened look at Dominic, grabbing for his younger brother's hand.

"She is safe," Dominic reassured him.

"She saw it," Franco whispered hoarsely, leaning forward. "She is not safe."

The ripple that coursed through Kira was one of sheer terror as the enormity of what she held in her hand represented. She leaned forward, holding the backpack out. "Franco…"

Dominic stopped her, pushing her arm back into her lap and issuing her a warning with his black eyes.

"You saw it," Franco repeated in Italian, fixing Kira with a glassy stare.

"I don't know what I saw," she skirted, remembering the glitter of gold in what she had thought was an empty cabinet after removing the grail.

"He is delirious," Dominic dismissed. "My brother needs his rest."

"Kira," Franco called, clearing his throat. He lifted an arm limply, then closed his eyes and lay back against the pillows. "You saw it."

There were tears in his eyes, but whether they were from pain or disappointment, Kira couldn't discern.

The nurse prattled off a string of Italian, eliciting a nod from Dominic. He took Kira's arm and led her out of the room.

Franco began to argue with the nurse in an agitated state, insisting that he had to speak to the couple leaving the room. Kira listened to him calling after her in a voice so full of pain it hurt her to hear him.

"He is very ill," Dominic assured her, ushering her out of the hospital. "I will see you back to Capri."

He did not look at her, didn't say another word. They rode in a taxi to the dock in silence. Gone was the overbearing expression of Il Padrone, replaced by something between grief and despair. He bore the unguarded expression of the dark man from her dream.

They sat side by side on the hydrofoil, Dominic's eyes closed against the wind that whipped his black curls straight. Kira watched him circumspectly, wishing for his strength to return.

As the Iron Island grew larger, Dominic finally spoke. "There will be a party Saturday night," he said, "a farewell for the team." His eyes settled on her, his expression carefully masking his feelings.

"I hope to be gone by then," she deferred.

"You are leaving, then?"

"It was your wish that I leave."

He stared across the water, his fingers clicking off against his thumb one by one. "I heard Franco invite you to stay. I thought maybe you had changed your mind."

Kira felt the lump in her backpack and looked down to acknowledge her package.

The hydrofoil settled back down in the water. Dominic disembarked, setting his stride purposefully. Kira followed quietly, knowing the time had come to surrender her find.

As they approached the villa, she called out to him. "Padrone." He stopped but did not turn. "I have to talk to you."

"What is it that you said to me?" he asked, turning to face her. "I'm not much in the mood for talking right now."

"Dominic, please," she entreated.

His shoulders dropped and he held an arm out inviting her into the villa.

Kira wished for the closed doors of the Casa. The Treasure had been such a well-guarded secret. It seemed important for it to remain that way.

Dominic conducted her into the stark salotto. She looked nervously around the room.

"They say Franco's recovery is nothing short of a miracle," he said almost venomously. "I am quite sure your presence had much to do with it. I should be grateful."

"A miracle," Kira repeated, opening the backpack. Her hands trembled uncontrollably, tears threatening.

"Dominic, I found something." She took the cup from its hiding place and handed it to Dominic. "It belongs to you, Padrone."

Dominic examined the grail carefully. "Why did you hide this from me?" His eyes were glistening.

"I haven't seen you since I found it."

He turned it in his hands.

Kira winced, not wanting to lose the cup into obscurity. "Do you know what it is?"

"I know." He leveled his eyes directly on hers. "And so do you." He fell into a chair opposite, staring at the cup. "I wondered what you would do with it."

His words felt like a slap in the face. "You knew I had it?"

He looked away from her.

"Then why did you give it back to me?"

"You would not have been able to leave the country with it."

"Why didn't you just have me arrested?" she asked sarcastically.

"I needed to know what you would do with it." He bowed his head and put one hand out to lean against the wall.

"Now you know, Padrone." She spat out his title angrily.

He spun to face her, matching her anger. "Why did you take it to Franco?"

"I suppose I wanted to test the legends."

"And?"

"And?"

He turned a hand, inviting her to continue.

"You may decide for yourself." Kira stood up and turned to leave.

"Wait." He reached for her arm. "You must have a drink." He wiped out the bowl of the grail and filled the cup with white wine.

"Lacrimae Christi," he said. "These grapes are grown on the side of Vesuvio. In English this means Tears of Christ." He took a sip from the cup and handed it to her. "Drink."

Kira took the cup and followed his example. She looked into the depths of his black eyes. He was searching hers as if trying to see into her soul. "Do you love my brother?"

"No." Tears stung her eyes as she fought to keep her true feelings to herself.

"You met him in England."

Her jaw tightened. "No."

His grip on her arm tightened. "Why here? Why not Herculaneum or Pompeii?"

"Fate? Predestination?"

He released her and turned away.

But Kira was just hitting her stride. "Why did you steal my purse?"

"You know I did not."

"Then how were you able to recover it?"

"Why did you not cry out for help when it was taken?" he growled back. "You may consider yourself fortunate that I saw the man who took it."

"You don't believe me. Why should I believe you?"

He caressed the cup in his hands, staring into the wine that remained in the bowl. "I believe you," he answered quietly. "When you drink the Tears of Christ from the Holy Grail you may speak only the truth." He raised his head to address her. "That's why Judas ran from the room that night."

His words sent a shiver through Kira. And then she remembered that he had taken a drink from the cup before her. "Then you won't mind answering a few questions for me."

He leveled a threatening glare. "I would not lie to you, Kira. But I would warn you not to ask me a question you do not wish to know the answer to."

Her throat tightened, his implication clear. Her next words were little more than a whisper. "I'm sorry. Maybe you should go now."

"Go?"

"Thank you for escorting me back."

"Go?" His eyes narrowed, the veins in his neck protruding visibly. "You do have a place to stay?"

Dominic slammed an open hand onto a table beside him. "Who's house do you think you are staying in?"

Kira took a step backward, afraid of the sudden intensity of his rage. "Maeve…oh, God." Realization struck a blinding blow. "This is your villa?" She felt the blood rushing from her head. "I didn't want to…she told me…she must have thought I wouldn't…"

He remained glowering before her, a tower of fury waiting to explode, his body trembling under the effort to contain himself.

"I didn't know," she answered feebly. "Maeve told me we were staying with friends."

"Go," he grunted quietly.

"But…"

"Go!"

Frightened, Kira ran from the room.

CHAPTER 24

Tourists flocked to the restaurant on the Marina Piccola. Sapphire waves caressed the shoreline. A little piece of heaven on earth according to the Capri guidebook.

"You should have said something," she told Maeve, shoes slung over her shoulders as she kicked at the hot sand with her toes.

"Would ye have come if ye knew?"

"Probably not."

"And where else do ye think ye'd have gone?"

Kira walked on, pensive. She chuckled briefly and looked at Maeve. "You should have seen his face when I asked him to leave."

"None too pleased, I'm sure."

"It can't be much longer before I can get a flight."

"So yer leavin' then?"

Kira shrugged. "Back home. Kira Ellison—history teacher. That's who I am."

"Didn't find exactly what ye came for?"

Kira gave a little snort, silently remarking that she had found everything she came for and more. Recovering herself, she smiled. "Well I was hoping for a small souvenir."

"The pieces, they belong in the museums. That's why Jean-Marc was here."

"And why are you here?"

Maeve remained silent, her shoulders slouched. "I was in love with Enzio Fioretti, but ye'll have guessed that by now."

"Tell me about their father," Kira prompted, following the older woman slowly. "He must have been quite a man to raise such strong-willed sons."

Her eyes twinkled. "Aye, that he was. Franco favors him, ye know." Maeve stopped and put a hand to Kira's shoulder. "Ye'll be knowin', of course, that he loves ye."

"Franco? Men like him don't fall in love. He's a hopeless flirt—throwing out bird seed like a cat to see what flies within reach."

Maeve laughed. "He wasn't the one I was referrin to. And the other?"

"The other. That's what Laura called him."

"She'll not have been referring to Dominic that way," Maeve said doubtfully.

"You still think I have to marry one of them? Even now when it doesn't matter anymore?"

The puzzled expression that Maeve wore gave her an air of credibility. "Ye needn't marry one of them, but 'twould be a shame to let go of the man ye love."

"I just want to go home."

"Yer certain there's nothin' else for ye here?"

"My family's there," she reminded herself. "My mother. My brother and his family. My students."

"And no man to warm yer bed at night."

There was Joe. Kira cringed at the thought of sleeping with him. Somehow she had never considered intimacy with Joe Cochran before. Thinking of it now repulsed her.

"Aye, I thought as much," Maeve chuckled. "I saw ye with himself at the ball. No other man will do for ye, Kira. It's as plain as that."

Kira lifted her head to look at Maeve Ryan, her face carefully masking the hurt and anger she harbored. It didn't matter what she wanted. "I think I'd prefer to be alone for a while," she said, moving toward an arriving tour bus.

"Will ye be all right by yerself?"

Kira gave a half-laugh through her nose. "Safer than I've been with everyone else I've met since coming to Italy." Kira looked up toward the Villa Jovis. "And I understand Tiberius has long since passed on. I don't think he'll be throwing me over the cliff."

Maeve took her hands, looking nervously at the bus that stood waiting. "If yer sure…"

Fifteen minutes later, Kira followed a small group of tourists, alone, hiking up the steep slope to the ruins. Looking out across the shimmering sea from the cliff, images of the ancient Emperor assaulted her from the history books.

Overhead, a bird cried out, answered by another, reminders of Tiberius' victims screaming out as they fell to their deaths on the surf below.

Kira closed her eyes and took a deep breath, overcome by desolation. What had she accomplished? Crossing the ocean in pursuit of a phantom, she had uncovered the most sought after artifact in the world. She had realized a dream and she had found love.

She gave up both to Dominic.

Dominic. A self-made man. A passionate man. A teacher, like herself. And from what Maeve had told her of Isabella Fioretti, mothering would be the last thing Dominic wanted from a woman. A sharp contrast to the man waiting at home for her.

Kira struggled to remember something of what Maeve had told her of Isabella Fioretti. There had been a scandal—a secret lover—and La Signora Fioretti had been asked to leave the Casa.

And now Kira had been asked to go.

A breeze rose from the sea lifting Kira's hair.

She walked across to the steep descent that branched off toward the Grotta dii Matromania in one direction and the Arco Naturale in the other. Watching her footing carefully, she descended toward the grotto until she came to the mouth of the cave.

He stood with his head turned toward the ceiling, his hair curling gracefully down his back. Kira's first inclination was to run away, and yet seeing him here he looked calm, at peace. In the fading light of the grotto, Dominic was the image of his ancestors, standing in the cave like a perfectly sculpted statue.

Maeve was right. No other man would ever compare to Dominic Fioretti.

"So you have come." He had not turned to acknowledge her.

Kira looked around, afraid she was intruding on a private conversation, but there was no one else immediately visible.

"I wanted to see the sights," she said tentatively. "This may be the last time I see Capri."

"That would be most unfortunate." He lowered his eyes so that they rested on her face. "Why did you choose this grotto? Certainly the others are more fantastic."

She pointed up the cliff. "I was at the villa, above."

"Then why did you not go to the Arco Naturale?" He approached her, gently pushing her out of the way of other sightseers following behind her.

Kira searched the floor of the cave. "I didn't really think about it."

"Do you know the origins of this cave?" He was standing close beside her, invading her personal space.

"It is where the people that celebrated life with Tiberius got married."

He scowled. "The tourist trade will promote that, of course."

"Does Matromania have another meaning then?" He was standing too close, producing a response from her body that she fought to suppress. She turned away under the pretext of examining the wall.

His voice was quiet, sending a thrill through her. "It is said to be a distortion of Mitromania. Do you perhaps know of Mithras?"

"A god?"

His breath was warm on her neck again. "Kira," he whispered. "Cyrus. Mithras." He pronounced each name slowly.

"The sun god?" Startled, she turned to face him.

He stepped back. "I thought that might have been the attraction for you." He formed a fist around something in his hand. "This grotto is the sight of pagan ritual. Worship of Mithras, god of the sun."

"I had no idea." Kira was watching the methodical movements of his fingers, turning a small coin in his hand. He offered the piece of gold to her.

"It was my father's," he explained. "He told me…my father was…" he shook his head. "He told me someone would come to me in this grotto." Dominic took a deep breath. "He gave me this coin as a reminder."

"That's a fairly easy prediction to make. Especially to an impressionable young boy."

His eyes were shining, yet his face remained unemotional, muscles straining to control his expressions. "It was after I returned from America. Ten years ago."

Kira turned over the coin he handed her. One side was imprinted with an image of the sun similar to some of those eroding on the walls of the grotto. "Il sole."

He was watching her intently. "I have not been back here since he gave it to me."

"Why did you come today?"

"I didn't realize I had until I stood here." He kept a safe distance from her, as if he were suddenly afraid of her. "How long do you think I have been standing here?"

She shrugged her shoulders. "I don't believe you would be a man to wait long."

"I have been here five minutes, and here you are: Kira, for Cyrus the god of the sun. The ghost called you by name, 'Il sole.'"

"So I have fulfilled his prophecy?" she taunted skeptically. "What happens next?"

He rubbed his forehead with his hand. "I could not say."

"Fine, I'll ask the ghost," she answered sarcastically.

"Is it possible to know the future?" he countered.

"How did I know about your father? How did either of us know about the grail?"

He turned away. "It is still not safe. I can trust no one."

Kira began to shake, struggling to keep her emotions in check. "When I came here, you accused me of being a pirate. When I found the hidden chamber you told me that if God had sent me to find the treasure then I must be the one to find it. You continue to insist that I can't keep my hands off your brother, a man who's methods I find repulsive by the way." She was pacing around the cave now, her voice echoing off the walls and bringing stares from curious tourists. "And if that wasn't enough, you humiliated me at that stupid ball." She stopped in front of him, demanding his full attention.

"I did not intend…"

"Then what was the point?" Tears threatened close to the surface. Kira's throat tightened so that she was afraid to speak.

He stood silent, unmoving, his expression curiously vulnerable. And then he turned away. "You could not understand."

"I understand much more than you think I do," she told him.

"Then that is a part of the problem, is it not?" His Italian inflection returned with the heightened emotion in his voice. "You, who knows much more than a stranger should coming into my home. You, who finds what my father lost his life trying to unearth, as if you knew where it was."

"I did."

"You did what?" he shouted angrily, throwing his hands down at his sides.

"I knew where it was."

He grabbed hold of her arms, resisting the urge to shake her. "How could you when even he did not know?"

A tear escaped from the corner of her eye. "The same way I knew he died." Her heart tightened with the pain she remembered from her dream of the dark man. Her voice broke to a whisper. "The same way I know you rescued Franco before you found your father buried alive." She raised a comforting hand to the side of his face.

His skin was warm, still smooth. She pressed her lips gently to his, cautious at first and then certain as he pulled her closer.

His eyes were soft and warm. The glow of the setting sun in the grotto transformed his features from those of the satyr to one of Michelangelo's angels. Kira gasped at the contrast.

"What is it?"

She continued to hold her breath, watching his face. The sun was shifting its position, taking the ephemeral glow from Dominic's face.

She reached out for one last embrace, not wanting to forget the sensation he had awakened in her. The touch of his lips was like wine to an alcoholic.

She pulled away from him, confused and afraid, and ran blindly from the grotto past the confused reverend Pastor Thompson standing on the stairway just outside the opening.

CHAPTER 25

The message was scrawled in flowery Italian handwriting laying on the table beside her journal. There was a flight to New York available on Monday.

Getting across the ocean was first priority. A connecting flight to Chicago would be a simple matter once she was in the U.S.

She was going home, but not before the final party for the archeologists.

She would see Dominic one last time.

※ ※ ※

The house was ablaze with lights and music. In one more day Kira would be back home, reacclimating to America and trying to explain to Joe Cochran why she could never marry him.

Tonight she would see Dominic, her last chance to engrain those dark features forever in her memory.

Kira took a glass of champagne from the tray making its way through the crowd, giving the waiter a smile and looking around the assembly.

As they had been during meals at the Casa del Fioretti, Kira noticed that the people segregated themselves into cliques: the professionals, the students, laborers, scholars…where did she fit in?

Kira spotted Laura, teasing coyly with some hapless Italian man. Her table-mate. Laura, Maeve, Jean-Marc…all of them there on some hidden agenda.

Guilt swept over her. Had Dominic been right all along? She was no better than a treasure hunter after all, as they all seemed to be in one form or another. Her archeological interests had only been the excuse.

"Kira?" came the Frenchman's voice beside her.

"Jean-Marc?" She wondered again what his secret was. He hadn't blended with the others.

"Come, let me introduce you to my sister." He nodded to a petite woman standing close by.

"Claudette," he introduced. "Kira."

The Frenchwoman nodded her. "I have heard much about you," she greeted in heavily accented English.

"Laura says you are going home on Monday," Jean-Marc said.

"Yes, I'm afraid all good things must come to an end."

"Perhaps we will meet again another time."

"Ah, mon ami, I do not think so, unless you will be coming to America."

"You may pass this way again, cherie," Claudette suggested.

"I don't think so," Kira replied politely. "My tour is over."

Jean-Marc stirred his drink, looking into the glass. "I hear you have found the treasure."

"You are mistaken."

"Your secret is safe with me."

"I do not have the treasure," she answered truthfully, having given it over to Dominic's protection. "You have been misinformed." She downed the last of her champagne and crossed over to a table of appetizers.

The guests laughed and chatted freely, celebrating life while they recalled the finds they had restored from the earth's womb.

"Kira!" Laura squealed, "I knew you'd come."

Kira ran a hand through her tousled hair, increasingly uncomfortable with the band of friends she had been drawn into.

"Kira?" Coming through the crowd, outstretched arms in front of him, was Joe Cochran. He looked older, his thinning blond hair showing more of his scalp than Kira remembered. His thick hands held hers, a smile lighting up his round face.

"What are you doing here?" she asked, unable to move.

"I was worried, what with the earthquake and all."

Kira scanned the room for Dominic's face. "You shouldn't have come."

"You never told me you had a boyfriend," Laura teased, grabbing onto Joe's arm.

"Joe Cochran, Laura Griffith," she introduced, pulling him away.

"Quite a party," he commented.

"A farewell party. The site's been closed." She smiled, seeing innocence in his gentle blue eyes. "What are you doing here?"

"Looking for you." He adjusted his glasses before he put his hands into his pockets. "You haven't written, or called, or…"

"I know. I'm sorry. I guess I owe you some kind of an explanation."

Laura came up behind them. "Kira, have you seen Dominic?"

A shiver ran up her spine, ending as she shrugged her shoulders. "Should I have?"

"I really need to talk to you," Joe insisted. "Is there somewhere we can go?"

Kira nodded toward garden doors that led outside. "How did you find me here? There isn't anyone left in Ercolano, is there?"

"The Italians are very friendly. And the Fiorettis seem to be well known. One of them is in the hospital, I hear. Bet you have quite a story to tell," he laughed a little nervously.

The night was dark beneath a new moon. The smell of algae hung heavy in the still air. Not even the familiar sounds of crickets broke the torpid silence after the earthquake.

"You shouldn't have come." She couldn't look at him.

He smiled and took her hands again. "I got to thinking, it was awfully quiet without you around. Then I was worried about you over here." He put a finger under her chin, tilting her head to look at him. "So I decided that maybe it would be fun if we got married here in Italy. We could have our honeymoon before we went back home and save the cost of another plane ticket."

She couldn't help but smile. "I can't," she whispered tears stinging the corners of her eyes.

"I know its kind of sudden."

She began to giggle. "Sudden?" She broke into laughter. "Sudden? Joe, I've known you most of my life." She wiped at the corners of her eyes. "You've never even kissed me."

He was taken aback. "Of course I have."

She pointed to the spot on her cheek. "This doesn't count. You can't be serious, Joe."

"I didn't want to offend you."

"Offend me?" She gave way to a fit of giggles.

"You've changed," he said quietly.

"Do you even love me?" she asked, daring him to say it.

"I'm very fond of you."

"It's not the same thing." She took a seat on the garden bench.

"I thought we understood each other. We agreed that love was something they made up to get to happily ever after."

"You're right, I have changed." Kira stood up, reaching out for the dark green leaves of an olive tree. "I knew what you were going to ask before I left. Maybe that was part of the reason I left." She looked at him standing defenseless in the moonlight. "I probably would have settled for the easy way out, too. But something's happened." The tears were falling freely down her face.

Joe sat beside her, putting his arm across her shoulders. "Don't cry, Kira."

"I never thought it would happen to me," She tried to laugh again.

"I'll take care of you," he offered. "I don't care what's happened to you. And if there are consequences, well we'll deal with that when the time comes."

"Consequences?" She repeated incredulously, trying to grasp his inference.

"You probably haven't had time to think about that," he patronized.

"Consequences?" She backed away from him. "You don't get it, do you? I'm in love, Joe."

"It makes it easier for the victim when she believes she's in love with her attacker."

Her eyes wandered to a shadow cloaked in white moving around the villa. And then Laura appeared in the door. "Kira?"

"I need another drink," she told Joe, scurrying back to the villa.

"Kira!" A voice beckoned her softly from the brush before she could walk back into the villa.

Hesitating, Kira squinted in the darkness, looking for the disembodied voice. "Not more ghosts," she murmured.

A face emerged from the shadows adorned in a long white robe emblazoned with a red cross. "Pastor Thompson?" she asked incredulously.

"Miss Ellison, how nice to meet you again."

"But what are you doing here?"

He lunged for her hand, pulling her around the corner of the villa. "You have something that I need."

Kira felt her heart pounding. "You're mistaken."

"She has no reason to lie." Jean-Marc appeared from the shadows. "I do not believe she has it."

The Pastor kept his eyes on Kira, a frightening look of near mania in his eyes. "She asked me about it, Brother. I am quite certain she does have it."

Jean-Marc assessed the situation before taking a step closer to the Pastor. "She is just a teacher. She has no need of it."

"And you are just a museum curator."

"Jean-Marc?" Kira asked nervously.

Jean-Marc took a deep breath, preparing himself for the confrontation he never expected to have. "Tell me, *mon frere*, why do we seek the grail?"

"To restore power to the order," Pastor Thompson answered immediately.

"To bring one man to power?"

John Thompson turned to look at the Frenchman, yanking Kira around in front of him. "You would go against Brother Ambrose?"

Jean-Marc took a step closer. "To guard the sacred relics," he said calmly. "To protect them from the sinful desires of men."

"That is Ambrose's goal."

"Ambrose desires power."

"Jean-Marc?" Kira asked again, an edge of hysteria rising in her voice.

"Release the girl."

"You have failed."

"She does not have the grail." Jean-Marc nodded an apology to Kira. "Her room and her belongings have been searched."

"Fool," Thompson hissed. "That does not mean she does not possess it."

"Release her."

Kira was thrown free in a surprising move of agility from the small Pastor. When she regained her balance, she gasped in horror at the sight before her: a red cross spreading across Jean-Marc's chest, random flashes of light glistening from the length of the sword the rotund pastor wielded in his hands.

"Oh my God, oh my God!" she cried, backing away, running toward the villa.

Laura met Kira at the door. "Come with me," she whispered. "Dominic's looking for you."

"Where is he?"

"At the excavation."

CHAPTER 26

❃

The Bay of Naples sent fingers of humidity into the mist that sprayed around the private boat as it sped back toward the city. Kira's hair hung limply, little curling tendrils tightening around the edges. She shivered in spite of the heat that still hung heavy in the muggy air.

She leaned heavily against the side of the boat, fighting back the nausea and the tears after seeing a man she had considered a friend murdered before her eyes. Was it her fault? Would he still be alive if she admitted to the grail's existence? Could she change the events of the evening if she had it still?

While her mind spun with all the questions and possibilities, fighting to suppress the reality of what she had witnessed, Laura stood unobtrusively beside the man piloting the boat. In a moment of what Kira considered normalcy, she allowed herself an almost hysterical laugh. In spite of the horror of what had happened on Capri, there was Laura, still making a play for the first available man.

And yet there was something hauntingly familiar about the man at the helm.

"Are you sure he's in Ercolano?" Kira asked again, wrapping her arms tightly around her to control her shaking. Laura had been avoiding the question since they left Capri.

Laura shrugged her shoulders again, leaning across the bow into the fine mist of water. "Maybe he's still trying to recover the treasure."

"He wouldn't..." Kira began, and then closed her mouth. She kept her eyes on the man piloting the boat, half hidden in shadow, still trying to place the rugged Italian features.

After docking in Ercolano, the captain followed them off the boat keeping his head down, the shadows still covering his features.

"I'm sure I've seen him before," Kira whispered, following Laura to a waiting car.

"Of course you have," Laura confirmed opening the car door and slid in.

"Why wasn't Dominic at the party?"

"Maybe he saw that guy that just sliced up Jean-Marc," Laura answered. "He must have decided he'd better find the treasure before someone else got hurt." She was picking at her fingernails, looking distractedly from her hands to the darkness outside the window.

Laura's cavalier attitude unnerved Kira further. She felt dangerously close to a full scale bout of hysterics.

The Casa was dark. Kira fidgeted nervously, becoming alarmed that there were no lights on in expectation of their arrival. "Are you sure he's here?"

The car came to a stop and Laura stepped out. "That's what I was told."

"It doesn't look like anyone's here."

"He said to bring you here," she insisted.

Kira walked into the shadowy house. How many times she had walked through the columned corridor in the dark, but this time she was afraid.

They emerged into the courtyard, eerie in the moonlight. "Dominic," Kira called out anxiously, her voice catching in her throat. The guard was not at his post. "Antonio? Where are they,

Laura?" When she turned again, she came face to face with the man who had brought them there.

"Paolo."

And then there was an explosion in the harbor. Flames lit up the western horizon.

❦   ❦   ❦

He was pacing again. They had been in the garden too long. She deserved a moment alone with her American friend, but he could not protect her when he couldn't see her.

He had waited long enough.

The American was sitting on the bench by himself. "Did she leave you?" Dominic probed, trying to make light of Joe's solitude.

"Joe Cochran," the American extended his hand. "Can you believe it? She's in love with someone else."

Dominic accepted Joe's hand hesitantly. "I am Dominic Fioretti. This is my home."

Joe stepped back and put his hand to his high forehead. "I'm sorry. I crossed the ocean to see her, I didn't mean to intrude on your party."

"You say she's in love with someone else?"

Joe laughed. "Can you believe it?"

"The man who asked her here?" Dominic suggested, making one last attempt to assure himself that Franco hadn't lured her here for his own entertainment.

"Asked her here?" Joe shook his head. "She's looking for the Holy Grail. Imagine looking for the Holy Grail in Italy. I can't believe…You say a man asked her here?"

Dominic shrugged his shoulders.

"She would have told her brother if she was chasing after a man," Joe assured him. "She tells him everything. And she doesn't chase men. That's not her style. Anyway, her brother didn't mention any man when I told him I was coming. In fact he slapped me on the back and wished me good luck."

Dominic was studying his hands. "So she left you?"

Joe waved his hand toward the house. "Said something about a drink. I saw her leave in a boat, though. I never thought she was that kind of girl."

"A boat?" Dominic tensed, silently berating himself for leaving her alone for so long.

"Yeah, that girlfriend of hers—and some guy. I suppose they had a late date."

Dominic could feel his pulse racing. "Which direction did they go?"

Joe pointed across the water. "What's over there? Naples? They seemed to be headed for those lights out there."

Dominic swallowed hard. "Ercolano."

"That's where they were staying, isn't it?"

Dominic nodded.

"Must've met him there."

"You must enjoy the party," Dominic told Joe hastily. "Perhaps you will find our Italian women somewhat more accommodating."

Dominic moved quickly past his guest toward the water.

His boat was floating out toward the Bay, the tow line released. He looked up and down the shoreline. There had to be another boat close by. She may have gone willingly enough, but Kira couldn't possibly understand the kind of danger she was in.

He raced to the villa, taking with him a ring of keys and a pair of binoculars. Back along the Capri shoreline, he located a speedboat and climbed in, apologizing to its unknown owner and promising to return it to the empty darkness.

With one hand on the rudder, he pulled the binoculars to his face, just making out the outline of his cruiser as it approached the opposite shore. He squinted, trying to see who disembarked, watching three figures climb the steps of the dock to the street above.

Putting down the binoculars, he leaned forward against the spray, willing the boat to move faster.

He didn't notice that he was shivering as the shoreline became closer, nor did he acknowledge the sting of salt water in his eyes. But the sudden flash of light in the docked boat made him cut the throttle and lean back just in time to shield his face as the explosion sent out shock waves that threatened to overturn his smaller craft.

He cried out involuntarily, praying that Kira had been one of the people he had seen go safely ashore.

※　　　　※　　　　※

Paolo's white teeth glinted against the shadows that covered his face.

"Where's Dominic?"

"Enjoying his party, I believe."

"Why did you bring me here?"

"I want the treasure," he answered immediately. "You will get it for me."

"But there is no treasure," Kira protested. "It's just a story."

Paolo reached up and pushed her shoulders with both of his hands and she teetered dangerously close to the edge of the pit. "You will bring me the treasure."

"You get it. It isn't safe down there."

He pulled a dagger from his waist similar to the one Kira had seen standing in her pillow. "It is not safe here, either," he pointed out.

"I didn't want to bring you here," Laura apologized. "He said we had to."

He hissed at Laura to be quiet. "I have already looked," he told Kira. "You know where it is. You will go down."

"How?"

He cocked his head sarcastically. "Jump."

Kira stared at him in disbelief. "You're not serious. It's six stories down!"

He shrugged his shoulders. "I push you," he offered. He waved toward the wooden structure.

"But there is no treasure," she persisted.

"Franco say you find gold," Paolo challenged.

"Franco?"

"He told me you found it," Laura supplied.

Paolo pushed Kira's shoulders once more and she took one step onto the staircase involuntarily. Her heart froze as she felt the structure sway uncertainly beneath her weight.

Weighing her chances, she closed her eyes, holding onto the railing. She put one foot onto the second step.

Her throat constricted while she wavered perilously. Turning her head skyward, she opened her eyes and looked up to the dark blue overhead. Stars winked, giving her the courage to continue.

Kira loosened her grip on the cool wood of the railing slowly, restoring the blood flow to her hands and continued down, one step at a time.

She reached the first plateau of earth. Halfway into the hole, she could see someone laying on the second tier. She leaned over to see who it was and the stairs moved threateningly. She closed her eyes again and gripped tightly to the wood.

"There is no gold," she shouted up once more.

"This is not what Franco say," the headstrong Italian yelled down again.

Kira stood still, staring at the figure laying on the shelf of earth. Forcing her feet to move, she took another step down. A cry escaped when she realized the body was Antonio, laying in a pool of blood. She recoiled, sending shudders through the unsecured structure. From the top came peals of Paolo's laughter.

"You have found the guard, no?" he called down.

Fully panicked now, Kira hurried down the remaining stairs, moving as carefully as she could to get off the unstable ride. A slap echoed in the darkness from somewhere beside her followed by the sound of a buckle.

Leaving behind the dangerously swaying structure, Kira jumped to the floor of the excavation and fell to her knees, sobbing uncontrollably after discovering another murdered man.

Her eyes darted through the darkness searching for another way out. There was no moon in the sky, and the starlight floated uncertainly behind clouds.

"No one to bother us," Paolo said breathlessly, appearing beside her. He released Laura and unbuckled a rope from his belt.

Kira turned to run away, but he tackled her before she could escape, weighing heavily on top of her. His belt cut into her back and she felt a trickle of blood making its way around her side. "You will get me the treasure," he hissed in her ear.

Paolo pulled her viciously back to his feet.

Laura was pacing off the square. "I was going to marry Franco, you know. But then you came and he said he was going to marry you."

Kira shook her head. "He's not the marrying type."

She smiled. "You're right of course. I suppose being so much older you'd know that right away." She looked up to the top edge of the excavation.

"So this is your idea of the perfect lover?" Kira cried out, fighting to regain some sense of poise.

Laura smiled, casting adoring eyes on Kira's tormentor. "He pursued me relentlessly."

Kira rolled her eyes, fully aware of how little pursuit was required.

"Oh Kira, he was so exciting. He promised me we'd be rich if I helped him. He's really nice when he's not angry."

"He just killed a man," Kira shouted. "That is not my idea of nice." Understanding dawned on Kira. She hit her head with her hand. "I saw you at the Casa—I passed you in the corridor that night." She turned to Laura. "He's the one that gave you that black eye."

"He was angry," Laura defended.

Paolo held his dagger under Kira's chin. "Now you will take me to the treasure."

"I suppose you're the ghost, too. There isn't any gold, you know," she insisted. A Corinthian column glinted white in the darkness. Kira saw a shadow pass behind it and gasped.

Paolo turned his head to see what had caught her attention. "Who is there?" He dropped to a crouch, turning nervously.

"The guard said no one was down here," Laura reminded him.

Paolo continued stalking in the darkness toward the atrium. Kira looked around for some means of protection, but there was nothing. Then she remembered the tools. Maybe they hadn't cleared out all the tools yet.

"Where is the gold?" Paolo demanded, still alert for another presence.

"There isn't any gold." She told him once more.

"Liar!" the man shouted, running up behind her and kicking her to the ground.

Kira doubled over as streaks of pain shot through her body. "See for yourself," she choked out.

"Franco said you found it," Laura reminded her.

"Franco's delirious. There is nothing here."

"Then you have it already?"

"You know," Kira pointed out, "if there's another earthquake we could all be trapped, suffocating or crushed like Franco. The volcano might even explode. The shift in the tectonic plates that caused the earthquake could trigger it."

"Then tell me where to find the treasure," Paolo responded coolly. He kicked at a support beam, releasing a flood of debris. "Maybe we leave you buried in here by yourself," he suggested. "No one will know what happened to you."

"If you don't tell him, he might kill you," Laura whispered urgently.

Anger took over where panic had subsided. "You left the dagger in my pillow," Kira accused.

"You will know I am serious this way." He kneeled beside her, holding the blade under her chin, applying just enough pressure to break the skin. "The treasure she is mine."

"But I told you already, there is no treasure."

"There is a treasure. Mi madre, she tell me about it. She say this will all be mine."

"Your mother?"

"Isabella Fioretti, she is my mother too. They are still married. She says this is mine, but Enzio, he say no." He stood over Kira, threatening. "I will have the Treasure."

He looked at the tunnel leading to the tablinum, cracked scaffolding still in place. Pointing with the dagger, he instructed her to move. "Now you will show me."

A blanket of claustrophobia covered Kira. "I couldn't get through," she choked.

Paolo smiled. "You are so unhappy that Franco is hurt that you return here and the earth buries you too. Another sad love story."

"You bet on the wrong horse," she mumbled.

His hand came crashing across her face. "There is no one to help you now," he said cruelly, wiping her blood off his hands.

"They'll miss me."

"Who will miss you?" He paced in front of Kira. "The Frenchman? Laura goes with me. And Il Padrone, he think only of Il Padrone. He will think you are gone with the American."

Paolo pulled her to her feet and pushed her toward the cavity in the earth. "You, go in," he demanded.

"It isn't there," she repeated weakly, holding her bloody nose.

"I don't believe you!" he shouted, causing an avalanche of debris inside the tunnel. He smiled, pleased with the results of his tantrum.

The knife went under her chin again. "I kill you here if you like, or you go in." He cocked his head, pressing the knife a little harder. "It is so easy down here, just like with the Signore." He moved his hand like a tree falling. "Down it goes and he is dead."

"You killed their father?"

"It should be mine!" he shouted again.

Kira closed her eyes, hearing the argument between the dark man and the other. The scenes from her dream, still vivid in her mind, showed her the identity of the man who had argued with Dominic, the man arguing for his birthright just moments before he caused the rock slide that took Enzio Fioretti's life. "He isn't dead," she told Paolo.

"I see him buried," Paolo argued, pushing her toward the tunnel.

Kira took a step forward. A breeze swept down, stirring the dust and cooling the perspiration on her brow. "*Kee-ra.*" The voice was as gentle as the wind calling to her, raising the hairs on the back of her neck.

"Who is there?" Paolo demanded, turning in circles. Again Kira saw a shadow gliding between the columns.

"It's just the clouds," Laura reassured him.

But Paolo stood fixed to his spot. "Signore," he whispered quietly, almost to himself. "It is mine," he cried out.

He shoved Kira firmly. "I will have the treasure," he insisted.

She fell into the warm scrapings that tried to close off the tunnel. Inside the chamber, she could see one of Jean-Marc's discarded tools laying on the floor. She shimmied through to the tablinum, trying to reach it.

Once inside, she saw a luminescent glow from the atrium beyond.

"Where is it?" Paolo demanded, still behind her.

Kira couldn't move. On the floor in front of her lay the cabinet that Jean-Marc had been restoring, displaced by a boulder of volcanic debris. In the shadowy light that came through the tunnel she saw where it had been sawed through, most likely to release the victim that lay under it, Franco Fioretti.

It was too much like the dream she had—the dream that had brought her here. She envisioned Dominic frantically trying to uncover his father not far from where she lay now and began to shake. "We have to get out of here."

Paolo pushed her so that she fell across the cupboard. "Take me to the treasure."

She reached for the ground to push herself up and felt the handle of a trowel. She closed her hand around it and rose slowly.

From the atrium came two electronic beeps of a wristwatch.

"Come out, Padrone," Paolo called, "or I will kill her now." He reached out and yanked at Kira's hair pulling her to her feet.

Kira swung around with the trowel, knocking the knife out of his hand. He cried out in surprise and took hold of her wrist before she could strike at him again.

Paolo's grip on Kira's arm tightened. "I will kill her now, Padrone," he threatened. "Come out."

A flicker of movement danced against the wall in the eerie light from the atrium. Paolo wrapped a forearm under Kira's chin as the silhouette of a man took shape in the shadowy room.

Then Paolo began to back away. "Signore," he whispered again less certainly. The apparition stood silently.

"Who is that?" Laura asked, putting a hand to Paolo's shoulder.

Paolo began apologizing in Italian, still backing away.

"Kira," the shadow spoke, "Come." He spoke in Italian, holding out his hands. When she hesitated, he shook his hands to emphasize his request. "Now," the wraithlike figure in the atrium demanded firmly.

"Franco?" Kira wondered quietly, shaking her head. She looked to Paolo, riveted to his spot. Knowing the danger that he represented, she decided to take her chances with the ghost.

She reached for the extended hands and was pulled back into the atrium where a candle continued to cast the ethereal glow. The flame went out with a gust of wind, while the phantom guided Kira expertly through the darkness.

"Who are you?" she asked him in Italian.

"We must move quickly," he responded.

With the sound of rumbling behind, Kira fell to her knees, instinctively covering her head. Dust rose up from the floor of the excavation, starlight streaming down where a wall section had collapsed.

The apparition coughed and stopped to catch his breath. "You're no ghost," Kira told him.

In fact, he was an old man, his hair white and his face marked by time. When he looked at her, his eyes twinkled, reflecting the stars overhead.

"So you are the one," he wheezed, trying to smile.

"Excuse me?"

"Come. We must move to safety." He stood again, taking her hand while leading her through the rooms beneath the Casa overhead.

He moved knowledgeably in the dark through the black tunnels beneath the earth. Kira followed him blindly, certain that they had traveled beyond the ruins of the villa.

When they stopped, he pushed her down gently until she sat on a boulder. "We can rest safely here." His voice echoed off invisible walls. Kira tried to see in the darkness, startled at the sudden weight of a piece of warm wool draped across her shoulders. The damp room was thick with the smell of seaweed and the acrid scent of kerosene.

"Where are we?"

"You will rest now," he instructed.

❦ ❦ ❦

Their voices echoed somewhere in the dark, confused, angry, frightened. Paolo seemed unsure about whether Kira had escaped or simply disappeared with the ghost. The more they searched, the more nervous his voice sounded.

After a while, she could only hear the sounds of the old man wheezing. She closed her eyes, and when she opened them again, light filtered into the cavern.

Jumping to her feet, the blanket fell off her shoulders.

"You are safe," the old man reassured her in Italian. He sat on a shelf of rock. His face was weathered and heavily creased.

"Where are we?" She asked again.

He put his finger to his lips.

The old man was sorting through a wooden box. From inside the box came the two quick beeps of the watch that had given him away in the dark.

"Dominic's watch?" she asked.

"He lost it saving his brother's life."

"Are you a gypsy, then? You make your home here?"

He just looked at her from the shadows, an enigmatic smile on his face.

Kira shook her head, frustrated. "I have to go. I have a plane to catch."

"You are anxious to leave?"

"Right now, the prospect of leaving Italy seems very enticing." She looked at the dried blood on her hands and put a hand to the soreness on her back. "And then again…" She dropped her weary head into her hands.

"Kee-ra." The old man stood behind her, placing a hand on her shoulder.

She looked up, startled. "It was you." She turned around to look at the old man. "I heard you calling me. Who are you?"

He smiled again and Kira's eyes opened wide at the unmistakable family resemblance. "Signore Fioretti?"

"KIRA!" Dominic's voice echoed in the cavern.

"Dominic!"

The old man took her arms and pulled her into a crevice in the rocks. "You must be quiet," he cautioned.

"But its Dominic."

"They are still there."

"We have to warn him," she insisted. She pulled away, moving toward the passage.

The path was cleverly hidden. The placement of the boulders gave the appearance of walls while providing only enough space to squeeze around them. The sunlight was getting brighter and the rocks gave way to the volcanic tufa.

"Kira," Dominic called again, his voice louder now.

She entered the remains of the villa cautiously, afraid to draw unwanted attention. Peering around the scaffolding, she searched out the reinforcements that remained intact.

She could see the courtyard. The tunnel that led into the tablinum was completely sealed off after the collapse in the night. Dominic was clawing at the debris, trying to clear the way.

She opened her mouth to call out, but a movement caught her eye. "No," she whispered as she watched Paolo snaking his way around the columns. "Dominic," she called out.

He stood up, turning in time to see Paolo come at him, leading with the dagger.

She moved guardedly around the perimeter of the villa, watching the two men struggle while she tried to get close enough to help.

The men fell to the ground in a tangle of arms and legs and blood. Kira moved quickly away from the shelter of the villa running toward the knife that still swung precariously through the air. She refused to allow another murder.

"No!" she shouted, stepping down onto the wrist that wielded the weapon. Paolo screamed in pain, releasing the dagger while Dominic threw a solid punch to his jaw.

Dominic sprang to his feet, his eyes blazing. He reached for a length of rope and tied Paolo's arms to the bottom of the broken staircase. Then he turned to Kira and grabbed her roughly by the shoulders.

"What are you doing down here?" he growled.

"Where's Laura?"

In response to her question Laura came running toward the staircase, clamoring up the swaying frame until it threw her off in one unpredictable shudder. She fell back to the ground with the sound of cracking bone.

Dominic looked back at Kira again. "What are you doing down here?" he asked again, his voice giving way under the strain.

"They told me you'd been hurt."

His eyes were wild with rage. He turned to look at Laura, a quivering mass of sobs on the ground. Paolo still lay unconscious almost beside her. Dominic began to laugh, a frightening hysterical sound that echoed around the courtyard beneath the earth's surface.

He walked across to a stone bench and sat down, his face turned toward the sky. "And you came to help me?" he asked. He held tightly to one of his arms, blood seeping between his fingers. "Look at what they've done to you!" He shook his head. "I will never forgive myself for leaving you alone."

"You're hurt."

"Now do you understand the danger?" He winced, tightening his hold and causing the blood to drip.

Kira yanked at his shirt sleeve, tearing away what remained of it to tie around his bicep. His skin was slick with blood and sweat. "Will you relax?" she scolded, fighting to pull the stained fabric around his tensed muscles.

"I am doing my best," he barked. His complexion was rapidly losing color, his face taking on an ashy hue. "You'll have to go for help."

"I'm sure your father's gone for help already. I'll wait with you."

Dominic rose to his feet, his face purpling with the exertion. "My father is dead!"

"You're wrong."

"I found him with my own hands." His voice broke, tears spilling from his eyes.

"And did you see him buried?"

"They brought me his ashes."

"Did you ever see his body after you uncovered him?"

Dominic dropped his head. "It was all over by the time they released me from the hospital, and Franco…" He shook his head, remembering.

"Then how can you be sure? I saw him, Dominic!"

"You saw someone trying to frighten you away." He slumped back down onto the bench. "If my father were alive he would come to me."

"He saved me last night. He is the ghost, but he's not. He's alive. Come with me. I'll show you," she urged.

She pulled him to his feet, leading him back beneath the mountain of earth. She directed him between the rocks and into the cavern where she had spent the night, but the old man was not there.

"He was here," she insisted. Kira walked over to the wooden box. "Your watch, it's in here. He had it last night." She pulled it out, holding it for him to see.

"It is not possible." Dominic's voice was raspy, blood still dripping from his arm. He dropped to his knees, groping for balance and slid against a large rock.

"Don't you pass out on me now," she commanded. "I'll never be able to get you out of here alone."

"Kira." The voice echoed from above. She looked up to see the old man scurrying down a series of rocks resembling a rude staircase. "He is hurt?"

"He needs help," she answered in Italian.

Enzio Fioretti hurried to his son's side, large hands touching Dominic's unconscious face.

"The police are coming," he told her.

She looked up to the top of the cavern. "How did you get out? Can you help me take him out?"

The old man nodded and wiped at his eyes. He supported Dominic's torso and pulled him gingerly from the floor. Dominic's eyes fluttered open. "Papa?" he whispered.

"Stand up," the old man told Dominic authoritatively.

Kira moved under one of Dominic's arms while his father supported the other side.

Dominic slipped in and out of consciousness providing little help for the two who struggled to lead him up the precarious ledges of rock.

The cave came out at the bottom of a hill. The Casa was several yards away, a short distance to cross after the rocky climb from below.

A team of paramedics came running from the house, quickly positioning themselves to redistribute Il Padrone's dead weight.

The old man led the way to Dominic's bedroom knowledgeably. He opened the door and the two stronger men eased Dominic onto the bed.

Kira watched his head fall gently onto the pillow, the sounds of sirens and flashing lights surrounding the Casa. She allowed herself to feel the pain in her back and the throbbing of her bruised face.

The old man held Dominic's hand lovingly. He held his other hand out to Kira, but she forced herself to keep her distance.

"You are the sun. You and Dominic, you are meant to be together."

Kira backed away, putting a hand to her neck. She felt the dried blood where Paolo's knife had broken the skin and began to gasp for air. "It is not…what…he…wants…" she wheezed. Then she closed her eyes and let the darkness envelope her.

CHAPTER 27

❃

She woke up in her room at the Casa, forgetting for a moment that she wasn't supposed to be there anymore. As realization dawned on her, she bolted up in the bed, immediately regretting the sudden movement.

She winced, putting a hand to the bandage that now covered the cut in her back. In the mirror her reflection seemed barely recognizable, a bandage across her nose and bruises on her cheekbones. She fingered the piece of gauze that was wrapped loosely around her neck, a tear falling down her cheek as she began to consider the extent of her injuries for the first time.

Her clothes of the night before were draped across the chair beside the desk, heavily soiled and tinged with dried blood. Kira looked self-consciously at her body, wondering who had cleaned and changed her.

She stood up slowly, feeling more aches than pains. She was wearing a pale pink dressing gown that stopped at her knees. "I wonder who this belongs to?"

She found her glasses laying on the dresser and decided not to try to put them on her swollen face.

Emerging into the corridor, Kira reached for the railing, leaning heavily to reduce the tightening of the bandage now covering the wound on her back with each step down.

The tiny tiles of the foyer were cool against her shuffling feet. The fact that she was wearing someone else's night clothes didn't seem important.

"Kirie! Ya shouldna be out o' bed!" Maeve reprimanded from the foyer.

"What....?"

Maeve ran to Kira's side, offering support to the tall woman beside her. "Kira, ye need yer rest! Just look at the sight o' ye!"

Kira closed her eyes, concentrating her efforts of building strength. Looking again at the dressing gown, she felt weak again and shook her head.

With a wry smile, Maeve helped Kira to the leather chair outside Franco's office. "It was me that changed ye, Kirie. I am sorry about the fit, but it was all that I could find. And in case yer wonderin', it came from Franco's room."

Still silent, Kira touched the guaze around her neck, almost afraid to speak and wondering how much of what happened the night before was real. Her strongest hope was that most of the events were only a nightmare.

"Dominic," she managed a hoarse whisper.

"He would not go to hospital." Maeve nodded down the corridor. "He's in his room."

Kira nodded. "The grail?" she asked quietly, tears streaming down her bruised face.

"The divil take the grail," Maeve cursed vehemently. "Jest look at all that its brought upon us!" The older woman's emerald eyes flashed. "Have I not seen enough of death and destruction? Was it not enough to see my man killed and then my two sons after him?"

Kira wiped at her cheeks gingerly. "Maeve...."

"I came here to get away from it. And then with Enzio I found a new hope—his search for the grail. I thought if it was truly the blessed cup it might put an end to the war in Ireland. And look at what's happened! Himself was murdered, Jean-Marc after him, and the two men who had become as dear to me as my own sons are both struggling for their lives as well."

Instinctively, Kira reached over to hug the woman beside her. So Dominic had been wrong after all. "It's over now," she reassured Maeve.

The Irish woman pushed away. "'t will never be over."

Fear tickled Kira's spine with the eerie words. "I want to see Dominic."

"Come along then," Maeve invited, rising to her feet. "But I'm goin ta help ye. I'll not have ye fallin' on these marble floors in the shape yer in!"

Reaching for each column, Kira pushed forward down the hallway.

Outside his bedroom, she took a deep breath before Maeve pushed the door open.

Dominic continued to sleep, still heavily sedated. Kira concluded that her own general lack of coordination probably resulted from a similar drug.

His arm lay outside the covers, the bandage over his stitches caked with dried blood.

"He is a strong boy," Enzio said, standing to greet her. "He will be fine."

"Enzio!" Maeve gasped, her momentum stalled.

"He is long past being a boy," Kira pointed out.

"You should not be up."

She shook her head. "I'm all right."

Dominic's father rose to greet Maeve, his uncertain smile reflecting his trepidation at the reception he was about to receive.

"Saints preserve us," she muttered, crossing herself.

"The banshee did not take me after all."

"Go," Kira suggested. "I will sit a while with Dominic."

❋ ❋ ❋

She closed her eyes to see it again, the tarnished gold sending out yellow rays of brilliance. She could still feel the electric charge it sent through her.

Still fighting in his sleep, the dark man jerked reflexively. Bruises discolored sections of his cheeks and forehead. Muscles continued to twitch involuntarily in response to private dreams.

Kira sat down where Enzio had been, resting her head against the wall behind her. Was Maeve right about the grail? Had it brought more harm than good?

❋ ❋ ❋

His legs jerked, startling him back to consciousness. He opened eyes bleary from medication and smiled.

"Kira." He swallowed with some difficulty and reached over for the glass of water that waited on the table beside the bed. Sitting up slowly, he sipped from the cup.

"I dreamt I saw my father," he told her.

"You did."

"My father is dead."

Enzio moved out of the shadows in the corner of the room. "I know you will understand," he told Dominic, "why I could not let anyone know I survived. Even you."

Dominic sat up straight, pushing back against the headboard. "Papa," he gasped. He looked at the bottle of pills on the table beside him. "Am I dead?"

Dominic closed his eyes struggling for clarity.

"You should rest."

"Kira." He said her name like an anchor holding him on the aware side of consciousness.

"It's okay," she reassured him.

He smiled, a drug-induced, lethargic grin. "I met your boyfriend. Joe? He said he saw you leaving." His face went dark again, although he was unable to force his features into the familiar scowl. "You could have been killed."

"Yes, well you saved me from the jaws of death once more."

He opened bleary eyes to look at her, squinting to focus. "Your boyfriend told me something else."

"He's not my boyfriend." Kira wrung her hands and pushed herself to her feet, squeezing her eyes tightly to fight the nerve impulses reminding her of her injuries.

"He told me you turned him down," Dominic continued. "He said you were in love with someone else."

"Can we leave my personal problems out of this?"

His eyes were glistening and a silver trail slid down his cheek. "I am in love with you, Kira, and when your friend told me you were in love with someone else, I was hoping that maybe it was me."

He slowly pushed himself up in the bed, aware once more of the ghost standing in the corner of his room. "She is the sun, isn't she, papa? That's why you are here, isn't it?"

"You don't know what your saying," Kira told him. She pointed to his father in the corner. "You talk to him like he isn't really there. Your father is alive, Dominic. He'll tell you. I'm just a woman—not some sun goddess that you keep imagining to appear. We tried, remember? If I was so perfect," her voice caught in her throat, "you would have known I went down there for you. Not for whoever the hell else came down after..." She looked through eyes filled with tears to the old man seated in the corner, her voice dissolving. "But then you were there, weren't you."

"You've asked me to leave, now please allow me some dignity."

He licked his lips, taking in a quavering breath. "I was wrong."

"Thank you for your hospitality, Padrone—Signore Fioretti."

Kira left the room, retreating down the corridor with tears falling freely down her face. She clutched at her back in agony, all of her wounds bleeding afresh.

CHAPTER 28

❈

The screaming of the jet subsided as the plane straightened out across the ocean leaving the coast of Italy behind like a boot dropped in the water.

The seat belt light went off, but Kira remained tightly strapped in, dark sunglasses covering her face while she continued to stare out across the endless expanse of blue below. She turned sharply when she heard the familiar voice address her.

"Do you mind if I sit beside you?" Joe Cochran asked, appearing in the aisle.

She gave him a resigned smile. "I'd be grateful for the company," she admitted. "Besides which I owe you an apology."

Joe slipped into the seat beside Kira, reaching up to adjust the small fan of cold air above him. "You don't owe me anything. Still friends?"

"I was so rude," she sighed, putting her hand over his. "You crossed the ocean to see me and what did I do?"

"Crossing the ocean was the smartest thing I've done in a long time." He let out a soft chuckle. "Those Italians have quite a lust for life."

Kira wrinkled her nose, catching the scent of stale fish that blew toward her from the redirected fan overhead. "It would seem life wasn't the only thing those Italian women lusted after."

Joe smiled, the top of his nearly bald head shining red. "No offense, Kira, but marrying you would have been like marrying my sister. We've been friends too long."

She sat quietly, turning again to look back out the portal. A tear slipped past the bottom of her sunglasses followed by a slow breath and a quick sniff.

"Must be hard for you, giving up everything you know," he offered.

Kira clutched the armrests beside her while the plane bumped through some turbulence. "I just want to get home," she answered very quietly.

"Anxious to get back to him, no doubt. Can't say I blame you."

She smiled, another tear washing down her cheek. "Don't expect I'll ever see him again."

He leaned across, taking her hand. "What about the love of your life?" Lines of concern etched furrows into his forehead. With his free hand, he reached for her sunglasses and pulled them from her face, shocked at the bruised eyes he uncovered. "What happened, Kira? Did he do this to you?"

She shook her head vehemently. "So much has happened…" she sniffled, her mouth pressed tightly closed to hold back the sobs.

A wry smile touched the corners of Joe's mouth. "I know it's none of my business, but do you want to talk about it?"

She waved a hand flippantly in front of her. "You know. Summer fling."

"You don't have flings," he reminded her, his expression empathetically reflecting hers. He sat watching her for several minutes, waiting for her to speak, before finally releasing her hand and relaxing into his seat. "I must have been mistaken. The guy I thought it was didn't look like the type to kiss you off." He cast a sideways glance at Kira. She sat quietly, wringing her hands in her lap.

"He didn't kiss me off," she admitted, barely loud enough to be heard over the loud engines of the plane. "I saved him the trouble."

Joe sat craning to look past Kira out the window while he chose his next words. "I've never seen you like this, Kira. All those conversations we've had over the years about happily ever after being the stuff fairy tales are made of—I'm not saying I believe in it, mind you, but I did learn something these last few days in Italy. Sometimes its worth taking a chance to experience something a little more substantial." He took her folded hands into his and looked sternly at her face, forcing her to look back.

"It didn't mean anything," she answered a little more surely, but her voice broke as she continued. "Just a crush. It'll pass."

"Keep trying to convince yourself. Maybe you'll believe it by the time we see New York."

Her body convulsed with a sob that refused to be contained. Joe reached out reflexively and held her against him.

"Is everything all right?" A stewardess asked, leaning across the seats.

"You must see this all the time," Joe replied cheerfully, giving her one of his best smiles, "leaving a loved one behind."

The stewardess answered his smile with a casual flip of her hair and tilt of her head. "Let me know if I can be of any help," she offered suggestively.

Kira punched Joe's shoulder, laughing through the tears. "I think I've created a monster. I've never seen you flirt before."

"Hey, I'm a free man now. My girl gave me my walking papers." He kissed Kira's cheek affectionately. "Are you going to be okay?"

She nodded, searching the pocket of the seat in front of her. Pulling out a tissue, she dabbed at her nose and gave Joe a reassuring smile before she started crying all over again.

CHAPTER 29

❀

"You might as well spill," Cindy Weatherhead encouraged as they walked back to their classrooms from the cafeteria. "Joe's already talking about it, so you might as well."

"There's nothing to talk about," Kira insisted.

"He's awful cheerful for someone who's just been dumped. What's the big secret?"

Kira half-turned, holding out her hands in a pleading gesture. "There's no big secret. Can we drop it?"

"Geez! He flies halfway across the world to propose only to be turned down and you say there's no big secret?"

Kira put an arm out to stop her colleague before they reached their classrooms at the end of the hall. "Look, Joe's okay with it. In fact, he agreed with my decision."

"And the other guy?"

"There is no other guy."

"But he said…"

"It was an excuse. There was another American girl there who's only reason for being there was to have a summer fling with some hunky European stud. It seemed like the right thing to say at the time."

Cindy turned away from her friend in disbelief. "Well he bought it—lock, stock and barrel. You must have put on one fine acting job."

The school bell rang and children began to pour back into the hallway. Kira and Cindy stood facing each other, a silent truce called for the moment.

"So who's your guest speaker?" Cindy asked.

"Guest speaker?"

"Yeah. Who's speaking to your class this afternoon?"

Kira rolled her eyes. "There's someone speaking to my class this afternoon? Why don't they tell me these things?"

Cindy laughed. "Well then who's the guy sitting in your classroom?"

Kira held out her hands, hurrying to find the answer.

"Miss Ellison!" the portly principal stalled her before she could walk into the room, his glasses low on his nose. Kira pushed her own glasses up reflexively.

Jack Schroeder was four inches shorter than she was and had great difficulty with the fact that he had to look up when speaking to a woman.

"Who's in my classroom?" she asked.

"Oh yes. Quite an enthusiastic man."

She put her hands to her hips. "Care to fill me in?"

"I knew you wouldn't mind. And Joe cleared it. Said he knew the man and thought it was an excellent idea." Jack clasped his hands together excitedly. "All fits together rather well, I'd say. Should fit right in with your lesson plan."

Kira bit her lip to keep from saying anything more and pushed past the smaller man into her classroom.

Behind her desk, the map of Europe had been pulled down covering the green chalkboard. She fumed silently at the invasion of this uninvited speaker into her classroom.

The new eighth grade girls seemed more social than those she had last year. Kira looked at the small clique gathered in a corner of the room giggling and nudging each other, looking nervously at the teacher.

"All right, girls, find your seats please," she suggested. She watched one of them sit down behind the captain of the basketball team and push teasingly at his shoulder. And then she saw him.

She felt the color rush from her face and felt dangerously close to fainting. The class bell rang, startling her back to her responsibilities.

"Okay people," she began, picking up a text book and clearing her throat to control her voice. "First, let me tell you what your homework will be for tonight, and second, are there any questions about yesterday's lesson?"

She looked at the faces of her students, anticipating hands from some of them but not being rewarded. "Good. Either you're all ready for a pop quiz or nobody did their homework." A slight titter went around the room which she silenced with a threatening "I can still give you a quiz" look. "For tomorrow, I want you to read through the fourth chapter about Etruscan civilizations. Why don't you get started now before I introduce our visitor."

There was an audible sigh from several of her female students and she somehow registered the fact that her male students were all sitting upright in their seats, trying to measure up.

"Good afternoon, Miss Ellison," he greeted with a soft Italian accent.

Kira closed the book, unable to take her eyes from Dominic Fioretti. She slid off the corner of her desk and to her feet, feeling suddenly light-headed. "Signore. Would you step into the hall for a moment?"

One of the basketball players hummed a cadence of doom for the unlucky man who had to "step into the hall" with the teacher.

Kira walked back through the classroom, nodding to Dominic to follow. "Read!" she commanded her students.

"What are you doing here?" she demanded once outside the room with the door safely closed.

"Sitting in on your class?"

She placed her hands on her hips defensively. "Jack Schroeder seems to think you're a guest speaker. Are you planning to address my class?"

"Am I not allowed to sit quietly in the back and observe my favorite teacher?" He reached for her hands.

She felt her face flush hot. "Why are you here?"

He stared into her eyes. "Have you seen Maeve?"

Kira shook her hands free of his. "Not since I left Italy."

"She has disappeared."

"Why shouldn't she?"

"You know why she shouldn't," he reminded her. "You know what happened to Jean-Marc."

"Maeve had nothing to do with that," Kira told him, a catch in her voice. She put a hand to her mouth to repress the renewed feeling of anguish.

"And the boat?" He took a step closer, standing inside her personal space. "That was meant for you."

"I understand you two already know each other," Jack Schroeder interrupted, walking down the hall. "A pleasant surprise, Miss Ellison? Do you mind if I sit in while he speaks to the class?"

Kira opened the door of her classroom. All heads turned immediately back to their text books. "Signore?" she invited, waving him through with her arm.

"People," she introduced, "I'd like to introduce Signore Dominic Fioretti, lead archeologist at a private excavation of Herculaneum, near Pompeii, and a scientist in the field of radiocarbon dating."

He stood beside her, smiling graciously. He bowed deeply. "Eet was my great honor to haf your teacher as one of my students," he told them, extending his vowels into exaggerated Italian pronunciation.

"You spoke better English in Italy," she muttered under her breath. "Please, Padrone, tell my students about Herculaneum."

Dominic stepped up to the chalkboard and cleared his throat. "I have promised your principal that I would educate you." His practiced English accent took over once more as he began to relate the eruption of Vesuvius and the burial of the cities beneath it.

Jack Schroeder sat beside Kira, in a chair at the back of her classroom. "Quite a speaker," he commented wryly.

"Why didn't you tell me he was here?" she whispered angrily.

"He wanted to surprise you. Didn't want to embarrass you or have you make a big fuss. He was very complimentary. Said you did quite well at the dig. Even found some significant relics."

Kira folded her arms stubbornly across her chest. "Amazing, don't you think?" she commented sarcastically. "And Joe Cochran? Where does he fit in with all this?"

"Well I couldn't just take the stranger's word for it. He said Joe could vouch for him."

"It is my classroom," she reminded him quietly. "You could have let me know."

"But it fits right in. You're telling your kids all about your summer vacation and in walks the expert."

Kira rolled her eyes. "The expert. Because of course I couldn't possibly know what I'm talking about."

"He does have qualifications you don't."

"And I have qualifications that he doesn't. This is my classroom."

"And you're teaching archeology. Unless I missed something on your resume, he can tell them more about that than you can."

"Then hire him."

"What's the matter with you, Kira? You don't seem yourself since you got back from Italy."

"There's nothing wrong with me. I am perfectly capable of structuring my own syllabus."

"What about you and Joe? I mean I knew you had a falling out…"

"Don't you have a school to run?"

Jack Schroeder rose indignantly from the desk beside Kira. "I was only trying to help." With a flip of his head reminiscent of a scorned woman, he went to stand in the corner of the room nearest the door.

She refused to look at Dominic, although she could feel his eyes on her. Instead, she turned her attention to the bank of windows while she took deep, measured breaths.

Closing her eyes, she rode the gentle waves of his lilting voice, deep and sure. It brought back memories of the ball—dancing in his arms, listening to the soft tenor of his voice in her ear, the strength of his arms wrapped protectively around her.

Checking herself, she looked at the man in front of her class, reminding herself of the hard realities. Summer was over and romance had no place in her life.

Dominic looked up at the clock over the doorway and wrapped up his lecture. "Does anyone have any questions?" he posed.

He pointed to each student as they raised their hands until the bell rang and the hour-long history lesson came to an end.

"Remember to read about the Etruscans," Kira reminded them from the back of the class.

He had been far too at ease for Kira's comfort, from the moment he first entered her classroom.

"Wonderful," Jack Schroeder applauded, advancing to shake Dominic's hand. "Sounds fascinating when you talk about it."

Kira rolled her eyes, feeling a stab of jealousy and wondering if her lectures were too dry.

"Do we have a few minutes before the next class?" Dominic asked Kira, politely ignoring the principal.

Jack Schroeder backed off, clearing his throat noisily. "Excuse me, I have other duties to attend to."

"You look well," he complimented. "Your wounds have healed?"

Kira's hands moved reflexively to her throat.

"And now you are afraid of me?" he suggested.

"No," she answered quickly, her voice cracking with the effort.

Dominic looked around the room and then moved to the chalkboard, inspired by an idea. He tugged at the map that hung over it, releasing it to roll back into the cylinder.

"I came to ask you something," he told her, still assuming his role as instructor.

Kira let out a sigh and moved slowly to the front of her classroom.

"My father told me once, and my father is a very wise man, that you should follow your dreams. Isn't that what you did when you came to Italy?"

Kira offered an accommodating smile, perturbed at his indirect approach. "Your point?" she prodded. And then she saw the uncertainty in his eyes.

He reverted to Italian, making Kira believe he was afraid she might understand what he wanted to say and leaving room for an error in comprehension. "Mi vuoi sposarmi?"

Kira felt the panic rising.

Dominic reached for a piece of chalk and scrawled the question across the green board in English. "Will you marry me, Miss Ellison?" Dominic asked, pointing to each word for emphasis.

Students had begun filtering into her room once more. Increasingly aware of their rapt attention to the question written on her chalkboard, Kira reached up for the map again to cover his proposal.

Kira picked up an eraser and slid behind the map, her hot face glowing bright red.

She slammed the eraser back into the chalkboard tray. "I can't believe you came all this way just to embarrass me again."

"You were right about one thing," he told her, leaning against her desk. "I do like a little fight in my women, but not when I'm proposing marriage." He straightened up and stood behind her, resting large hands on her shoulders.

"You can't be serious," she barely whispered, her voice strangled with emotion. "After all, it was just a summer thing, you know." She feigned nonchalance. "A game, remember? So the others would think you too distracted to attend your duties."

His lips curled upward into a sardonic smile. "So you care nothing for me?"

The tips of Kira's ears were burning now. She made a move to escape and was quickly halted.

"You left Italy without saying goodbye." He took her arms firmly, forcing her to face him.

"You asked me to go."

"It was very dangerous for you then…" He lifted her face toward his, demanding her attention. "I love you Kira. I never want to be without you again." Dominic took her hands in his. "You told your American boyfriend you could not marry him and you told him why. If you don't love me—if you love someone else…" he pulled her hands up to his chest, "I will not use jealousy as a shield against you any longer. If I am not the one you love, I will go. But if you do love me," his voice caught momentarily, making him pause before he continued…"if you do love me, my *sole*, please say you'll never leave me again. Marry me."

A round of applause broke out around the classroom. Startled, Dominic straightened, looking sheepishly at the seventh graders looking on.

Red faced with embarrassment, Kira placed one hand to the side of Dominic's face, regaining his attention, and replied in intimately subdued tones. "There could never be anyone else. You know that line '…what God has brought together…'? Kinda takes on a whole new meaning here." A tear slid down her cheeks. "I love you, Dominic."

Epilogue

The man who had introduced himself to her as Pastor Thompson continued to strike out with his sword in her dreams. Kira thrashed around helplessly until two strong hands brought her firmly back to consciousness.

The dark man held her close, drying her tears against his shoulder. She clung tightly to him, afraid that he would disappear again as he had so many times upon waking, a phantom of her imagination.

"Cara Mia," he purred into her hair, his deep voice reassuring her that he was real. He stroked his fingers through her outgrown tresses.

Outside the windows she could hear the soothing waves of the Mediterranean Sea lapping against the shoreline, the scent of lemons carrying on the gentle breeze.

With a deep breath, she relaxed, settling back against the pillows. She twirled the dark hairs on his chest, admiring the physique of the man beside her—her husband.

His black eyes set deep inside the recesses of his face showed small wrinkles at the corners lending character to his olive skin. There was a hint of gray creeping into the black curls around his ears.

His hand went to the side of her face while he spoke to her in Italian, the way he had that night in the excavation, gentle, caressing words that needed no translation.

His transition into English was almost seamless, taking her by surprise. "Another dream?"

"Yes."

"He has been brought to justice," he reassured her once more. "There is no more reason to fear."

She nodded, shaking loose the last fragments of the nightmare. "Do you miss the excavation very much?"

Dominic exhaled deeply, closing his eyes. "It was my home. And yet…" he rolled onto his stomach, fixing his dark eyes on Kira's, "I think it is much better this way. My father's goal has been attained, the risk had become too great…" he nodded certainly. "It is better this way."

"And the grail?"

"In the Museo in Napoli where it should be. Just another treasure uncovered from civilizations past." He kissed the tip of her nose. "Like the Hope Diamond or the ancient mummies. Always there is a legend attached to such artifacts. This one will remain lost in obscurity."

"So many people looking for it. So many hopes and dreams pinned on one piece of the past."

"Like your own?"

"And yours."

Dominic held her close. "Cara mia. Never did I dream I would find such happiness." He kissed her fervently. "Mi corazon. You are my heart."

She smiled, touching his rough shaven face in the dimly lit bedroom, smelling the essence of the man she had pledged the rest of her life to. "How could I have known that in coming to Italy I would discover more than I ever dreamed could truly exist."

0-595-23363-5

Printed in the United States
6025